MURDER AT THE COOK-OFF

"Why would it matter if he had words with other guests? It has to have been an accident with no one at fault but Fitz himself," Sherry said.

"Sherry, you may fancy yourself an accomplished amateur sleuth, due to past successes at finding a killer or two, but right now your guesses about Frye wandering the grounds, tumbling into a pool of cold water, and drowning are way off base."

"Enlighten us, will you, Detective?" Erno said.

"Frye had blunt force trauma to the back of the head, inconsistent with someone accidentally falling forward into a hard object, which is the way he was found. There was also a calling card left at the scene. A fishhook, a multiple-barbed, bait-holder hook, to be specific, that was meticulously maneuvered into the back of Frye's neck in such a way that the man could not have possibly managed it on his own, even if he had fallen backwards onto it in a mishap. He was also clutching a handful of illegible soaked papers."

"Sounds like murder to me," Erno surmised.

Books by Devon Delaney

EXPIRATION DATE

FINAL ROASTING PLACE

GUILTY AS CHARRED

EAT, DRINK AND BE WARY

Published by Kensington Publishing Corp.

Eat, Drink and be Wary

Devon Delaney

KENSINGTON BOOKS
KENSINGTON PUBLISHING CORP.
www.kensingtonbooks.com

Chapter
1

"So many merlots, so little time. How are we going to make a selection?" Sherry continued her walk down the domestic reds aisle.

"Not we, you," Pep replied. "And it's not my fault you spent so much time meeting your neighbor's new cat. We could have been here an hour ago."

Sherry peered over her shoulder and caught sight of her brother checking his phone. "Expecting something important? I've seen you pull that thing out of your pocket every two minutes since we've been in here. When you have time to focus, I could use your help choosing the right wine."

Pep lifted his gaze from the phone screen. "Message received. I'm all yours. I just didn't realize signing up to be your cook-off sous chef meant I had to be in on all the recipe decisions."

Sherry noted his sweet smile hadn't changed a bit since childhood. But the scruffy, day-old stubble he sported was a change she hadn't yet fully embraced. The whiskers aged him more than she was willing to accept. Even after not having seen her brother for nearly a year, his handsome features left Sherry's heart warm every time she looked his way.

"It's important you're familiar with all the ingredients and how they work in the recipe. The problem is, the merlot I used in the recipe's sauce was a gift from a previous contest. I can't seem to find the maker here in Augustin." Sherry sighed. "I'm looking for something light and fruity that pairs well with seafood."

Sherry faced the wall of bottles. As she reached toward a domestic red, her fingers collided with an arm. "I'm sorry." Sherry retracted her hand. "We seem to have the same taste in reds." She giggled. "Go ahead, you take it."

"I'm not too particular. I just like the design of the label and the fact that it's from a Massachusetts winery," the tall woman with wavy red hair explained. "I'm in a recipe contest tomorrow, and one of the prizes is a trip to the Mass winery, Risky Reward. I thought drinking a glass later might bring me good luck."

Sherry heard Pep clear his throat with extra emphasis. She glanced his way, and sure enough, he tossed her a smirk. For a split second, she was ten again. Sherry let a snicker escape, despite trying to suppress it.

"Did I say something funny?" the woman asked.

"My brother and I are in a contest tomorrow, too. I'm assuming we'll all be competitors in the New England Fall Food Fest?"

The woman gave Sherry a look that lingered. "Are you by any chance Sherry Oliveri?"

Sherry nodded.

"I'm in big trouble now." The woman lowered her

head. "I thought I had a shot at winning with my Surf and Turf Shepherd's Pie, but not now." She lifted her head and cupped her hands around her mouth. "Donnie, come here a sec. I have someone I'd like you to meet."

Sherry watched a man make his way from the other side of the liquor store.

"I'm Day Paulson, and this is my brother, Donnie, although he prefers Don. I'll never see him as anyone but my little brother, Donnie, who bugged the heck out of me growing up, so that's what I call him."

Sherry pumped Day's extended hand. "I don't think we're in the same category, unless you've found a way to make shepherd's pie a portable food that needs no utensils to eat it. That's the category I'm competing in. Hands-On Foods. You must be in the One-Pot Wonders category."

Day swept her hand across her forehead. "Phew."

"Where are you two from?" Sherry took note of Don's resemblance to his sister, especially his height. His gaze shifted her way. She felt a flush sweep across her cheeks.

"I'm from just outside of Chicago, and Donnie lives on Long Island. He wasn't thrilled when I asked him to be my sous chef, but he nicely agreed." Day pinched Don's cheek.

"I'm beginning to reconsider. She's getting pretty bossy," Don added. "Nice to meet you."

"There aren't many contests that allow a sous chef. The Fall Food Fest is such a prestigious contest, I think the sponsors want to ensure the contestants put out their best work without getting tripped up in the details." Sherry put her arm on Pep's shoulder.

"Not sure how thrilled Pep was to be asked, either. Lucky for me, he's Mr. Nice Guy."

Day stepped back from the wine shelf and handed Sherry the wine bottle. "Take this. I'm not choosy."

"Thanks." Sherry read the label. She returned the bottle to Day. "Can't use this one. I need a merlot, this one's a blend. I'm looking for light and fruity."

"If those are the qualities you have in mind, may I suggest another?" Don walked a few steps down the aisle. "I'm not a great cook like you and my sister, but I know something about wines." He pointed to a bottle with a minimally decorated label. "This merlot's also from Risky Reward. It's fruity, not overly so, though more so than the one you're holding." He pulled the bottle from the shelf. "Can't hurt to have the bottle in a prominent position on the table during the cook-off either."

"I owe you one," Sherry laughed. "I'm not completely comfortable with my sauce. One more practice session should nail it. Merlot's the secret ingredient."

"Competitor helping competitor. The world needs more of that," a woman dressed in a blue pantsuit commented as she approached the foursome.

"Patti, so good to see you." Sherry smiled at her friend. "This is a hopping place today. Let me introduce you to these nice people."

Patti set down her shopping bag. "No need. Day Paulson from Illinois, Sherry from Connecticut, and these are your sous chefs, Pep Oliveri and Donald Johnstone."

"Donnie, actually," Day corrected.

"Don, actually," Don corrected. "And you are?"

"Patti Mellitt, food writer for the *Nutmeg State*

of Mind and podcaster. I'm covering the cook-off tomorrow. I've studied the contest literature, and it's safe to say I can put a face to a photo for all the finalists and their seconds in command."

"That's why you make the big bucks," Sherry laughed. "Devil's in the details."

"From your mouth to my boss's ears," Patti replied.

Out of the corner of her eye, Sherry saw Day nudge Don with her elbow.

"We're gonna keep moving," Day announced. "We'll see everyone tomorrow morning at the cook-off." Day took a step backward.

"Aren't you going to the contestant gathering at the Augustin Inn this evening?" Patti asked.

"I'd like to," Don responded. "But when my brother-in-law's not with her, Day gets shy about going out. But hey, I'm single and ready to mingle."

"I'll be there. I'd highly recommend you attending, Day," Patti said. "You didn't hear it from me, but all the sponsors and judges will be there. Doesn't hurt to let them see you at the scheduled events, even for a quick check-in."

"I'd skip it if I could." Pep placed his phone in his pocket.

"Sounds like we'll see you there," Day said, then turned and headed to the cash register with her purchase.

"Thanks for the wine advice," Sherry called after her new acquaintances.

"Happy to oblige. All I ask in return is that you don't use my knowledge against me." Don gave a casual salute and followed his sister to the register.

"If only all competitors were so nice." Sherry

observed Pep tapping the toe of his hiking boot. She faced Patti. "Are you on duty tonight or can you let loose?"

"I'm not really a let-loose kind of gal. I'd think you'd know that about me by now. That's why we get along so well." Patti winked at Pep. "Am I right?"

"Yep. Sherry's not as buttoned up as she used to be, but she'd still rather be the caterer to the party than the life of the party," Pep said with a gentle tone. He reached for the bottle of wine in Sherry's hand. "I'll check us out while you guys finish up. See you tonight, Patti." He waved the bottle of wine overhead and headed toward the front of the store.

"Your brother is so handsome. A young version of your dad." Patti's gaze followed him.

Sherry grinned. "And a few inches taller. Dad would deny he was ever that handsome, but I agree with you."

"Erno is still handsome. I'm assuming Pep's off the market? If I were only ten, maybe fifteen years younger."

"Your guess is as good as mine. Getting information on his private life is more difficult than getting meringue to set up. He's only been in town twenty-four hours, so I haven't gone too deep with him. He lives the life of a single guy, that's for sure. Over the last year he's lived in Europe, followed by Nova Scotia. He's currently working and living in Maine. He studied geology in college."

"Good profession. Can't find too many places without rocks." Patti picked up her shopping bag. "I'm off to review the new café in town, The Hunger Dames. It was started by three ladies—one a widower, one a divorcée, and the third, a spinster. Supposed to be fantastic."

Sherry patted her stomach. "My dream profession. Restaurant reviewer."

"Not always my dream. Last week, I got food poisoning from the new diner in Eastport. Fingers crossed for today's assignment. Gotta squeeze a review in before I switch gears and begin full coverage of the Fall Food Fest. See you soon."

On the way home, Pep was quiet. Sherry drummed on the steering wheel as she considered how to enter the uncharted waters of her brother's love life. She held her tongue until they approached a red light.

"What did you think of Amber? She's been such an asset for The Ruggery. You know the whole story—how she and I met at a cook-off and became fast friends. Fast forward a few months, she moved down here from Boston. Left her family therapy practice behind after her divorce and traded it all in to work with Dad selling the Oliveris' famous hand-crafted hooked rugs. Did you know she also writes a family therapy advice column? So well rounded. Funny thing is, I think you and her would make a good match." A quick side-eye Pep's way revealed nothing but the back of his head. His sights were aimed out his window. A honk from behind nudged her attention back to the road.

Pep pointed at the windshield. "Green means go. Mind if we listen to the radio?" Before Sherry could respond, Pep tapped the knob, and the sound of seventies rock filled the car.

Chapter
2

Back in her kitchen, Sherry watched the timer tick off the final seconds. She plunged her wooden spoon in the saucepan and removed the thyme sprig. "Look how the spoon is coated with the deep red goodness." She waved the blushing spoon in front of Pep's face.

"Is it done?"

Sherry lowered the heat. "Not yet. Can you hand me one tablespoon of butter and the cream?" Sherry tipped her head in the direction of the dairy products gathered on the counter. "Those two additions will make the sauce creamy and glossy and perfect. Added too soon, it might curdle, too late, and the sauce won't be blended."

Sherry stirred until the cream was incorporated and the butter was melted. "Taste this balsamic merlot reduction and see what you think." Sherry thrust the spoon toward Pep's mouth. Bits of shallot dotted the creamy sauce. One bit fell to the floor, only to be lapped up by a furry Roomba.

"Thanks, Chutney." Sherry smiled at her dog, who remained under foot to wait for more spills.

Ding, ding, ding.

"Time!" Pep took a taste and licked his lips. "Wow, that's good. Maybe a touch more salt and pepper. I'd advise using the sauce sparingly, so it doesn't overpower the shrimp."

"Phew. Perfect timing. The sauce will be warm and fresh for the plating if tomorrow's prep goes as well as today. Glad there are no problems with the sauce and happy the merlot Don picked out worked. You're right about the amount to put on. I wrote 'drizzle on lettuce wraps' in the instructions. The judges who picked it to compete must have liked the result." Sherry loaded the spoon in the dishwasher and rolled up the sleeves of her shirt. "Ready to move onto the other steps in the final practice session?"

Either Pep didn't hear the question or was too engrossed in scrolling through his phone.

Sherry raised her voice. "Pep?"

"Sorry, did you say something?" He didn't lift his head.

"We're going to run through the recipe prep, minus the sauce, since I mastered that." She held up a piece of paper. "It's not as easy as reading the recipe and getting it right the first time. If you could put down the phone for a bit, we could get the run-through completed from start to finish, and we'll all sleep better." Sherry eyed Pep's phone as if the device was a worm in her spinach salad.

Pep lifted his gaze from the phone and met Sherry's. "I'll be sleeping fine. Take a deep breath, and you'll realize you made the right choice when you picked me. Time's ticking away. Let's not waste a second even talking about my phone." His voice had a bit of an edge to it.

"I apologize for losing my patience. If you'd come a few days earlier, we'd have had more than a few hours to prepare."

"I couldn't, so let's make the most of the little time we have. I'm sorry, too. Don't, for a minute, think I take your favorite hobby lightly." He clicked the side of his phone. "Mute. I'm putting you in the naughty timeout corner." Pep walked over to the edge of the kitchen counter. He set his phone down and gave it a mild whack. "You've been a bad boy." He sidled up to Sherry. "I'm ready."

Sherry groaned before resettling her attention on her written list. She tapped into the compartment of her brain crowded with the experiences of competing in recipe contests and cook-offs. "I need to remember, practicing at the last hour has served me well. Things seep into my short-term memory, so tomorrow I'll be able to recall tiny details quickly. You'd be surprised, I'm still learning what works best. If I hadn't made that sauce just now, I wouldn't have learned cream before butter, rather than the other way around, makes for a better blended sauce."

"How do you know when enough is enough?" Pep asked. "Practice, I mean."

Sherry scanned her list of steps needed to execute a winning recipe in two hours. "I wish I knew the right answer. Once, I was in the finals of a cook-off with the theme Cake-Mix Creations."

"Let me guess. Was that when you were in your Cake-Mix-Kitchen-Sink-Cookie phase?"

"Exactly. Sounded like such a fun contest, until I was notified I'd made the finals."

"Nothing wrong with that good news," Pep commented.

"The finals were in Denver. How was I going to practice for high-altitude baking here at sea level?"

"You love challenging cooking conditions. What you don't love is lack of control, but I sense something is different about you. Dare I say you have given up some control in favor of less stress and anxiety?"

"Don't try to overanalyze the situation. I'm working on going with the flow, as they say. But, like the perfect dry-aged steak, good things take time."

"I like what I see. Continue with your Denver story."

"I've competed at an underequipped and undersupplied pro football stadium at halftime in front of a crowd who only wanted more beer and hot dogs, in an outdoor tent with no additional outlets other than the one the single burner unit we were allotted was plugged into, and in the back alley of a television station in the driving rain with no protection from the elements. Denver was the toughest."

"I don't remember how you did."

"Not well. Baking isn't my strength. It's too precise. The cookies were bumpy and uneven. The edges were burnt, and the center was raw. The winner was a Denver native, surprise, surprise. To answer your original question—I was never going to be prepared for that contest, but I vowed to step up my prep for the contests I'm best at. Oh, and I'm staying away from high-altitude contests."

Sherry ran her finger down the paper in front of

her. "As sous chef, your job is to be my equipment and ingredient supplier, workspace tidier-upper, chopper on demand, recipe place checker, timer watcher . . ." Sherry drew in a deep breath before continuing, giving Pep a chance to interject a thought.

"What the heck is your role? There's nothing left after I do everything else. Perhaps testing the merlot for fruitiness?" Pep hummed a note of question.

"If I may continue. I know it sounds like grunt work, but since the cook-off is a two-hour contest, your help will cover a range of tasks. Very important tasks, may I add."

"I'm kidding. I wouldn't have agreed if I didn't feel needed. That, and I haven't seen you and Dad in so long. Killing two birds with one stone."

Sherry stole a look at her brother, and a recurring thought entered her head. She'd never lost hope he would one day move back to Augustin. After college, he became a man consumed by wanderlust, often losing touch with her for months, but the sibling bond had always managed to pick up right where they left off when he reconnected.

"I'd be happier if you weren't gone for such a long span next time, please. Doesn't this time in the kitchen make you yearn for the good old days when you, Marla, and me played Recipe Piggyback? We'd take turns adding a surprise ingredient to a Dutch oven until an interesting casserole was born. Admit it, those were fun times."

"Agreed. The best times were spent with my two sisters. Now, let's keep our eye on the prize and get a move on."

"The contest begins at the stroke of ten, tomorrow morning at the pavilion at Oyster Bed Harbor.

It's over at the stroke of noon. You're in charge of watching the time."

Pep nodded. "Time keeper—check."

"Pretend you heard the opening bell. Team Oliveri is now in go mode. First on the agenda is laying out and measuring all the ingredients for the Savory Shrimp Lettuce Wraps in order of usage." Sherry turned to her brother. He was running his finger down the list of ingredients and acting out putting them side-by-side on the counter.

Pep stopped at one listed ingredient. "Will the shrimp be peeled with tails off?"

"That's a potential problem." Sherry pointed to a line on the recipe printout. "In the recipe I submitted to the contest—the one chosen for the finals—I listed, 'one pound large shrimp, peeled, heads and tails removed' in my ingredients. Right here, though, is the recipe they have in their contest book. Only 'one pound large shrimp' is specified." Sherry waved a flyer in front of Pep's face. "Not much I can do about that now. Are you ready to deal with deveining, peeling, and, possibly, chopping the head off if you have to?"

"No worries. I'm an old hand at shrimp cleaning. It was one of my many jobs over the years."

"Remind me to ask you about that later." Sherry paused for a moment. "Onward we go. If they only provide us with one measuring cup, you'll have to be the wiper-outer before we can measure the rice. That involves paper towels and a trip to the sink, where there's sure to be a line waiting for a turn. Thank goodness we have two hours, right?"

Silence.

Sherry's attention left the recipe and traveled to

Pep. "Pep? Are you with me?" Sherry squeezed her eyes shut for an instant and took a deep breath.

"I've rinsed a measuring cup before. I can do it again."

"You seem preoccupied."

"Nope, I'm with you every step of the way."

They continued on, through each item on her list. After an hour of reenacting the steps of the recipe in double time without any actual ingredients, Team Oliveri was satisfied.

"There's a fine line between being prepared and being overprepared." Sherry folded her information sheets. "Let's quit while we're ahead."

Pep tiptoed over to his phone. "Okay to touch my phone now?" He held his hand hovering over his connection to the outside world.

"All yours. FYI, Dad should be stopping by any minute to say hi. After that, we need to get over to the Augustin Inn for the contestant cocktail hour at six-thirty."

In the next room, Chutney began a barking tirade.

"Speaking of the devil, he must be here." Sherry let the tall, slim man in his early seventies in, accompanied by Ruth Gadabee, who was wearing an unusual wardrobe choice. The sight of the woman, nearing seventy, wearing overalls, came as a bit of a shock. Sherry's gaze lingered on her father's girl-friend's baggy, denim farm fashion.

"Where's my son?" Erno called out. He gave Sherry a passing hug. He continued onto the living room, leaving Ruth at the door.

"Good to see you, too, Dad."

"He's so excited to have Pep home. Too bad it's

not for longer." Ruth tugged at one of the straps that slid off her shoulder. The stauesque woman, whose overalls were missing the mark of full ankle coverage, extended Sherry a broad smile. "You're probably wondering why I'm dressed in these duds."

"Overalls are a left turn from your normal pretty dress, but I'm not one to talk. Sweatpants and T-shirts are my preferred outfits. Overalls could be an upgrade." When she observed Ruth's brow rise, Sherry hoped she hadn't offended her in some way.

"Actually, these'll be my working clothes. Tomorrow, I'm volunteering at the Fall Food Fest. I thought I'd give the outfit a test drive. All the volunteers are required to wear this getup, in honor of the region's farming history. Now that I've been wearing it for the past hour, I have one question. Do farmers ever use the restroom? I mean, it takes the flexibility of a contortionist to get the straps unbuckled, the bib pulled down, and the sides unbuttoned before you can get down to business. If time is of the essence, there could be some accidents."

Sherry surveyed Ruth's overalls from neck to ankle. "I see what you mean."

"I didn't get assigned to the cook-off, but I'll pop in as often as possible to see how you and Pep are doing. I'm so excited it's an Oliveri family affair," Ruth said.

"Hey, Ruth. Get in here and see how handsome my son is," Erno called out from the next room.

Ruth hooked her arm around Sherry's elbow and led her to Erno. "You're pretty, too, dear," Ruth added as they traveled to the living room.

"Pep, this is my dear friend, Ruth Gadabee." Erno untwined Ruth from Sherry's arm. "Ruth, this is the son I was hoping would one day return to Augustin and take over my ruggery store, but I've had no luck so far luring him back. Sherry, maybe you can perform some magic to get Pep to set down an anchor here."

"I'm not doing such a bad job at the store, am I?" Sherry asked. "Why are you trying to replace me?"

"Sweetie, you've only expressed interest in a part-time position all these years. I'm happy to have you a couple days a week. But that's not gonna get the entire job done. Besides, you love your editing work on the town hall newsletter, your cooking takes up so much of your time, and you volunteer at the community garden. You may also inherit a pickle business when Frances Dumont retires. I need a full-time working family member if we're going to keep The Ruggery in the family if, and when, I decide to retire." Erno's voice trailed off toward the end of his thought.

"Do we have to discuss this right now?" Pep extended his hand toward Ruth.

Ruth swatted Pep's hand down in jest before she wrapped her arms around him. "I've heard so much about you and your travels, dear."

"All good, I hope." Pep's words were barely audible, muffled by Ruth's embrace.

"Mostly good, but there's an air of mystery about you. I've heard you're putting your geology studies to use. I've also heard you're self-employed with property investment in some of the places you've traveled to." Ruth dropped an arm to her side, hiking up a fallen strap with her other hand as she did so. "How people wear these things on a daily basis has me baffled."

Sherry giggled. "The people that do probably wonder how you can be comfortable in a dress every day."

"Touché," laughed Ruth.

"Let's have lemonade on the porch before we have to say good night. Pep and I have to be cleaned and polished for our contestant cocktail hour by six."

Sherry led the way to the kitchen, where she loaded a tray with her always-on-hand pitcher of lemonade. She gathered some glasses to complete the tray.

"I'll be there in a minute." Pep exited the room, staring at his buzzing phone.

"I'm really worried about Pep being able to focus on his duties as sous chef tomorrow. All he does is study that blasted phone. I need him to be dialed in for one hundred and twenty minutes with no interruptions." Sherry sighed.

"He's a bright boy. He can multitask." Erno poured himself a drink and lifted the glass in the air. "Here's to a cook-off victory for my two favorite contestants."

Ruth lifted an empty glass. "I second that."

"I hope you're both right," Sherry added.

"As I always say, even with eight eyes and eight legs, a spider still needs to spin a web to catch his dinner." Erno pursed his lips.

"If you always say that, why have I never heard that little maxim?" Pep let out a hardy laugh as he walked into the room. "And what does it mean, anyway?"

Ruth cleared her throat. "Your father's words of

wisdom are subtle in their meaning. I believe he's saying things get done, even though they don't always happen with the most obvious tools available."

"Ruth, have you heard from Frances?" Sherry asked. "How's she liking the cruise?"

Ruth frowned. "I got an email from her, but I haven't opened it. I'm afraid she's telling me she'll never return."

"Ruth, bite your tongue," Erno scolded. "She likes her family. She loves us. After two weeks confined to a cruise ship with her kids and grandkids, she'll love and appreciate us even more."

"Best friends, confidantes, partners in crime," Sherry added. "Frances, Ruth, and Erno. Without the wit and wisdom you three pass on, life would be very dull."

"I feel out of sorts when Frances is gone." Ruth's lower lip jutted forward.

Erno gave her a hug.

"She deserves a vacation, if you can call it that. Now that she's taken her Dumont pickle business back full-time, she's had to work hard all summer season. I'm ready to take over when she retires for a second time, but I'm not holding my breath," laughed Sherry.

"See? You'd make time for selling pickles again, even with your packed schedule. All the more reason Pep is the man for The Ruggery job," Erno said.

After some quality time spent talking about the hooked-rug business, Chutney's new relationship with the cat adopted by Sherry's ever-inquisitive neighbor, Eileen, and Ruth's expectations for the

Fall Food Fest, it was time to dress for the cook-off cocktail party. The visitors made their way to the front door.

On his way out, Erno paused. "I'm assuming you won't be in the store tomorrow afternoon?"

Sherry scooped up Chutney before the Jack Russell could scamper out the open door. "I will. And Pep said he'd love to come along, since he'll be riding a wave of post cook-off energy." Sherry peeked behind her to check her brother's expression. "The look on his face confirms his enthusiasm."

"I have no recollection of saying that. Why rest, when my family can run me ragged? And remind me why I thought this visit would in any way be relaxing?" Pep asked.

Chapter 3

"You know the last time I was inside the Augustin Inn?" Sherry asked.

"For me, it was your wedding reception." Pep threaded the leather belt through the last of his pants belt loops. "Speaking of weddings, thanks for scavenging Charlie's belt from the back of the closet. Haven't had to wear one in forever."

"You're quite welcome," Sherry sang out. "Did you know the Augustin Inn wasn't our first choice of venues?" She buttoned the lower half of her black cashmere cardigan. "Charlie was adamant about being close to the beach. Unfortunately, a nor'easter a month prior took out every potential venue within a twenty-mile radius of Augustin. When you get a location stuck in your head, it seems like nothing else will do."

"Maybe that was a sign of things to come. An omen you and Charlie weren't meant to be."

"Actually, I think we had a stroke of good luck when Clarence Constable, the owner of the inn at the time, heard of our situation and offered up his place.

Not on the beach, but we were certainly beggars who couldn't be choosy at that point."

"His daughter is the owner now, right? What's her name?"

"Ginger Constable. She never married, I believe."

"Wasn't there talk of the inn being haunted?" Pep asked.

"The barn behind the inn is supposedly haunted by the ghost of a man who arrived at the inn on horseback over a hundred years ago. While he was putting his horse in the barn for the night, he was trampled when something spooked the animal. That's the local lore." Sherry checked her face in the front hall mirror.

"Didn't a guest have an accident during your reception? Was it a run-in with the ghost?"

"All a misunderstanding. One of Charlie's cousins claimed he heard screams from the barn, ran inside, tripped, and broke his arm. The hospital tested his blood-alcohol level, and, sure enough, it was sky high. Only ghost he saw was most likely a figment of his pickled imagination."

Pep took a step closer to the mirror. Sherry saw his reflection peer around her head. He stuck out his tongue.

"I know you don't want to come tonight, so thanks for making an appearance."

"It's fine. I'm going to take my own car, though. I need to run a quick errand. Plus, everyone wants a piece of Sherry Oliveri. You'll be required to hang out longer than I'm willing to. I need a getaway car."

"See you soon, boy." Sherry gave Chutney a farewell cuddle. "I won't be late. Hopefully just an hour, two tops." She set the dog down on the couch by the bay window, where he curled up and closed his eyes, then she plucked off the white fur that had transferred to her black sweater.

"I don't think he can measure time," Pep suggested.

"Nonsense, of course he can." Sherry picked up her car keys and opened the front door.

Pep scooted through the doorway. "I'll see you there."

The short drive to the Augustin Inn provided Sherry just enough time to let the nerves creep in. *Why does Pep have to take his own car to the party? Why doesn't he suggest we do his "errand" together? If he decides to go out afterward, he may be too tired to be of use to me at the cook-off. Maybe he's not even coming to the party.*

Sherry's concerns vanished when she parked the car. She spotted Pep's car a few spots away. "That's a good sign," she whispered. "Must have decided against running his errand."

The brick path leading to the whitewashed colonial building was worn and moss covered. Sherry's canvas wedge shoes wobbled with each step, and she began to question her shoe choice. A sprained ankle would make maneuvering the cook-off platform difficult. She slowed her pace to a near crawl, taking care to set her foot on a level brick with each step.

"Passing on the right," a couple called out as they strolled past Sherry at a fast clip.

Sherry began a reply, but the words fell flat as the couple strode out of earshot. Sherry followed the signs to the reception, which took her past the stately columns framing the entrance. She navigated around to the side of the inn. She stepped up to the covered porch and took her place in line, waiting for what, she wasn't sure. As soon as she stopped walking, the breeze chilled any exposed skin. She regretted not choosing to wear heavier protection from the cooling autumn temperatures.

"Name tags are on the table if you're a contestant," a voice on the porch directed.

Half the people reassembled themselves to form another line in front of a long table.

"You have to be Sherry Oliveri," a broadly built man with a mustache and short beard suggested. "I saw you at the back of the line and grabbed your tag for you. You're just as pretty as you were when we competed against each other at the Iron Skillet Cook-off in Nashville."

Sherry gave a subtle glance at the name tag the man had attached to his blazer. With his fingers obscuring half the name, she was left guessing.

"I'm sorry. Can you remind me of your name?"

"I guess you block out the names of the cooks you've lost to," he laughed.

Sherry studied the man's face. "Fitz Frye? I didn't recognize you with all that facial hair."

"And a few extra pounds." Fitz patted his belly. "What do you expect? It's been five years." His gaze scanned Sherry from head to toe. "You're putting us all to shame—how wonderful you look. Life is treating you right. I should have retired when I beat you. Guess I'm a glutton for punishment. I feared you'd be competing tomorrow, but I showed up anyway."

"You're too kind." Sherry's gaze dropped to the floor. "Thanks for retrieving my name tag. Guess I don't have to be in this line anymore." Sherry stepped to the side of the line. As she did, the man behind her advanced to the spot she left vacant.

"Nice to see you, Sherry," the man said.

"Uh . . . hi again. Don, right?" Sherry adjusted her sweater to let cooler air hit her suddenly heated neck. "Is Day with you?"

"She's on her way. She made a pit stop in the ladies' room."

A waitress carrying a tray of wineglasses offered a beverage.

"Thank you." Don accepted a glass.

Sherry held up her hand. "I'll wait until I get inside, thanks."

"See you later." Fitz backed away from Sherry. He tossed out a wave and turned on his heels toward the side entrance.

"I didn't get a chance to meet him. Fitz Frye, right? There certainly is some stiff competition. I hope Day's up to it." Don rotated toward Sherry as the next contestant in line reached across the table, knocking him off balance. He bumped Sherry's forearm, jarring his wineglass and spilling its contents. "I'm sorry. You okay?"

"My fault. I'm in the way." Sherry glanced at her wine-soaked sweater sleeve.

Don offered assistance with a cocktail napkin. "I shouldn't have accepted a drink from the waitress before I faced the crowd here. You were smart to wait." Don dabbed at the spill until it looked acceptable.

"Thank you." Sherry took a look around the porch. "Have you seen my brother? The guy with me at the wine store?"

"I haven't. If his name tag is gone, he's most likely stepped inside."

Sherry scanned the table and saw no name tag for Pep Oliveri. "Inside is my next stop. I'll follow you."

The inn boasted a large meeting room adorned with dark wood paneling and wide-plank pine floors so worn in spots, the wood was littered with dips and valleys. Seeing it would be impossible to easily cross the crowded room, Sherry pulled out her phone and texted Pep to meet her by the appetizer table. That seemed the most accessible location. When she lifted her gaze from the phone, Don was gone.

"Sherry Oliveri?"

Sherry jerked her head in the direction of the question. A woman's smile beamed Sherry's way. As she approached, the ashy blond topknot of hair on her head bobbed with each spirited step. The name tag secured to her lapel was embellished with hand-drawn multicolored stars, easily spotted from a distance.

"I'm Ginger Constable." The woman extended her hand. "I'm not sure if you remember me from your wedding reception. I was the bartender slash waitress slash cleanup crew for my father in those days. Probably didn't see much of me. I ran around like a chicken with my head cut off at the inn's special events. Still do. Welcome."

"So nice to see you again. You're the manager now, if I'm not mistaken." Sherry watched person after person pass Ginger and either pat her back or wave a hello.

"Owner-manager's my job title. Basically, I do the same jobs I've always done. When Dad did all those tasks, he made it look a lot more glamorous than it really is. But I love my job," she added in haste, drawing up the corners of her mouth.

"My brother, Pep, is supposed to meet me over by the food. I wonder if you've talked to him?"

Before Ginger had time to respond, an imposing figure of a man, with what Sherry imagined was a very expensive haircut and wearing what looked to be a very expensive suit, settled himself next to Ginger. A rosy blush danced across Ginger's face, giving her sparsely applied makeup more radiance. If there were a photo to go along with the definition of the word "dashing" in the dictionary, it would be a portrait of the man next to Ginger.

"Uri, I'd like you to meet Sherry Oliveri. As you probably know, she's a contestant in the cook-off, and, you didn't hear it from me, but my money's on her. Sherry is Augustin's celebrity chef, and we're lucky to have her call this seaside stomping ground home." Ginger guided Uri forward until he was within arm's length of Sherry.

Uri picked up Sherry's hand and clasped it in his. "Uri Veshlage, president of Maine Course Foods." He pumped her hand. "So nice to meet you."

The warmth and power of his grip weakened her knees. She shifted to a more solid stance. Uri stared into Sherry's eyes.

"Maine Course, and our Shrimply Amazing Division, are proud to sponsor this year's cook-off. Our goal is to supply the contest with the finest ingredients and, after that, may the best home cook win."

Uri gently lowered Sherry's hand to her side. He picked up Ginger's and lifted it to his lips. "I must continue to welcome contestants, judges, and sponsors. So, for now, I say good evening, ladies." He bowed and backed away until he blended into the enlarging crowd of partygoers.

"Uri is as smooth as butter and just as delicious." Ginger giggled.

"He seems very nice. By any chance, have you seen my brother?" Sherry asked again. "I was hoping he and I could make the rounds together."

Ginger blinked away the glazed look in her eyes. "Yes, as a matter of fact I have. He's quite a tall specimen of a man himself. Hasn't changed hardly a bit since your wedding, except for the better."

"That's not what I mean. I mean, do you know where he might be? I need to find him so we can mix and mingle with the guests here, as a team."

"A few minutes ago, I saw him with the contestant Fitz Frye, my brother, and one of Uri's employees, Roe. Back by the food table. It's getting so crowded you can't even see the table from here. I'd imagine they couldn't have gone too far in this tight space."

Sherry peered into the mass of men and women milling about. "Thanks. I'll head over that way. And thanks for hosting tonight."

Sherry spotted her brother. Pep was leaning on the appetizer table with one hand. As she moved closer, she observed his inflated cheeks. His free hand wagged an index finger in front of Fitz Frye's nose. Addison Constable and another man seemed caught up in the conversation, too. As she neared, Sherry heard Pep's serious tone. When Pep caught sight of her, he removed his hand from the table, stood tall, and stopped talking. Beside him, Fitz and the unfamiliar man held an unwavering stare toward one another. Addison's head swiveled between the group.

"Hey, Sherry, you found us." The edge to Pep's voice made the hair on Sherry's forearm spring up. "Do you remember Addison Constable? Fitz is a fellow cook. He said he saw you at the check-in table. And this is Roe Trembley."

"Hi, everyone. I hope I wasn't interrupting. Nice to meet you, Roe." Sherry reached across Pep and helped herself to a smoked salmon toast. The caper garnish took flight when her hand bumped into Addison's, who was also helping himself to an appetizer.

"Let me get that for you." Roe's lengthy bangs floated across his eyes as he dipped to the floor in search of the runaway appetizer. "On second thought, let me get you a fresh one." He reached behind Sherry with arms equipped with such pronounced muscles, they were visible through his tight cotton shirt. Roe plucked a salmon toast off a tray. He handed the appetizer to Sherry with a grin that revealed a chipped front tooth.

Sherry's line of sight stalled on the injured tooth, until Roe pinched his lips together. She turned her attention to the man in the flannel shirt. "Addison. Long time no see." She remembered Addison as a wiry young man. Seems he'd bulked up over the years.

"Thanks for coming, Sherry. I'm a big fan," Addison replied.

"I'm so excited to be here. And we meet again, Fitz," Sherry added. "Pep, we need to keep an eye on

Fitz. He's our toughest competitor in the Hands-On Foods category."

"That's not the only reason we should keep our eye on him," Pep muttered.

"You're not going to keep this up, are you?" Fitz huffed a breath. "Excuse me, I need to find someone." He turned his back and disappeared into the crowd.

"Everything okay?" Sherry examined her brother. "Fitz didn't seem thrilled with your conversation. Have you two met before?"

"We've met in passing." Pep's curt reply stalled Sherry's inquiry.

Addison and Roe exchanged glances and began a private conversation.

"I wonder who his sous chef is for the cook-off. He doesn't have to have one necessarily, but a helping hand is invaluable if the rules allow," Sherry said.

Pep shrugged his shoulders. "No idea."

Addison and Roe separated to include Sherry and Pep in their huddle.

"Sherry, Addison and I are here on behalf of Shrimply Amazing Seafood, which is owned by Maine Course Foods. We're experts in sustainable fishing practices. I've been a fisherman my whole life, and I enjoy sharing my knowledge with customers. Do you have any questions about the salmon you're about to eat?" Roe asked.

"I do. Where does this salmon come from?" Pep watched Sherry take a bite.

"I'm guessing Alaska?" Roe responded with a question rather than an answer.

"Shouldn't you know that?" Pep widened his eyes.

Addison puffed out his chest. "What he meant to say was, while wild Atlantic salmon is under conservation restrictions, we supply the freshest aquaculture salmon. Grown and harvested under pristine conditions on farms off the coast of Maine."

Sherry's gaze shifted from Addison to Roe, who popped an entire salmon toast into his mouth.

"Pep, I think you're coming on a bit strong," Sherry whispered.

Chapter
4

"I'm back to make sure you're learning about my company's practices from these fine gentlemen." Uri leveraged himself into the circle. "Sherry, if your recipe uses any seafood, it'll be supplied by our Shrimply Amazing Division."

"Yes. I do use shrimp," Sherry said.

"Shrimply Amazing supplies only the finest, locally sourced, whenever possible. Right, guys?" Uri looked at Roe.

Roe nodded with vigor. Addison held a rigid stance.

"Addison may not be agreeing," Pep inserted.

"New England shrimp is making a comeback, but most shrimp, at the moment, is from the Gulf of Mexico. And they're beauties, right?" Uri added in haste. "Our fish is so local it roots for the Red Sox."

"Local is relative, I guess. You guys should get your story straight." Pep crossed his arms in front of his chest.

"Roe and Addison, if you both wouldn't mind, I'd like to introduce you to a journalist covering the cook-off. Ms. Mellitt is over by the ice sculpture waiting for us. That is, unless you need more time with these fine cooks?"

"We're good," Pep said.

Sherry nodded her head in agreement. She watched the men leave the food table. They parked themselves next to Patti Mellitt and a giant ice sculpture of a bowl filled with what, from her vantage point, appeared to be various forms of sea life.

"Have you said hello to anyone else in our Hands-On Foods category?" Pep asked.

"It's tough to tell who's in what category unless you get so close to the name tags, you're getting into personal space," Sherry laughed. "These icons indicating the categories are practically microscopic." She pointed to the tiny picture of a hand holding a wrap sandwich in the corner of her name tag. "See what I mean?"

Pep squinted and studied Sherry's name tag. "Barely. Maybe I need glasses. Not getting any younger."

Out of the corner of her eye, Sherry spotted Don Johnstone closing in.

"Care for the glass of wine it appears you never got?" He was double fisted with two wineglasses. He handed one to Sherry. "Sorry, old man, I don't have a third."

"I'll help myself. See you in a minute." Pep skirted around a petite woman who was making her way toward Sherry.

"Sherry? Is that you?" The woman shrieked with a voice squeezed from the depths of her being. Her glossy brown hair danced across her shoulders as she closed in on Sherry. "I was hoping I'd see you here. I follow your cook-off successes in the paper."

Sherry made eye contact with the excited woman. "Kelly Shanahan, it's been forever." Sherry glanced at Don. He seemed fixated on Kelly. "Don, Kelly was a classmate of mine from Augustin High School. I don't think we've seen each other since graduation. Amazing how easy it is to lose touch." Sherry turned her attention to Kelly. "Do you still live nearby?"

"I loved growing up in Augustin. Southern coastal Connecticut was a kid's paradise but way too sleepy for me as an adult. I live in New York City."

Sherry cocked her head to the side. "Are you in the cook-off?"

Kelly generated a belly laugh that jostled her hair-band loose. "I could never do what you do. Probably why we didn't spend much time together in school. You were so domestic, and I was, well, I was . . ."

"Uninhibited?" Sherry suggested.

Don coughed. His wine splashed over the rim of his glass.

"I prefer explorative," Kelly responded. "The thought of me cooking under pressure makes me ill. If I didn't have my boyfriend, I'd die of starvation or go broke from ordering out. I don't know how you do it. Let alone, how you win so often. I'll just stick to rooting for my honey."

"Your boyfriend is in the cook-off? Do you know what category?" Sherry asked.

"Hands-On is the category. Recipes that don't re-quire a fork, knife, or spoon to eat. Like a sandwich," Kelly explained. "He's making the most delicious recipe. He's practiced it a million times, and I'm still not sick of it."

"By any chance, is your boyfriend Fitz Frye?" Sherry asked.

"That's right. You know each other. I forgot all about that."

Sherry studied her former classmate, who she didn't necessarily believe had no memory of Sherry and Fitz knowing one another. The thought of the stubby man, with eyes like dark marbles, matched up with Kelly, gave Sherry pause. Sherry's memory of Kelly involved her being a hardcore cheerleader in the perkiest sense. She was popular with the elite athletes and rewarded their interest by adorning herself with layers of makeup and skimpy outfits. She dated the quarterback of the football team and the basketball team captain, and there were even rumors of a teacher liaison. Fitz didn't fit her dating profile, but the possibility that Kelly had exhausted the state's supply of overachieving jocks and was forced to fish in unexplored dating waters, was a real one.

"We've cooked off against each other in the past," Sherry added.

"Come to think of it, Fitz mentioned he'd beaten you in a previous cook-off. From what I've heard and read, that's not easy to do. But, you're probably not even in the same category tomorrow." Kelly unleashed a toothy grin.

"We are," Sherry responded in a near whisper.

"Well, his shrimp wraps are in for a tough battle," Kelly chuckled.

"Shrimp wraps," Sherry repeated. The words tasted like week-old fish. "Of course, Fitz is my toughest competitor. I always read his published recipes because he's so creative. He's taught me a lot." She raised her head and peered behind Kelly.

"Just don't steal his ideas." Kelly winked.

"Sherry, is this woman bothering you?" Fitz laughed as he wrapped his arms around Kelly from behind. The man's arms easily enveloped her tiny stature. "She may be a petite morsel, but she's loaded with flavor. Right, sweetheart?" He gave Kelly a kiss on the cheek.

"Fitzy, you didn't tell me Sherry was such a gracious competitor." Kelly winked at Sherry. "Let's face it. In high school I had other things on my mind, so I didn't give the bookworms, I mean the studious group, much consideration. From what Fitzy's been telling me about your success in cook-offs, I was picturing a ruthless villainess willing to stop at nothing to win."

Sherry shot a gaze at Fitz. Don coughed again and went in for another sip of wine.

"Hardly," Sherry laughed. "The minute I get that obsessed about my cooking, it's time to throw in the competition apron. Don't get me wrong, I love to win, but not at all costs."

"Fitz Frye?' A man with a kind face, in a plaid vest and rolled-up sleeves, tapped Fitz on the shoulder.

Don whispered in Sherry's ear. "Boy, it's hard to finish a conversation tonight. I'm dying to hear more about these two."

Sherry leaned away from Don to get a better look at the vested man.

"Yes. Do I know you? I don't see any category on your name tag." Fitz squinted. "Lyman St. Pierre. You must not be a cook."

"I'm a spice representative. I'd like you to read about my products." Lyman reached around to his backside. He presented a brown business envelope from his pants pocket. He slid papers from the open envelope. "Our company has selected you as someone who could benefit from what we offer."

Lyman stepped between Sherry and Fitz. She could no longer see Fitz's face, but the tone of his voice soured.

"Not interested." Fitz put his arm around Kelly.

"Shouldn't you take the information from the nice man?" Kelly questioned. "He said you were hand selected. That's quite an honor."

"I'll take a look," Sherry offered.

Lyman ignored Sherry. Her ready hand was left hanging in midair.

Don shifted closer to Sherry. "He must not have heard you."

"Or I didn't qualify," she added.

When Sherry returned her attention to Fitz, she saw the envelope and folded papers being held to Fitz's chest, at arm's length, by Lyman. Fitz snatched the papers, backed up abruptly, and bumped into a woman behind him. The papers scattered across the floor. He lowered himself to his hands and knees to collect the mess.

When he was done, Fitz picked himself up off the floor and took off.

"Fitz!" Kelly called after him. She was left to apologize in his absence. When she was done, she traced his footsteps into the crowd.

Don dipped down to collect the last paper and the envelope. He waved them at Fitz who never turned back. "This one's blank." Don displayed a white sheet of paper.

"Just chuck it, thanks." Lyman fanned his fingers in the air. He walked away.

The single speaker mounted on the wall behind the ice sculpture crackled to life. "Ladies and gentlemen. May I have your attention, please? If you would, direct your attention over here by the exit sign."

The din inside the room faded, and bodies rotated toward the double French doors leading to the porch. Ginger stepped up onto a small podium. "I hope I've met most of you. If not, my name is Ginger Constable. I own and manage this historic building. Welcome."

Applause erupted throughout the room.

"My brother, Addison, and I . . . now, where is he . . . would like to welcome everyone associated with the New England Fall Fest Cook-off. Hopefully you can all see the gorgeous cook-off apron I'm wearing. Contestants, you will all be receiving yours tomorrow at the event." Ginger showcased her red apron with a giant spatula embroidered on it.

Someone in the crowd catcalled.

"I should wear this more often," Ginger remarked with a shy smile. "Thank you to the sponsors for providing me with an apron. All four categories are represented tonight, and we look forward to sampling the fantastic recipes tomorrow. All four judges are present, but, in the name of fairness and honesty, we haven't made their identities public."

"Is that the usual procedure—keeping the judges' identities from the contestants?" Don asked.

"Not really," Sherry answered. "More often, the judges are featured. Guess the organizers thought this would be a fun twist. Hope everyone behaves, since the judges could be anyone in here."

Ginger waved her arms over her head. "Addison, would you raise your hand so I can locate you?"

Sherry scanned the crowd but saw no hand raised. A low murmur swelled but was quickly drowned out by what sounded like a thunderous argument to Sherry's left. Sherry's eyes widened. She realized one of the participating voices was a familiar one. She could make out four words delivered with venom. "Sponsor stays, I walk." Another voice dripping with desperation cut in, and soon silence followed. A moment later, two men entered the reception room, faces lowered, chests heaving.

"Gentlemen. I hope everything is okay?" Ginger's question was amplified throughout the room.

Fitz and Pep lifted their heads, exchanged glances, and presented the room with painful smiles.

"What in the world was that all about?" Day asked as she approached Sherry and Don.

"If I only knew . . ." Sherry's voice faded away as the words struggled to emerge. She took a look at her brother, who had arrived at her side.

Ginger cleared her throat. Heads turned in her direction.

"My brother has the perfect antidote for any contestants who may be letting the anticipation of a kitchen battle for the ages get the better of them." Ginger held her gaze on Fitz. "If you'd all direct your attention to the doors leading to the porch, Addison is overseeing a giveaway featuring coupons from our spectacular sponsor, Maine Course Foods, and jams and jellies from Sweet Art Brands, and I've just been

advised samples of spice packets from Spice Attitude
will be included. Glorious!"

Sherry swiveled her head toward the other side of
the room but was only able to see a hand wave over
the heads of the crowd migrating to the porch.

The hubbub in the room increased until Ginger
spoke. "Have a good evening, everyone, and I'll see
you bright and early in the morning over at the
Oyster Bed Harbor Pavilion."

Sherry pulled her phone from her linen pants
pocket. "I think it's time to head home. Day and
Don, we'll see you bright and early." She looked
around the room for a place to set down her empty
wineglass. "Pep, you set? I'm going to run this glass
over there, then grab a parting gift." She pointed to
the large table behind the ice sculpture.

Pep was scrolling through his phone and didn't
lift his head to acknowledge her.

"You have your own car anyway, so I'll see you at
home." Sherry paused before leaving Pep's side.
"Are you coming home now?"

Pep heaved an exhale. "Yep."

On her way out of the reception room, Sherry
encountered Uri speaking with Roe and Addison.
She slowed her pace in hopes of a break in their
conversation. When it didn't come, she poked her
head into their huddle. "I wanted to say have a good
evening, and it was nice seeing you all."

Uri beamed a smile, while the other two men
looked as if they had bitten into a moldy lemon. "We
feel the same way, right, guys?"

Sherry didn't wait for their responses. She tossed
a wave their way and continued onto the porch. A
few steps away, a woman parked by the wall reading

a notebook caught Sherry's attention. "Patti. I was hoping I'd see you here. I'm on my way out. Will I see you tomorrow?"

Patti was holding a paper bag decorated with images of seagulls and seashells. "You couldn't stop me from attending." Patti winked. "Especially since I'm getting paid to cover it for the paper." She held up her bag. "Nice goodies. The spice addition is a bit weak, unfortunately. I had high hopes for some interesting flavors. Looks like someone ran to the bulk spice bins at the grocery store and filled Ziploc bags with whatever they could find. The labels are incorrect, too." She reached inside her gift bag and pulled out a tiny baggie. "This is labeled cinnamon but is most definitely nutmeg."

"I wonder if this man I met, Lyman St. Pierre I think his name was, had anything to do with that. Come to think of it, he was one of many here tonight I wonder about."

Chapter
5

"So convenient. The Oyster Bed Harbor Pavilion is only a few towns east of Augustin." On the drive to the cook-off, Sherry's thoughts drifted to the time she'd spent surveying the venue's sitemap online. "I checked out their website to get a feel for potential cook-off layouts."

Pep kept his attention out the windshield. "How does it look? How much room will we have to work?"

"I didn't get a good sense. The photos of the pavilion were from last year. The area had the remnants of a hurricane come through after the pictures were taken, and I know they had to rebuild the structure. I had every intention of driving over there. Never got around to it."

"We're going in blind." Pep put his hands over his eyes.

"No matter what, there won't be much excess room to maneuver. That's par for the course in any outdoor, or even indoor, cooking contest. Add the sous chefs to the mix and we've got ourselves culinary gridlock."

"Now you're making me nervous. I'm kidding. I'm not worried one bit."

Sherry was glad they arrived early enough to find a parking spot within reasonable walking distance to the event. "We have two hours to prepare my Savory Shrimp Lettuce Wraps with Balsamic Merlot Reduction." Sherry turned the car off and faced her brother. "That's a luxury. Usually, it's sixty minutes or less."

"There you go. That's the spirit." Pep unbuckled his seat belt. "You're a master at this."

"Not always," laughed Sherry.

She opened the car's liftback, and, together, they gathered up her supply bags. They headed out of the parking lot toward the boardwalk.

"Once I was in a sixty-minute cook-off and had technical issues with the oven. Plus, the food processor was wonky, and I was supplied with gritty spinach instead of prewashed. Managing all those problems, the time drained away faster than I could believe. The result was undercooked chicken roll-ups and no spot on the awards podium. From that contest on, my motto became 'less is more' when it came to the recipes I considered for contests."

"I repeat, I'm not worried."

"You're going to have to run back to the car and grab my sunglasses after we check in," Sherry said. "This autumn sun is at such an extreme angle, I think it's going to be a factor the whole morning."

"I'm here to serve. Be thankful it's not pouring rain or thunderstorming. Thank you, Mother Nature."

Sherry scanned the beach in front of the pavilion. "Look at all the people claiming a good viewing spot."

"I hope the contest organizers know when high tide is. Half the depth of the beach will be gone by then," Pep laughed. "Won't bother us, but half the audience will be set adrift."

Pep helped Sherry carry the items she was allowed to bring from her kitchen, which included her favorite knives, preferred sauté pan, a large platter, and theme-appropriate serving plates— one for each of the four judges. They walked up the gray boardwalk that led them to the pavilion entrance.

"We have to check in and pick up our identification," Sherry advised.

While waiting in line to pick up her contest credentials, Sherry observed a woman collect a badge indicating she was competing in the Just Desserts category.

"I drove up from North Carolina in one shot, and I'm a bit sleep deprived," the woman told the contest official.

The man in front of Sherry chose his ID badge from the column of tags labeled Edgy Veggies. When Sherry's turn arrived, she noticed her category, Hands-On Foods—No Utensils Required, had the most IDs yet to be claimed.

"Hi. I'm Sherry Oliveri, and he's Pep Oliveri." Sherry set her load on the table decorated with a red-and-white plaid tablecloth. She scanned the four columns of laminated name tags on lanyards.

"Nice to put faces to names," a plump woman, not much taller than the table, chirped. She smiled. "My name is Sophie Jefferson. You've surely seen my name on the emails the contest has been sending out, advising you on all the ins and outs and whatnots leading up to today."

"Of course. So nice to meet you," Sherry said.

Pep's hand jutted out and enveloped Sophie's hand in a robust shake.

"Oh, my goodness, you're strong." Sophie swayed slightly. A Southern twang was discernible as she pronounced strong as if it were a two-syllable word. *Ster-wrong.* "You Northerners are certainly a hardy bunch. Have to be, with the nasty winters I've heard you get up here. The last two contestants I met were from Minnesota and Vermont. I can't even begin to imagine what their winters are like. A sun worshipper like myself would never survive. I only made the trek up north to attend the Fall Fest before the cold weather sets in. Figured I'd volunteer while I'm at it." She checked out her clothing. "Didn't realize I'd have to wear these dang overalls."

"You look nice," Sherry fibbed. Truth was, the ill-fitting overalls were swallowing the woman whole.

"White lies don't suit you, sweetie," Sophie cackled. "By the way, you're in the category with the extra contestant. Last minute addition, or so I'm told."

"Huh," was all Sherry could counter with.

Sophie reached under the table, an act that didn't involve much bending for her because her short stature held her so low to the ground. "Please enjoy these gifts on behalf of the New England travel bureau. Your contest aprons are in the bags, as well." She placed two tote bags next to Sherry's supplies and pointed to her right. "Just follow the boardwalk in that direction and you'll find stove number nine. Good luck."

Sherry and Pep picked up their supplies and headed to the pavilion. Once under the sun canopy, Sherry searched for her designated prep area. She was wary of her footing as she made her way past the first eight workstations. The stoves were set up side by side, powered by a strip of wiring that ran across the pavilion floor. When she reached her station, Sherry went about laying out her utensils and cookware in order of usage. Pep was silent as he watched.

Nearing the end of her organization exercise, Sherry checked the digital clock that rested on a table in front of the audience. "We have thirty minutes until cooking begins." She turned to Pep. "Would you mind grabbing my sunglasses from the car? I'm going to pick up our food from the cooler. We're allowed to organize everything but no prep work until the starting bell. There's not much else to do for now."

"I'll meet you back here in a few." Pep tied on his red contestant apron. "Fits like a glove." He twirled once, fashion-model style, and trotted away.

"Hey, Sherry, over here, on the boardwalk."

Sherry blinked the sun glare from her vision as she peered across her stove to locate the voice beckoning her. When she recognized who it was, Sherry waved with vigor to her friend and coworker. "Amber. Thanks for coming. You've got a prime viewing location. Lucky you."

"It's not exactly my spot."

The couple next to her, with the no-nonsense stances and serious expressions, implied the two feet of sand was merely on loan.

"This nice couple said if I could get you to say hi to them, they'd let me stand here for a minute."

Sherry lifted an eyebrow. "Sure." She smiled at the couple. "Hi, I'm Sherry Oliveri. Thanks for coming to watch."

"Herb, she remembers us from the plane ride we took home together with her after the Taste of America Cook-off." The woman pumped her fists overhead. "Good luck, Sherry," she bellowed.

Herb raised two thumbs in agreement.

"I do remember you both. Thank you, and thanks for coming." Sherry turned her attention back to Amber. "Pep's somewhere in the area. Have you seen him?"

"I just passed him on the way to your car. I wished him good luck and told him I'd see you both after the cook-off. Good luck. I'll be watching." Amber tossed Sherry a salute and surrendered her coveted spot back to its rightful owners.

On her way to retrieve her cooking supplies from her designated cooler, Sherry took note of some of the other contestants. Heidi Keimer, from the Pennsylvania Dutch region, was a remarkable home cook with a talent for anything potato. Sherry had tasted her gnocchi, latkes, and croquettes at the National Spud Recipe Championships and had fallen in love with each recipe. The woman was even built like a potato, oval and thick in the middle, with a beige, sun-kissed hue to her skin. As Sherry passed Heidi's prep area, she wasn't surprised to see an abundance of red potatoes on her cutting board.

"Good morning, Sherry." A man with a New York Yankees baseball cap tipped his head toward Sherry as he unloaded a basket of utensils. "Go easy on me. I've been absent from cook-offs for a while."

"Bernie," Sherry said, "you could create a five-star meal in your sleep. You're the one who should go easy on the rest of us."

"Nice of you to say, but hands-on foods aren't

really my thing. I mean, who really likes to eat with their hands after the age of five? I entered this category thinking it would have the least entries. Just my luck, it's the category with the most finalists." Bernie's hat toppled off his head as he enjoyed a robust belly laugh. "Good luck."

Next to Bernie sat an empty workstation. No food, no utensils, no sign of a contestant having staked out a territory. "Time's a ticking. That person better get a move on," Sherry whispered to no one in particular.

Sherry arrived at the contestant coolers and was surprised and pleased that there was no line. "Two bags of groceries, Ms. Oliveri. Everything you listed on your recipe should be inside. Please eyeball the contents so I can mark you off on my list as complete." A young man checked off a box on a clipboard as he handed Sherry her supplies. Under his watchful eye, Sherry rummaged through the bags while visualizing her recipe ingredient list.

"Looks good." She glanced at the clock. A rush of adrenaline surged through her core. Her hands trembled, ever so slightly, as she recognized the cook-off was moments away from start time.

On the return trip to her station, she caught up with Pep. "Is that mustard on your lip?" She pointed to a glob of the thick yellow condiment above his mouth. "Where did you get that?"

"I figured we wouldn't have time to eat for the next two hours, so I grabbed a hot pretzel with some dipping mustard at the concession stand. I haven't eaten since breakfast."

"Let's get this stuff sorted out." Sherry sucked in

a deep breath and held it for the count of seven. "Focus," she mumbled.

"Five minutes, cooks. The contest begins in five minutes," a voice announced.

"Here we go." Sherry's words tripped over each other. She paused midthought and caught her breath. "You ready?"

"Not sure how many times I can tell you I am, but I'll do it again. Yes, I'm ready." Pep put his hand on Sherry's and squeezed. "We've got this."

One glance out to the audience and Sherry was swamped with another adrenaline rush. The gathered audience, Sherry estimated as twenty rows deep, delivered cheers and applause. Sherry tied her contest apron around her waist and wiped her palms down the sides, leaving a perspiration streak on the red fabric. She unfolded her recipe printout and propped it up against the edge of her sauté pan.

"Don't you know the recipe by heart at this stage?" Pep threw his hands in the air. "Should I be nervous?" He winked at his sister.

"Doesn't hurt to take a peek when my mind goes blank. And that always happens about halfway through the contest for me. My mind starts to wander, so I need to reel it in. I've seen contestants go into panic mode even after tons of practice. I'm taking no chances."

"Five, four, three, two, one. Time to cook," proclaimed a contest official.

"Let's kill it," Pep called out.

Chapter
6

"Watch the cables and wires," Pep advised. "I'll wait here. Good luck."

Sherry stepped cautiously as she carried her tray of plated lettuce wraps to the judges' table. Name cards revealed the four judges were nationally recognized chefs from California, New York, Texas, and Illinois. With essentially all four corners of the country covered, she hoped her Savory Shrimp Lettuce Wraps would appeal to the palate of at least one, but hopefully all four, culinary experts. She admired her vibrantly colored creation, from the green butter lettuce and pink shrimp to the burgundy-hued balsamic merlot glaze. She was happy with her choice of a white, scallop-shaped platter to present the lettuce wraps on.

"Please wait here until you're called," a cook-off official told Sherry.

Sherry stood ready to set down her platter of food on the chefs' table. She watched carefully as they scored the previous cook's recipe. Hard as she tried, she couldn't make out any of the scores they assigned to Heidi's crab-stuffed red potato bites. A moment later, Heidi was given the go-ahead to collect her platter. She circled in from the other side of the table and gathered her platter. Her hand was visibly shaking.

"Good luck," Heidi whispered as she passed Sherry. Sherry mouthed a thank you before returning her attention to the judges, currently involved in a conference huddle. When the huddle broke, a cook-off official waved Sherry forward.

"Sherry Oliveri. Please bring your Shrimp Lettuce Wraps to the judges."

"I've been looking forward to these since I read the recipe," Judge Number One exclaimed. He patted his stomach as he spoke. "Set those right down in front of me."

The toe of Sherry's comfort sandal dragged and curled under as she began her journey to judgment. She lurched forward. A collective gasp filled the air. With a swift, and somewhat lucky move, Sherry regained her balance and landed at the edge of the table, tray first.

"While it was a great recovery, no points for a dramatic entrance," Judge Number Two said.

Sherry attempted a retort. Instead, her brain retreated from the situation, leaving her mute. She focused on her lettuce wraps. No time for a poker face. Present a beaming smile. She knew it was important for the judges to see her pride.

"Thank you, Ms. Oliveri. Your shrimp lettuce wraps are beautiful. Please wait over there." Judge Number Four assigned Sherry a location over to the side with a point of the finger.

Sherry settled into the spot Heidi had vacated.

She had a frustratingly obscured view of the judging.
From her vantage point on this side of the judges'
table, she could only make out a portion of each
judge's face. The judges helped themselves to a
plate from her platter. Sherry leaned in, hands
clasped at her aproned waist. Not much chance of
reading their reactions to the taste of her dish.

The judges' tablecloth is white. I would have provided a
pop of color instead of the white platter had I known. The
wrap going to Judge Number Three has a garnish that's
gone rogue. Too late to fix. Can't rush the table and adjust
the lemon slice with my bare hands in front of the judges.
Is that a tear in the lettuce on plate two? If the filling
falls out, that defeats the purpose of a secure lettuce
wrap needing no utensils. Phew, crisis averted. That's the
corner the judge bit first. I'd give anything to see those
notes they're taking. It's over. They're done.

A murmur rose throughout the collective audience, positioned in front of the judges.

"Sherry, you may collect your platter."

As she scooped up the platter and plates, she side-
eyed the judges' score tally sheet. She was unable to
decipher any of their chicken scratch. Sherry made
her way back to Pep at their cooking station. "That's
too bad. Someone must have had a last-minute
emergency," Sherry noted as she passed the contest-
ant-free workstation.

When she arrived at her stove, the area was spotless, and all her pans and utensils were bundled up
in their bags.

"Pep! Thank you." Sherry's head pivoted side to
side as she took in the spotless scene.

"We were such a well-oiled machine this morning,
I had to continue the flow." He folded his apron into

a square. "Your precision must be rubbing off on me. I've never folded anything this neatly in my life."

"I think the judges were happy with the wraps. Heidi's red potato bites looked delicious, too. Seems like there were no hiccups for any of the cooks today, so it's an even playing field. Kudos to the sponsors for providing great ingredients."

Pep put his hand up to mask a yawn. "Now, we just wait."

"Sherry, can I have a moment with you?" Patti Mellitt guided Sherry away from the reporter she and Pep were speaking to. "Vilma Pitney has some nerve showing up here, after I told her I was granted first interview rights by the organizers."

"Patti, you're squeezing my arm. Ouch!" Sherry winced. She retracted her assaulted arm from Patti's grip.

"Sorry. She makes me so mad. That woman is insufferable."

"Sherry, would you mind posing for a group photo next to the other category winners, please." Sophie Jefferson steered Sherry and Pep toward the other cooks lined up in front of the judges' table.

"Hold up your checks and say cheese."

The photographer got the desired shots, and the winners dispersed with their winnings in hand. Sherry and Pep returned to Patti.

When they reached her, Pep asked, "Do you need me, too?"

"Not on this round," Patti answered.

"Great. I'm going to see if Amber can give me a ride back to the house."

"See you soon, Pep. And thanks again." Sherry blew Pep a kiss. "That was so much fun."

Pep snatched the kiss out of the air and returned a smile.

"That Pitney woman. What was she even asking you?" Patti asked through gritted teeth. "Never mind. Forget I asked that. Must play nice, even if she doesn't." Patti plastered a grin across her face. "I have a few questions for you. The winner of the Hands-On Foods category is our local gal. Readers need to get their Sherry fix."

"Hey, Sherry. Congratulations. We knew you'd take your category," Day called out as she, Don, and Bernie filed past. "We'll be gunning for you next year."

"I will be, too," yelled Heidi. She rolled her supply case past Sherry, a netted sack of potatoes dangling from the handle.

"I got lucky. Thanks." Sherry's gaze lingered on the passing contestants. "If anyone's staying around Augustin, come visit our store, The Ruggery, and we can grab a bite to eat or see the sights."

"Will do," a male voice responded, but she couldn't be sure who the voice belonged to.

"Do you mind if we sit down to do the interview? I'm pooped after the morning's activities." Sherry led the way to a picnic table beside the boardwalk. Her shirt was splattered with balsamic merlot reduction where her apron didn't provide coverage. She lowered herself to the bench with a moan. "That feels better."

Patti sat across from Sherry and opened her notepad to a blank page. "Did you hear any details about Fitz?"

"Nothing special. Why?"

"You haven't heard? Surprised Vilma didn't tell you."

"I didn't talk to her for more than a minute."

"Fitz Frye is dead."

"What? No!"

"He never made it to the cook-off. You didn't notice the empty cook station?"

"This is the first I've heard of it. I'm in shock. I didn't even put two and two together that the empty contestant station was his. I never get social with the other cooks on cook-off day. Everyone is locked into business mode. I didn't take inventory as to exactly who was missing."

"I understand completely," Patti replied. "Word of his death was kept under wraps until after the awards ceremony."

"I'm so sorry. What a shock." Sherry organized her thoughts with a shake of her head. "How did the poor man die? Physically, he seemed in good shape last night. His mood was a different story. Something was upsetting him, and he had some harsh words for a few people. Wonder if he had a heart attack."

Patti narrowed her eyes. "If he did, he went out with a splash."

"What do you mean?"

"He was found unresponsive in the melted remains of the seafood ice sculpture at the Augustin Inn." Patti tapped her pen on her notepad. "Goes without saying, our dear Ginger is beside herself."

Sherry lowered her head. "Awful. The answer to your original question is, since this is the first I've heard of this, I have no details to share."

"I'm not touching on the death in my article. Just thought I'd ask. I'll leave that to the news bureau. I have lots of story content, but, as always, I'd love your perspective on why you think your dish beat the other portable recipes."

"Let me get the image of Fitz and the ice puddle out of my head. You know, I considered him my greatest threat. The last time I competed against him, he was flawless, all the way down to the exact number of trailing sauce dots circling his Fresh Tuna and Spinach Strata. He's the reason I never check out my competitors during a cook-off. I took one look at his perfect presentation and lost focus, knowing he set such a high standard."

"Interesting that his recipe today was supposed to be a shrimp wrap." Patti held up the cook-off recipes handout. "Two shrimp wraps versus each other. How exciting it would have been to see the judges' notes when they picked the winner. I'm sure it still would have been yours, but his would have provided good competition." Patti met and held Sherry's gaze.

"I admit I wasn't thrilled when I heard we were both cooking off shrimp wraps, but I was up for the challenge. You never know who or what you'll be up against in a cook-off. Almost anything goes."

"I'd like to use that in my article, if it's all right with you." Patti held her pen poised to begin writing.

"Sure." Sherry paused over a thought. "Wait, maybe leave out the part where I'm not thrilled about Fitz and I both preparing shrimp wraps. It wasn't too long ago when I was the suspect in a murder investigation. I don't want any connections made between our friendly rivalry and his heart attack, or whatever took the poor man's life."

"Do you think the pairing of you and your brother inspires you to seek out more contests with a team theme in the future?"

"Might have been a one and done scenario. Pep's got other interests. What made me so happy was how well we worked together. I was unsure if his head was in it before the cook-off began. He's been so distracted since he arrived in Augustin."

"Well done, Sherry," Heidi called out, as she passed by a second time. "Guess not every judge loves potatoes as much as I do."

"Your dish looked fantastic. Better luck next time," Sherry said, then turned back to Patti. "Let's see. What was I saying?"

"Your partnership with Pep?" Patti suggested.

"Right. It was a good morning. All the stars were aligned. I was pleasantly surprised by Pep's attention to detail. Having his full participation gave me confidence in my dish's timing. I didn't get tripped up with small mistakes. While being allotted two hours was divine, sometimes having too much time to cook and plate works against you. Hands-on food doesn't need to be oven hot. That was in everyone's favor."

"You won a trip for two to a winery in Massachusetts. How lovely. Any idea when you might go and who you might bring? I do love wine, if you don't have anyone in mind." Patti delivered a reinforcing smile.

Sherry nodded as she considered Patti's proposal. "I'll keep that in mind, my friend. I'll offer the spot to Pep first and go from there, if he declines. Not sure how excited he'd be to take a trip with his big sis. Is there anything else? I'd give anything to go home and change out of these clothes. I still have to work at The Ruggery this afternoon."

Patti stared at her notepad. "Last thing. Were you aware of the fact that the Augustin Inn will be closing its doors forever at the end of the year?"

"You're the bearer of bad news today. That's awful. It's been in the Constable family for something like a hundred years. I had no idea. Ginger certainly didn't let on last night."

Chapter 7

Sherry couldn't think of a time when she walked into The Ruggery and her senses weren't overloaded. The odor of the newly dyed wool permeated the air with must, a smell she likened to the tolerable side of wet dog fur. It was a pungent, organic smell that enlivened her and provided her continued appreciation for the craft her family had practiced for generations. Customers often asked if they should air out the rugs when they brought them home, but Sherry was always hesitant to recommend. She knew the scent of the lamb's wool would soon take on whatever the dominant smell of the owner's household was, which she considered a shame.

Pep was leaning on the counter when she approached.

"If I'm on the team for your next cook-off, I vote for one with a sixty-minute time limit, not another two-hour extravaganza like we just survived." Pep plopped down in a chair he had dragged in from the store's tiny kitchen.

"Duly noted," Sherry said. "I just heard the most awful news."

"What?" Pep asked. "It's been such a great day so far, I hope you're exaggerating."

"I wish I was. Patti Mellitt told me, as I was leaving the cook-off, Fitz Frye is dead."

"That can't be. We just saw him last night. He seemed healthy and especially ready to compete against you."

"I don't have any details beyond what I've told you. I feel so sorry for his family and friends."

Amber's dog, Bean, jumped up on Pep's lap.

"Me, too," Pep said, with a marked lack of enthusiasm. "I'm exhausted. Bean and I'll take a rest." He shifted his attention to two women as they entered The Ruggery.

"You're making me feel guilty I left Chutney at home. I could have brought him, since I stopped off to change my clothes. I should have known Amber was leaving Bean here with Dad while she was at the cook-off." Sherry cocked her head as she watched her brother and her friend's cuddly Jack Russell share a mutual admiration moment. "My baby brother needs to work on his stamina. With those bulging biceps, I would think shuffling pots and pans on and off the stove for two hours wouldn't be any problem."

"Different set of muscles involved. The mental ones." Pep laughed.

Sherry eyed the women, who marched up to the sales counter and set down their purses, side by side. "Good afternoon, ladies. Ruth, I see you've had a chance to change out of your Festival overalls."

Ruth spun around and her floral dress billowed.

"Hello, dear. Yes, I'm back in my street clothes. My shift is over. I'm so glad you're here, too, Pep, my dear." Ruth rubbed her shoulder. "My doctor says my shoulder wouldn't be sore if I didn't ferry my purse around all day."

"Hi, Ruth." Pep hoisted himself and Bean from his chair. He sat back down as quickly as he rose. Bean settled back down on his lap.

"He also mentioned you needn't carry the entire inventory of a mini convenience store inside the purse, if you want to lighten the load," added Beverly Van Ardan. "Good afternoon, Sherry. Is this your dashing and debonair brother?"

"Yes, though I've never used those exact words. My parents referred to him as 'cutie patootie.'" Sherry turned toward Pep. "Pep, this is Beverly Van Ardan. She's dear friends with Dad and Ruth and Frances. They usually travel in a pack, but Frances is on a trip."

Beverly's silver updo held firm as she rotated her head to see behind her. She adjusted her turquoise silk scarf when the front knot shifted with her movement. "I don't see Erno."

"Here I am," Erno called out. He made his way across the wide-plank wood floor, drawing creaks and groans from the old wood with each step. "Finishing up my lunch. What a nice group of friends and family. To what do we owe this honor, ladies?" Erno planted a kiss on Ruth's cheek.

"We came in to congratulate Sherry and Pep on their win this morning," Ruth said.

Sherry tipped her head. "Thank you so much."

"I wasn't able to watch much of the cook-off," Ruth continued, "as I had the very important job of handing out Fall Fest brochures. I did manage to sneak a peek at the action every now and again. Sherry was as intense as always. I caught Pep glued to his phone while Sherry was sautéing the shrimp. I gather that's what young people do these days."

Sherry shot a glare at her brother.

Pep's breath caught in his throat with a gasp, and he coughed. "For one or two seconds I was checking texts. No big deal," he said when his cough died down. "Sherry had my full attention when she needed it."

"Except maybe that one time when I asked you to dice the red pepper and you diced a red onion," Sherry added. "Better keep that detail to ourselves. I gave an interview to Patti Mellitt singing the praises of my worthy assistant. Wouldn't want her to think I embellished my brother's contribution to our win."

"Rookie mistake," Pep laughed.

Sherry didn't join him in his amusement.

"Ruth Gadabee can keep a secret," Ruth announced. "Especially concerning the Oliveri family." She winked at Erno. "He was all hands on deck when time came for stuffing the lettuce leaves. A thing of beauty to watch."

"Aren't my kids talented." Erno sent an air kiss Ruth's way.

Beverly turned to Pep. "How long are you visiting for?"

Pep remained silent until Beverly repeated the question. "A few more days, I think. I'm heading back up to Maine. My employment is in a transitional stage, shall we say. Changes are on the horizon."

Ruth hummed a note of consideration. "I like a man of mystery."

"I don't see the attraction," Sherry commented to her brother.

"We're happy you're here for as long as you want," Erno added. "Any hand at the store is a welcome hand."

Ruth fished in her purse for something. She pulled out folded papers. "Getting back to the cook-off, I was looking at the recipes you cooks prepared." She unfolded the contest recipes booklet. "The contestant two stoves down from you, who never showed up, had a remarkable recipe I'd have loved to have seen prepared. When I took my first break, I stopped by for a gander, but the spot was empty. Wonder why the man didn't show up? Did he fall ill, do you know?"

"He passed away after the party last night," Sherry offered in a hushed tone.

"Heavens! Dead?" Ruth sounded incredulous.

"Now I'm not as sorry I couldn't make the cook-off," Erno commented. "I've been to one too many cook-offs that involved a death."

The bell over the store's door tinkled, and heads rotated in that direction. Detective Ray Bease, wearing a battered tan hat, entered the store. As he approached the sales counter, his rubber-soled shoes screeched across the floor.

"Hello, Sherry. How have you been? Mr. Oliveri. Mrs. Gadabee. Mrs. Van Ardan. I hope I'm not interrupting anything important." He removed his hat and tucked it under his armpit. His short-sleeved shirt was in need of a steam iron, as were his khaki pants.

No one spoke. The store, full of people, was as

quiet as if it were after hours. Sherry's gaze bounced from person to person until it landed on the detective. His face was expressionless. She knew it was his job to make her feel as if she couldn't respond fast enough.

"Ray. It's been a while. How have you been?" Sherry's words were cautious. She studied the Hillsboro County detective, hoping to read his mood. As in the past, it was an impossible task. "In the market for a colorful rug to brighten up your home?" Sherry laughed. "Imagine after all we've been through; I'm helping you decorate your home. I'd never have considered we'd be friends, or even share a pleasant conversation, for that matter. Our first meeting had you suspecting me of murder. If that wasn't enough to tarnish any potential relationship, you followed up with putting my father on top of a murder investigation suspect list."

"Just doing my job," Ray said.

Sherry knew Ray well enough to know he wasn't going to elaborate. He was a man of few words when the subject was not of his own choosing.

"I have a bit of business to attend to first, but sure, I'll take a look at a few rugs while I'm in here." Ray peered toward the rug showroom. On display were autumnal-themed hooked rugs in various shapes and sizes, blooming with reds, browns, oranges, and moss-colored lamb's wool yarn. Rug designs ranged from root vegetable cornucopias to antlered deer roaming through dramatic fall foliage. He returned his focus to Sherry. "Very nice."

"What sort of business?" Sherry's words rolled off her tongue faster than she intended. "Does this involve all of us, or would you like to step into the other room?"

"Actually, some, not all." Ray reached around to the backside of his wrinkled pants and his hand returned holding a small spiral notepad. He flipped it open with a jerk of his wrist. He scanned his notes. "Is there a Josep Primo Oliveri in your family?" Ray kept his focus on the page.

Sherry grinned at Ray's method of note taking. "Done away with your computer tablet?"

"It's in the car. Notepad's still my preferred field-recording device. More of those metal contraptions come back soaked from rain, shot up by perpetrators' bullets, or run over in a car chase than the department would like to admit. I think I'm onto something with my three-dollar-fifty-cent notepad." Ray waved his notepad. "Josep Primo Oliveri?"

"That would be me," Pep answered. "And you are?"

"Pep, this is Detective Ray Bea . . ." Sherry's voice trailed off, making Ray's last name indiscernible.

"Nice to meet you. What can I do for you?" Pep stood and set Bean down on the floor. His hand launched toward the detective.

"So you prefer Pep, not Josep?" Ray asked.

"Pep's been my name since I began walking at fourteen months. I've been in constant motion since then, or so the story goes. Right, Dad?"

Erno's eyes lost focus. Sherry imagined he was visualizing baby Pep toddling through his memories.

"Yep. You were a Pep, not a Josep. Name still sticks. Always on the go." Erno lifted his vision sky-ward. "No offense, Grandpa Josep, your namesake."

"Got it. Pep, were you at the Augustin Inn the

night of the New England Fall Food Fest contestant cocktail party, which was last night?" Ray flipped his notepad shut and stored it back in his pocket.

"Of course he was, Ray. He was my sous chef at the cook-off. We're a team," Sherry said before Pep had a chance to respond. "What's this all about?"

Ray ignored Sherry's interjection.

Ruth and Beverly edged closer to Erno, sandwiching him as they hooked their arms through his elbows.

"You seem awfully serious, Detective Bease," Erno commented. "You're not here to congratulate Team Oliveri on their win, are you?"

"Ray?" Sherry implored.

Pep stepped to the side. "I'll answer his question. I was at the cocktail party, yes."

Sherry studied Ray, who was studying Pep.

"Pep, did you have any interaction with another partygoer? A man named Fitz Frye?" Ray asked.

"Whoa, whoa, whoa," Sherry waved her hands, as if she were attempting to stop traffic on a busy freeway. "Ray, please explain. You don't just show up out of the blue and start asking questions about someone who has passed away unless you're gathering information. If anyone knows that, it's me. Poor Fitz died of a heart attack or something like that. Why are you involved?"

"Sherry, take it easy. He asked a simple question." Pep put his arm on his sister's shoulder. "Fitz and I know each other. I haven't seen him for a while, so we caught up on current events. Believe me, I was horrified to find out he had passed away hours after I had spoken to him."

"I see," remarked Ray. "How did you find out he was deceased?"

"Sherry told me when she got home from the cook-off."

"Sherry, how did you find out Mr. Frye was deceased?" Ray asked.

"I found out from Patti, who was covering the cook-off for the newspaper. She said word was only getting out after the competition ended, which was a calculated move by organizers for obvious reasons," Sherry replied.

Ray's attention landed back on Pep. "Why did your sister wait until she got home to tell you about the death of another contestant?"

"We left the cook-off at different times. Sherry stayed to do some interviews, and I took off. I got a ride home with Amber. I knew Sherry would be in hot demand from media and well-wishers. I was exhausted, and she didn't need me to hang around with her. She heard about Fitz after I left."

"That begs the question, did you ride together to the cook-off party last night?"

Pep sucked in a hefty breath. Before he could exhale, Sherry broke in. "He took his own car last night in case I was obligated to spend more time there than he wanted to."

Ray curled up one side of his mouth. "So, Pep came right home after the party, which I've been told by the Augustin Inn's owner was cleaned up after its last attendee exited at ten?"

Sherry held her breath.

"I arrived home sometime after midnight. Maybe a bit later," Pep answered in a voice so soft Sherry could barely understand the words he spoke.

"I was wondering what had Chutney all in a bunch last night," Sherry commented. "His barking woke me. I didn't even bother looking at the clock. I was so tired, I turned over and fell back asleep." She tried to assume a nonchalant tone, but the pitch of her voice stung her own ears. "Glad I didn't know you were out so late the night before the cook-off."

"The boy's young. He can stay out late and not be phased, like us old folks," Erno said.

"Dad, I'm not much older than the young boy." Sherry shrugged. "But, I admit, I get tired. By the way, he wouldn't be so exhausted now if he'd gotten more sleep last night."

"We're getting off track here," Ray said.

"What track? Are we on a track?" Ruth asked.

"Really, this is becoming a riddle with no answer," Beverly added. "Pep went out after the party, and Sherry got tired and went to bed. What of it?"

Ray glared at Sherry. "That doesn't bother you, knowing he went out late the night before one of your important events?"

"I thought he was home when Chutney was barking. This is the first I've heard of him being out so late. Dad's right. Pep's a grown man with more stamina than me. As long as he brought his A game to the cook-off, that's all I'm concerned with. And, obviously, he did, or we wouldn't have won."

"The way he was slumped in that chair when I came in the store doesn't exactly boast a young man with stamina. Probably wishes he wasn't out so late now," Ray commented.

"I'm fine," Pep explained. "Staying up late requires a certain type of stamina. Cooking in a timed competition requires another. Sherry's used to the latter, and I'm not. I did the job required of me this morning, and that's what counts. Yes, next time getting to bed earlier would make more sense. Why are we talking about my sleep habits? This is getting ridiculous."

Ray looked at everyone gathered around him. "Fitz Frye was murdered. I'm gathering information about anyone who may have had a conflict with the man." His gaze stalled on Pep. "You were seen having a heated discussion with Mr. Frye. A discussion more than one partygoer described as contentious."

"Murdered?" Sherry gasped.

"Frye was found with his head submerged in the pool of water that had collected under a massive ice sculpture. An ice sculpture of seafood. Shrimp, lobster, a swimming salmon."

"The sculpture was in the inn's big gathering room. Wouldn't someone have noticed him in there as soon as he fell, or however he landed in the pool?" Sherry asked.

"The sculpture was on a wheeled base. After the party, it was rolled into a barn in the back of the Augustin Inn. Apparently, the owner had neglected to turn off the newly installed space heater in the barn and the warm temperature made fast work of destroying the icy artwork. By the time Frye was found, shortly after midnight, three quarters of the sculpture had melted into the tub below, providing a deep enough pool for a man to drown in. Or more accurately, be drowned in." Ray lifted his gaze to meet Sherry's.

"Tragic accident. He didn't appear intoxicated

during the party, but he must have had a few more cocktails after the party ended. I'm guessing he wandered around the inn's grounds, found his way into the barn, tripped, hit his head, and fell in. So sad." Sherry reinforced her version of the accident with a nod of her head.

"Sherry's right," Ruth agreed. "The grounds of the inn aren't well lit. I can see how someone unfamiliar with the layout could get disoriented."

"Why would it matter if he had words with other guests? It has to have been an accident with no one at fault but Fitz himself," Sherry said.

"Sherry, you may fancy yourself an accomplished amateur sleuth, due to past successes at finding a killer or two, but right now your guesses about Frye wandering the grounds, tumbling into a pool of cold water, and drowning are way off base."

"Enlighten us, will you, Detective?" Erno said.

"Frye had blunt force trauma to the back of the head, inconsistent with someone accidentally falling forward into a hard object, which is the way he was found. There was also a calling card left at the scene. A fishhook, a multiple-barbed, bait-holder hook, to be specific, that was meticulously maneuvered into the back of Frye's neck in such a way that the man could not have possibly managed it on his own, even if he had fallen backwards onto it in a mishap. He was also clutching a handful of illegible soaked papers."

"Sounds like murder to me," Erno surmised.

Sherry shot a side-eye glare toward her father.

"And an eyewitness has come forward with word

she saw Pep submerge his hand in the ice sculpture's base toward the end of the party," Ray added.

Sherry studied her silent brother, who was analyzing his shoes. "So? What eyewitness?"

"Some might believe he was measuring the depth," Ray said with a hint of provocation.

"Their guess would be wrong." Sherry forced her statement on the detective, and he winced.

Pep shrugged his shoulders. "I had cocktail sauce on my hand and a dip in what little water there was under the ice sculpture was enough to wash it away."

"We have to get back to work. Is there anything else?" Sherry rubbed her pounding temple.

Ray turned to Pep. "Where you went after the party is the difference between you becoming a suspect in the murder investigation of Fitz Frye and my preliminary research moving in a different direction. Can you answer the question as to where you were between the hours of nine and midnight last night?"

Pep kept his head down. "I left the Augustin Inn sometime after midnight and came right home."

"*After* midnight?" Sherry exclaimed before she could censor the question.

Chapter
8

"You realize your answer puts you squarely in the crosshairs on the suspect list, unless you can prove exactly what you were doing at the Augustin Inn." Ray spoke as if he were addressing a child. "Witnesses are a plus."

"I had nothing to do with Fitz's murder. Dad, I'll be in the stockroom separating the new shipment of yellows." Pep shimmied through the circle of people and out of the room.

Bean accompanied his friend.

"Ray, can I see you in private for a moment?" Sherry wasn't presenting Ray with an option to decline. "Right now." She poked Ray's forearm. "Excuse us." She shouldered past Beverly and Ruth.

When Sherry and Ray reached the display table, which was covered with the latest collection of small oval fireplace rugs, Sherry spun around to face Ray. "What do you think you're doing?"

"My job. You know the drill. There's been a murder. My department is investigating. The process begins with building a list of suspects."

"Pep talked to the man. That's it. I talked to him, too. Am I a suspect?" Sherry regretted her spontaneous question the moment the words passed her lips.

"Not at this time. If someone were to offer up credible evidence that Frye and you had a beef, well, then you would be. I'm giving you the benefit of the doubt. Killing every cook-off contestant you compete against would take a lifetime, and you're getting an awfully late start, if this is your first murder."

"Not a good time for bad jokes." Sherry backed up against the table and used it to steady herself.

"The investigation has to begin somewhere."

Sherry began to fidget with a rug decorated with puppies playing on a checkered pillow. Her breathing slowed as she manipulated the soft wool loops between her fingers. She raised her gaze and caught Ray squinting at her.

Ray tilted his head and softened his tone. "Your brother hasn't said much that assures me he wasn't anywhere near the murder scene last night. Do you know of any reason he won't speak up in his own defense?"

Sherry sighed. "Pep's going through something. He's been very guarded since he arrived. I imagine he's reached the age where his wanderlust way of life needs to come to an end. He's having trouble embracing the idea of a grown-up world. He'll come around. The moment he does, I'll give you a call."

"I can't grant special favors just because we have a past," Ray whispered. "I don't mean a past, that's not what I meant."

"I'm fully aware of how you operate, Detective

Bease," Sherry huffed. "You had no trouble putting me, and then Dad, at the top of the suspect lists in your prior murder investigations. Why should my brother be any different?"

"It's early days, but I would advise Pep not to leave the area for a while. Until he's willing to cooperate, I'll give him some space. If I have to chase him down, things could go from bad to worse very quickly." Ray topped his head with his hat before taking a final look at Sherry. "I've got some stuff of my own I'm going through, so I feel for Pep. But it's not enough to keep me from doing my job as best as I know how. I'll be in touch." Ray headed to the front of the store. Sherry shadowed him until he reached the door.

"Have a nice day," Ray offered as he left the store.

"Pleasant fellow," Beverly said.

"Not that pleasant," Sherry replied.

"Could be a tad more updated on his fashion sense," Beverly added.

"That's an understatement if I've ever heard one," Sherry said.

"Are we going to get any work out of you today, Sherry?" Erno laughed. "Or are you off to solve another murder?"

"Very funny, Dad. But"—Sherry paused and Erno groaned—"there are a few folks who were at the cook-off party that I wouldn't mind having a chat with. You know, just to clear the air and get Pep off the detective's radar."

"Uh-oh," Ruth said. "Sounds like Sherry's got a plan."

"Not at all," Sherry said. "Pardon me, I'm going

to have a word with little bro while I help him sort inventory."

Before she could leave the room, the bell over the front door sounded, and a woman pushed her way inside. The amount of vibrantly colored makeup the woman wore made it difficult for Sherry to estimate her age. She always liked to fit her new customers into appropriate demographics in order to best fill their needs. This woman might be as young as late thirties or as old as late forties, give or take. Sherry wasn't feeling confident enough to guide the potential customer to the modern rug design section, so popular with the younger crowd. If her heavily applied makeup were doing its job of disguising a decade or two and the woman was nearing fifty, Sherry would show her the retro rugs first. Better not to risk judging this book by its cover. As the woman neared, Sherry realized she knew her.

The woman lowered glasses from the top of her head and rummaged through a shopping bag. When she was done, she raised her head and repositioned her glasses above her hairline. Her accent confirmed her identity. "Good morning, Sherry. I hope you remember me. We had a brief interview following the cook-off this morning." She turned toward Erno. "This must be your father, judging by the strong resemblance." She made her way over to Ruth and Beverly. "I know you. You're Beverly Van Ardan." She returned her gaze to Ruth. "I'm sorry, I don't know your name. I'm Vilma Pitney."

"I'm Ruth Gadabee. Nice to meet you, Vilma. You have such a pretty accent. I'm a great admirer of all accents."

"Thank you. I spent a fortune trying to suppress my Russian accent. I was told it was a bit harsh and turned people off. Lately, I've thought twice about that decision. It's fun to throw in a rolling *R* every so often, to keep people on their toes," Vilma chuckled with conviction.

"Oh, yes." Sherry said. "Nice to see you again."

"You granted me the first interview. It was so amusing to see the expression on Patti's face when she realized she got sloppy seconds," Vilma responded.

Sherry swallowed the words she considered saying in defense of her friend Patti. Instead, she changed the subject. "And you know my father and Beverly?"

Vilma shifted her bag from one arm to the other. The heft of the tote left an indentation on the sleeve of her sweater. "I don't exactly know your father. Researched your family, that's how I recognized your dad. I sent my résumé and an audiotape of one of my interviews to Beverly's husband in hopes of landing a job in one of his media outlets, but it's been in the under-consideration pile for a year now. I googled the Van Ardans before I took that step, for a better level of familiarity. You have a lovely photo online, Beverly. You'll see it if you search yourself."

"Oh dear, no thanks. I shudder to think how I might look if I'm caught unaware my picture's being snapped." Beverly sidled up to Ruth. She whispered something in her ear.

Sherry recognized the smirk on Ruth's face as one she'd seen many times, shared between Ruth and Frances when the ladies disagreed with someone's opinion.

"Would you mind if I put my bag on the counter? It's killing my arm." Vilma lowered the bag.

"Please." Sherry cleared a spot for the bag. The weight of its contents made a solid bang when it hit the wooden counter. "May I show you some rugs? Or perhaps you hook your own, in which case I can show you some beautiful hand-drawn canvases and the associated wool."

"That sounds lovely. First, though, I was wondering if you and your brother would be willing to answer a few more questions. I'm putting the finishing touches on my cook-off article. Is that adorable sous chef of yours anywhere nearby? I can come back later, if that's more convenient."

"I don't know about adorable, but I'm the sous chef." Pep emerged from the stockroom. "Doesn't look like I'm getting much help in there. I might as well come out here where my helping hands have stationed themselves."

Erno put his arm around Ruth. She made a subtle head gesture toward the door. "Maybe we'll go grab a cup of coffee and see you back here in an hour. Let's go, Beverly. Nice meeting you, Vilma."

Pep put his hands on his hips as he approached Sherry. "Oh, sure. Now it's time for a coffee break."

Ruth and Beverly gathered their purses, and each of them took one of Erno's elbows in the crook of their own. The trio slipped out the doorway with Ruth in the lead and the other two links in the friendship chain following close behind.

"Did I scare them off?" Vilma asked. "Was it something I said?"

"No. My dad is only working part-time nowadays,

so he makes his own rules as to his comings and goings," Sherry explained. "He was spotting us all morning, while we were at the cook-off. Amber, my coworker, came to watch, so he worked solo."

"Family business can get messy. Glad yours works so smoothly."

"Ha, not always," Sherry replied. "What else would you like to ask us for your article?"

"One minute, while I open up my iPad." Vilma reached across the table and slid her tablet out of her bag. She tapped on the screen and the device lit up. "I'm satisfied with the answers from your interview this morning, Sherry, but, Pep, if you wouldn't mind answering a few questions for the readers, I'd be very appreciative."

"Who exactly are your readers?" he asked.

Vilma raised her line of sight to meet Pep's. "Anyone and everyone."

"And what publication do you work for?" A ting of exasperation crept into Pep's voice.

"This is a big story. The New England Fall Fest Cook-off takes eleven months of planning and every year attracts a broader pool of the country's finest home cooks. This year there were cooks from all four corners of the US and a whole bunch of states in between."

Sherry nodded. "That's right. That's what I love about cook-offs. I meet cooks from everywhere. We all share the love of recipe creation."

"And the sponsors! More and more are jumping aboard. Risky Reward Winery, Maine Course Foods, Shrimply Amazing, Sweet Arts, Spice Attitude—all eager to sponsor the prestigious competition. To answer your question, Pep, I'm not going to sell the story that encapsulated the drama, intrigue, and heart of the cook-off to the first two-bit publication that comes along."

"Besides, Patti's got Connecticut covered," Sherry said. "Her newspaper's circulation is the largest in the state." She was glad to put in a good word for her friend.

Vilma didn't acknowledge Sherry's attempt to bolster her friend's reputation. "That's the beauty of freelance journalism, and maybe the curse also. I have to sell it to the right market at the right price without pricing myself out of contention. Time is of the essence, because Patti will have her story out ASAP. Haste makes waste. Her content is consistently shallow, but she's still my competition, so I have to keep my work timely."

Sherry side-eyed Pep as he checked his phone. He kept his attention on the small screen until Vilma addressed him.

"So, Pep. First question. Is the Fall Fest your first foray into the cooking competition world? I, of course, mean as a competitor, not as a cheerleader for your sister."

Sherry watched her brother shift his weight from one leg to the other. "Growing up, our sister, Marla, myself, and Sherry used to play a game called Recipe Piggyback, whenever Dad would let us. It wasn't exactly a competition, but it was a test of our creativity in the kitchen. Other than that, no cook-offs for me. Honestly, I've only seen Sherry compete live in one cook-off, maybe seven years ago. I've been traveling so much I can rarely squeeze in a pleasure trip.

This cook-off was perfect timing. Sherry caught me by surprise when she asked me to join her as sous chef. How could I say no?"

"Nice answer." Vilma typed. She looked at Pep. "I was saddened to hear of the passing of one of the contest cooks, Fitz Frye. Did you know him?"

"Not well." Pep thrust the words at Vilma.

"I could have kicked myself when I didn't get an interview with him at the contestant party." Vilma stared across the room. "I wonder if Patti got one?"

"Anything else?" Sherry asked, in hopes of bringing Vilma's attention back to her iPad.

"He had a sweet girlfriend that I had a chance to speak to. She was rushing past me on her way to find Ginger when I intercepted her for a few words. Kelly, I think her name was. She was his sous chef."

Pep didn't respond.

"She was very nice when I spoke to her," Sherry added when the silence became unbearable.

"She did her best to answer a quick question but was all consumed with putting out a fire between Fitz and a man named Lyman. I'm going to find out more about this Lyman fellow. Pep, you had an argument with Fitz, too, if I'm not mistaken? If there were a dustup between cook-off teams, that would make for interesting reading. Care to elaborate?" Vilma's eyebrows lifted, revealing more of the purple-blue eye shadow curtaining her eyelid.

"No story there. Only guy talk. Fitz said something about my sister, and I came to her defense. I'll do that every time." Pep's words were clipped.

"What did Fitz say about Sherry?" Vilma glanced at Pep before returning her attention to her tablet.

Sherry crossed her arms. "He doesn't have to answer that." She turned to Pep. "You don't have to answer that. I know the answer. Fitz mentioned he wanted to beat me again after a solid win at the last cook-off we competed in. I'm sure that's all he said. And it wasn't only Pep and Lyman who argued with Fitz. Ginger's brother and his coworker, Roe, were involved in a heated discussion with Fitz. So, you see? Put a bunch of testosterone in one room and you get some showboating."

"Yep," affirmed Pep. "That's all."

"Hmmm." Vilma held her fingers in the ready position over the tablet. "Okay then. One more question."

"Sherry," whispered Pep, eyes pleading for her intervention.

"I'm sorry," Sherry said. "It's part of the process. We can't say no to interviews."

"I'm trying to get into the head of the secondary chef, if you don't mind me calling you that. It wasn't you who submitted the recipe, and unless your partner decides to split the winnings with you, the sous chef can walk away with nothing other than a thank you. What's the arrangement between you and your sister?"

"I don't feel comfortable discussing how we're splitting the ten-thousand-dollar prize, but suffice it to say, Pep is happy with his cut. He deserves every penny," Sherry said.

"Fitz's girlfriend said she expected nothing in return for her efforts. She said she was helping him to a victory he felt was in the bag."

"Doesn't sound like she was getting a fair deal," Pep added.

"Question is, when you spend some time with the other competitors in a supposedly relaxed atmosphere, but, instead, there's contentious behavior in the room, is that a performance motivator for the cook-off or are you so taken aback that you don't know how to handle the situation?" Vilma held a steely gaze on Pep.

Pep squared up his body to Vilma's. "Ms. Pitney, it appears you're looking for some story line that just isn't there. Guys get together and sometimes don't play nice. We're not aware we come off prickly until it's pointed out to us. My cook-off motivation comes from helping my sister do the best job she can. End of story." Pep dusted his hands together, rotated a half circle, and headed to the stockroom.

"I need to get back to work," Sherry said. "Is there anything else I can do for you?"

Vilma pushed out her rose-colored lips. "If what I hear is true and Fitz was murdered, the guilty party may have acted out in defense of a loved one's reputation."

"Hard to say without speculating what the motivation was. And speculation is risky." Sherry pictured Ray giving her a judgmental look.

"Word is also out about Pep's argument with Fitz. Kelly, his girlfriend, is making sure of that. She's told everyone from Ginger to Uri, the head of Maine Course Foods, to a detective fellow who has begun an investigation."

Sherry's stomach heaved.

"If he were my brother, I would see what more that Lyman St. Pierre fellow has to say. He was in the midst of the commotion last night. Lyman told me he's staying in town for more business opportunities. From what I've witnessed over the last few minutes, Pep isn't speaking up for himself. Is he always this quiet? If so, he might want to choose now to open up, unless he's got something to hide."

"Thanks for the advice." Sherry's words died slowly from lack of effort.

"You've been involved in other murder investigations. I know, because I've followed each one very closely. You're good, or maybe lucky. Nonetheless, let me know if I can be of any help." Vilma collected her tablet and inserted it into her bag. She turned toward the door. Without glancing back, she added, "I'd hate to see your sweet handsome brother behind bars."

Vilma reached for the doorknob. "When he's in town, Lyman St. Pierre kiteboards at the Town Beach whenever the wind kicks up, my sources tell me. It's a nice breezy day today." As she finished her thought, she was knocked back a step by someone coming through the doorway. "Oh, excuse me, I didn't see you coming."

Amber made her way inside the store. "I'll hold that for you." She leaned against the open door until Vilma slipped past her. "Hey, Sher. Hope that was a paying customer with an unlimited budget," Amber laughed. Her animated comment ended as fast as it began when she met Sherry's gaze. "Uh-oh. That look on your face doesn't jive with a sale."

Chapter 9

"Hi to you," Sherry said. "You're right. No sale. That was a woman writing a story about the cook-off."

"That's fun. Right in your wheelhouse. Cooking, competing, winning. It's your thing, and you're the best." Amber tucked her purse behind the sales counter. "Thanks for texting me about the poor cook-off contestant who died. Is there any new information on the guy?"

"Uh, yeah. Ray stopped by, and it wasn't a social visit." Sherry shook her head.

"Oh, no! Are you saying the contestant was murdered?"

"Yep. Ray was info gathering, but I'm not going to let him spoil my victory. Now that he's gone—out of sight, out of mind."

Pep emerged from the back room, followed by Bean. The dog overtook the man to reach Amber and ply her with enthusiastic jumps against her leg.

"Hi, Amber."

"Hi, Pep, and hello to you, boy." Amber reached down and tussled her dog's neck fur. "Thanks for filling in for me, Sherry. You saved me. I didn't real-ize I was obligated to pick up the tennis team's new shirts by lunchtime today. Yours is in the car. Pep, go get some much-needed rest."

"Well, actually," Sherry began, "I was hoping Pep could stick around for an hour or two longer, while I run an errand. I know you can get the job done on your own, but why not take the help when you can get it? Also, I'm pretty sure Dad will be returning in around an hour. Can't be sure, though. When he's with his girls, he loses all track of time." She sent Pep a sweet smile.

"I repeat. Why was I under the false impression that at least part of my visit to Augustin would be relaxing? It's getting less relaxing by the minute."

"Come on," Amber pleaded, "admit you enjoy your time with me. We had some laughs on our way home from the cook-off, right? I mean, who else is going to give me the inside scoop on these contests. Heaven knows, Sherry isn't willing to share more than the published recipe with me. I've been in one contest myself, but I'm still fascinated to learn what makes the perennial contestant tick."

"Wait, Pep shared information with you?" Sherry threw her hands up in the air. "I can't get him to tell me more than the bare essentials."

"The answer is yes, I'll pitch in here, with Amber, while you do your quote, unquote, errands."

The front door burst open, announced by the dull thud of a bell hit too hard.

"I'll take one of each," announced a man dressed in madras shorts and a gray sweatshirt. He pointed to the rugs on display.

"Me, too!" a woman in navy sweatpants and a white sweater called out. She followed a step behind the man.

"Day! Don! I'm so glad you made it to the store."
Sherry offered each a fast hug. "My new cook-off
friends, this is Amber, who basically runs The Ruggery. And you know my brother, Pep."

"Who, also, suddenly basically runs the store,"
Pep muttered.

"The rugs are beyond gorgeous," Day gushed.
"Would anyone mind showing me a small area rug
in lavender and greens? That's the color scheme of
my front hallway."

"Amber, would you mind? I was just on my way out
to run an errand on the other side of town," Sherry
said. "We could meet up for a drink before dinner, if
that works out."

"Is this too far to walk?" Don rotated his phone
and showed Sherry a map of the town of Augustin.
He zoomed in on the Town Beach. "Day wants to
shop until she drops, and I need some fresh air."

"It's a bit of a hike. Let me give you a lift." Without waiting for a response, Sherry grabbed her
purse from behind the sales counter and hoisted it
over her shoulder. She marched to the door and
turned the handle. "We'll figure out a drink spot on
the way and text you guys. All are encouraged to
attend. Amber and Pep, I should be back in an hour,
give or take."

"Guess I don't have a choice. I'm right behind
you." Don trotted to the door before it closed. "Happy
shopping," he called back to his sister.

Sherry drove the scenic route to the beach, instead of her usual, more direct route. The lengthier
drive took her and Don through the reasonably
priced neighborhoods on up to the extravagant and
exclusive enclaves, closer to the sound. She pointed

out landmarks that had special meaning to her, such as the majestic oak tree, survivor of numerous storms. The centuries old, hand-built stone walls marking property lines were her absolute favorite because they'd stood the test of time. By the time they reached the beach, she was filled with a renewed sense of pride to be an Augustin citizen.

"Thanks for the lift and the tour of your town. Hope I didn't take you too far out of your way," Don said.

"I was on my way to the Town Beach, actually. I didn't want my brother to know. He might think I'm goofing off." Sherry forced a laugh. She wasn't convinced Don would accept her explanation when it was only a partial truth.

"An errand at the beach on a beautiful day. Who would question the legitimacy?" Don chuckled.

Sherry parked her car in the beach's lot. There were a surprising number of cars for a Saturday in autumn. Sherry seldom made it to the beach on Saturdays, no matter what the season. Maybe she was missing out.

"I'm hoping to find someone over at the north end. That's the windy side of the beach and kite surfers flock there on breezy days, like today." Sherry pointed to a group of people in wetsuits gathered around boards and sail lines a few hundred yards away.

"Mind if I tag along?" Don asked.

"Not at all." She swept her arms forward. "This way."

They walked along the boardwalk until it ended on the beach. Don removed his sneakers. Sherry laced hers tighter. Their footsteps were heavy and cumbersome in the dry sand. Sherry stopped once to shake out some pesky granules that had hitched a ride in her sock and scratched her skin. Don dug his feet in deep until they were covered.

"Why don't you just take those off?" he asked. "The sand feels so good."

"I'd have to rinse and dry my feet before we get back in the car, and I'm too tired," she moaned.

"Winter's coming fast. You may not get another chance."

"On my next day off, I promise I will." She reached behind her back and crossed her fingers.

As they approached the group of kite surfers, Sherry scanned each person for any signs of famil-iarity. With their wetsuit hoods pulled up over necks, ears, and hair, she found making a positive identifica-tion of someone close to impossible. The suits offered so much compression she could barely tell a male from a female.

"I'm going to talk to that guy who's unloading his equipment. I want to pick his brain. I might have to take up this sport." Don trotted toward a Jeep that had four-wheeled to the top of the beach.

"Have fun." Sherry neared the group, most with their backs to her. "Excuse me," she said to the first person she approached.

The body in front of her holding ropes with gloved hands made no move to respond.

"He can't hear me," she muttered. "Excuse me," Sherry shouted. Her words cut through the roaring wind and startled the kite surfer.

A whiskered man jerked his head in Sherry's direction. "Yup?"

"I'm sorry, I thought you were someone else," Sherry retreated a step and caught her foot on the edge of a board someone had just set down. Her other leg collapsed under a mistimed step. She tumbled onto her side. The coarse sand broke her fall, but the granules made themselves known in every accessible clothing opening. When she stood up to dust herself off, the sand sprinkled out of her pant cuffs, her waistband, and her sleeves.

"Might as well have taken off my shoes at this point," she laughed.

The kite surfer wrinkled his nose and refocused on straightening his ropes.

Sherry sidestepped a huge sail canopy as it lay in wait on the sand. "I'm looking for Lyman St. Pierre. Do you know him?" she asked a surfer dragging a board toward the water.

The surfer, who she assumed was a woman after assessing the delicate physique, made a head bob toward the water. Sherry's gaze followed the direction of the head bob. Bouncing from whitecap wave to whitecap wave was a kite surfer in full flight. The colorful canopy billowed overhead, catching the wind to power him forward. Sherry walked to the edge of the surf. The next thing she remembered was crawling out of knee-high water.

"That's the worst place you could have chosen to stand. Are you okay?" another neoprene-protected body asked her. "These canopies are hard to control. I'm learning the technique as we speak. This is only my third time out. Lucky you weren't dragged out any farther."

Sherry crawled to dry land then chose to sit on the sand where she could safely monitor how see-through her soaked pants had become. "No problem. My fault."

"Coming in!" shouted a kite surfer as he sped toward shore.

Before Sherry had time to leap to her feet, she was nearly face-to-board with Lyman and his equipment.

"Phew, that was close. Glad you saw me. Quick, grab my kite."

Sherry swiveled her head in hopes an expert kite grabber was in sight. Seeing no one facing the surfer, it became clear the directive was aimed at her. She beelined for the canopy and held on for dear life. The wind tried its hardest to rip the sail from her grip. Sherry held her breath as she watched lines and harnesses being unhitched. Finally, the edge of the canopy was deflated. It fell to the sand, limp.

Lyman thanked Sherry for her service. He peeled his tight hood down to his neck. "Have we met? I'm sure we've met." He surveyed Sherry's soaked clothing. "You were dressed a bit differently. It was at the cook-off reception last night. I never forget a face, but I'm not coming up with your name, sorry."

Sherry wiped her hand on her pants, which only served to sand them up further. "Sherry Oliveri. I was one of the cook-off contestants."

"What a coincidence running, or should I say, sailing into you down here. I hope you'll enjoy the spice samples included in your goodie bag. Spice Attitude only imports the finest."

"Actually, I live in Augustin, so it's not that much of a coincidence. I don't get to the beach as often as I'd like, but today was so lovely, I couldn't resist playing a bit of hooky from my work. Needed to relax after the cook-off."

"Ha," he chuckled. He studied Sherry from head to toe. "You might want to consider the other side of the beach where the action's a bit slower."

"I learned that lesson the hard way. Are you staying in Augustin long?" She handed Lyman a stray cable. "Where are you from?"

"I'm staying at the Augustin Motor Lodge for a few days. A few more business appointments to attend to. I'm from the northern hill country of Connecticut. Close enough I had to bring my kite board, which I don't get to use as much as I'd like, due to travel obligations. I spend a fair bit of time in Maine, where our distribution plant is located."

"Maine is such a foodie paradise. Seafood, produce, craft beers. Everyone is about organic and sustainable up there. I'm jealous." Sherry waited until Lyman's full attention was on her and off his equipment. "Wasn't that awful about the contestant, Fitz Frye? I was looking forward to cooking alongside him."

Lyman squinted and gazed past Sherry's head. The wind caught his hood and pushed it halfway up the back of his head. "Poor guy."

"Did you know him well?"

"Nope. The few minutes I spent with him I got the impression he was kind of feisty. Maybe that's a characteristic of the creative."

"Honestly, I heard he had angry words with some at the party." Sherry took some time to scan her surroundings. Twenty people, at least, were milling about the beach. The closest person to her looked as if he or she could subdue Lyman if need be. She could see Don making his way down the beach toward her, as well. Sherry decided to go for it. "As a matter of fact, I specifically remember you and him arguing over something."

Chapter 10

Lyman resumed packing up his equipment. "Unfortunately, that's true. Goes to show, pick your battles. It was a silly argument over dried herbs versus fresh herbs. As an importer, I choose dried spices and herbs because that's what I represent, so that's the side I'm on. Fitz was Team Fresh Herbs all the way. So silly, right? Never know what will set someone off. I'm guessing he's got a few skeletons in his closet if he angers that easily."

"Someone was angry enough with him to kill him." Sherry sucked in her breath, bent down, and collected the rope Lyman let fall from his grip.

"Kill?" Lyman spat out the word. "He was murdered? Makes sense why all the questions. Some lady came looking for me just before I set sail. Never seen anyone wear so much makeup to the beach in my life. She had a lot of questions. I admit I ran out of patience with her prying. When did his death happen, exactly?"

"After the party. Sometime around midnight last night." Sherry handed Lyman the rope.

"Hey, you're the spice guy from the cook-off," Don said as he trotted up to Sherry. "I watched you come in. You're amazing. I need to take up this sport." Don's hand jutted out and shook Lyman's, ropes and all.

"Thanks. You should. It's a blast. Gotta get going. Nice to see you both. Write a review of the spices on our website, if you enjoy them." Lyman turned and hauled his board and harness up the beach.

Don transferred his attention to Sherry. "I wasn't aware kitesurfing was an audience participation sport."

Sherry inspected her pants again. "I wasn't either. I hope Amber has a change of clothes I can borrow back at the store."

"Probably should have taken your shoes off."

"Definitely will next time," Sherry agreed. "Would you like a ride back to the store?"

"I think I might go for a walk. Maybe someone can text me if we're getting together for a drink." Don glanced up the beach in the direction Lyman was headed. "Was seeing Lyman St. Pierre the errand you needed to run?"

Sherry sighed. "It was, and I didn't even get any spices out of it."

"I'm going to go watch that guy sail. I can't get enough of this sport." Don headed down the beach. "I'll catch up to you later."

Sherry attempted to dislodge more sand from her pant cuffs, but the wetness of the fabric held the sand tight. She gave up the task, sighed, and made her way back to her car. As soon as Sherry put the vehicle in reverse, her phone rang. The backup camera on the center console overrode the incoming call information. "Hello?"

"Sherry?"

"Yes?"

"I got your number from a very nice woman named Amber when I called The Ruggery. This is Vilma Pitney." The caller paused.

Sherry stepped on the brake pedal. "I need to have a word with Amber about handing out my phone number."

"Speak up, dear, I can't hear you."

Sherry raised her voice. "Hi, Vilma. What can I do for you?"

"When I called the store in hopes of finding you there, she mentioned you were out on an errand. I called to tell you to run, don't walk, to catch up to Lyman St. Pierre. He's down at Town Beach surfing across the ocean while being dragged like a puppet by a flimsy kite sail thingy. He's the one who can get the suspicion off your brother."

"By any chance, did you have a conversation with Lyman within the last hour or two? I found him, and he mentioned someone had asked him questions. Presumably about Fitz."

The phone crackled. Sherry pictured Vilma repositioning it.

"Yes, I did. I went right after I visited your lovely store. I felt like you might not have taken my suggestion to seek him out seriously, so I found him myself." Vilma's tone was a blend of apologetic and annoyed.

"I appreciate your suggestion."

"If you have any information to share, please let

me know. He didn't have any time to speak to me. In midsentence, his sail caught wind, and he took off."

"Why are you even interested? I thought your article was about the cook-off." Sherry put her car in gear and drove out of the beach parking lot. She caught a last-minute sighting of Don waving to her.

"You, of all people, should realize a murder connected to a cook-off makes for great reading. I want to be current with my information in case the story explodes. I want a leg up on that Mellitt woman." Vilma's *w*'s began to sound more like *v*'s as her accent crept in.

"I've arrived back at the store," Sherry fibbed. "Yes, I'll be sure to keep you updated."

"And I, you."

The remainder of the drive back to The Ruggery wasn't phone-free for long.

"Call Ray Bease," Sherry ordered.

The voice-commanded dialer connected.

"Sherry, is there a problem?" Ray asked.

Sherry was caught off guard by the urgency in his voice. "No, no. I wanted to run something by you. Hold on for one second." Sherry heard a groan on the other end of the phone. She wedged her car into the narrow parking spot beside Amber's car in the back alley of The Ruggery. "Are you still there?"

"No rush. I've got all day." Ray's sarcasm made Sherry cringe. "You could have called when you had your ducks in a row."

"Don't get ornery, Ray. I've done some legwork on Lyman St. Pierre. While he appears a happy-go-lucky spice rep, the brief conversation I had with him revealed a different side to his personality. He didn't mind sharing that he and Fitz had had an argument about dried versus fresh herbs." Sherry stared at the phone display on her dashboard and watched the timer tick off seconds of dead air. "Ray?"

"You'll have to do better than that. Witnesses say it was a full-blown altercation between the victim and Mr. St. Pierre. I highly doubt a spice controversy initiated much more than a debate."

"I knew you wouldn't be happy with me doing some investigating," Sherry admitted. "I'm bracing for your lecture to stay in my lane and let the long arm of the law clear my brother. And a bunch of euphemisms from past decades blended in for good measure, Detective Bease style."

"On the contrary. Don't get me wrong. If you want to search for the murderer in order to clear your brother, feel free."

"Is this Detective Ray Bease I'm talking to? The man who, on three separate occasions, went above and beyond to try to keep me from any involvement in a murder investigation, even when I, and then my father, were the prime suspects? What's gotten into you?" Sherry watched a blue jay land in a bush outside her open car window, only to be spooked by her voice.

"Frankly, I don't mind the assistance right now." Ray's voice dropped to an almost inaudible level.

"Is everything okay?" Sherry matched his tone.

"It's been a tough few months for me. My mother is on her last legs. I'm the caregiver. The situation has taken a toll on my work schedule, and, as much as the department tries to support me, I know I'm on thin ice if I don't wrap up this murder investigation in a timely and successful manner. I feel like the young detective vultures are circling my decaying carcass in hopes of picking my bones clean and claiming my job."

"I'm so sorry about your mother. Maybe you're being a bit dramatic about the status of your job being in jeopardy?"

"My job is most certainly on the line, to some degree. If I'm demoted, well . . ." Ray sounded winded, as if he were fighting surfacing emotions and losing the battle.

"That's not going to happen. As annoying and prickly as you are sometimes, you're the best at what you do. You've always said your street smarts can beat out the new crop of detectives' book smarts any day."

"Huh." Ray's tone picked up energy. "I do want to tell you I'm getting pressure to formally question Pep. Time's ticking. You didn't hear it from me. Anything else?"

"I wish I had more, but I don't. Chin up, old friend." Sherry ended the call. "I'm starving," she muttered to herself. She reached into the crevices of the car's center console and pulled out a stick of gum. "Beggars can't be choosers." She crumbled up the foil wrapper and set it in one of the cup holders. "What's this?" She lifted two business cards wedged in the adjacent cup holder. "Well, what do you know? Now I remember putting these here after the contestant party."

One card read: SPICE ATTITUDE, FINEST IMPORTED DRIED SPICES AND SPICE BLENDS, LYMAN ST. PIERRE, SALES REPRESENTATIVE.

The other read: FITZ FRYE, PERFECT LOCATION INC. PROPERTY MANAGEMENT.

Sherry tucked both cards in her purse and exited the car.

"I'm back," Sherry called out as she entered the store.

Erno was with a young couple at the rug hooking demonstration table. He was punching the sharp metal hook threaded with luxurious yarn through a hand-drawn canvas tacked to a wooden frame. The couple watched in amazement, as most did, while her father crafted his artistic magic. He tossed a hand in the air as a greeting. Bean scampered across the store with a more ebullient welcome.

Amber trailed behind her four-legged companion. "Erno made it back right after you left. He said Ruth and Beverly snubbed him in favor of a spontaneous bridge game. No men allowed. Was your errand successful?" Amber pinched her eyes nearly closed.

"What's that look you're giving me?" Sherry asked.

"You went in search of that Lyman fellow, admit it."

"How did you know that?"

"A woman called here looking for your cell. She told me to urge you to find the killer. She was pretty assertive. Judging by the soaked outfit, ocean water smell, and dots of seaweed on your pants, you found him in the Long Island Sound." Amber laughed. "I'm not a bad little detective, am I?"

"Bingo." Sherry pried off her wet shoes behind the sales counter.

"It helped that the lady looking for your number mentioned the importance of finding a certain Lyman St. Pierre who was kite surfing. You're being extra careful, I hope."

Sherry swept her open arms across her body. "Extra, extra careful. Any chance you have a change of clothes here or in your car?"

"Yep. I'll go get them and meet you in the restroom. Oh, and Day said she and Don would be at the Lobsta' Taproom at five-thirty, and we should please come." Amber nodded her head and flashed a broad smile.

"Perfect. This stick of gum is all I've had to eat since the cook-off. I might splurge for a celebratory lobster roll in honor of my cook-off win. We'll close up promptly at five and hustle over there." Sherry raised her sleeve to her nose and sniffed. "No time for a shower. I should be plenty ripe by then. Is Pep interested in joining us?"

Sherry glanced at Erno. He was plunging a hook threaded with a long strand of lavender yarn through the framed canvas.

"Pep told Erno a few minutes ago that he had somewhere to go. I didn't hear where, and I didn't hear how long he'd be gone. He was checking his phone every few minutes like an anxious parent while you were gone. As much as I enjoy his company, it was kind of a relief he took off."

"He gets in his own world sometimes and won't tell me where that world is." Sherry shrugged. "I can only pry so much before his shell snaps shut and he retreats. I'll text him the plans and hope for the best."

Only one task remained before closing time. Sherry collected the last bits of yarn from the floor and marveled at the array of colors in her hand. She packed them neatly in the half-full canister under the demonstration table.

"That should be full by Tuesday." Erno picked up the canister and peeked inside. "Love that nothing goes to waste around here."

"The kids at the Kid's Klub Daycare Center make the coolest projects out of the bits of yarn we donate. Honestly, the gratitude alone of the group over there makes the twice-a-month trip something I really look forward to."

Erno nodded and stirred the basket contents with a loving hand.

"Are you sure you don't want to come out with Amber and me? I'm not positive Pep will join us, but I'm hopeful." Sherry lifted her jean jacket from the coatrack beside the door. "If not, we'll see you tomorrow when we get some plans made. No one plans too far ahead around here."

Amber sidled up to Sherry.

"I think not for tonight," Erno replied. "Ruth and I might paint the town red on our own. I haven't seen her since lunchtime. Absence makes the heart grow fonder."

"Have fun, Dad. Amber, I'll meet you at the Taproom in a few."

Erno exited through the back door, as did Amber. Sherry took one more look around the store. When she was satisfied everything was in its proper place, she turned off the lights, with the exception of one hallway light, which remained on twenty-four seven.

On a whim, Sherry decided to take the longer route across town and drive past the Augustin Inn. A truck parked under the inn's columned overhang caught her eye. She slowed her car to a crawl. Two muscular men were loading a large tabletop into the back of the truck.

"There goes the appetizer table," Sherry commented to herself. "Must have been a rental."

"Sherry? Is that you?" the woman standing by the driver's side door of the truck called out. Ginger. She motioned Sherry to pull into the inn's driveway. "Over here."

"Doesn't pay to be nosey." Sherry sighed. She parked her car behind the truck and opened her window. "Hi, Ginger. I was on my way to meet some people down at the Taproom. How're you doing? Thank you so much again for hosting the contestant gathering."

"My pleasure. It was certainly a plus to be booked to capacity during the event. Wish business was always this brisk." Ginger's lower lip protruded as the sentiment left her mouth.

Sherry leaned out her window. "I was so sorry to hear about what happened to one of the party attendees."

"The occurrence certainly isn't helping business. I hope the mess gets resolved quickly and my potential customers have short memories."

"Excuse me, lady. The set of chairs is ready to be packed in the truck," a burly man barked from the inn's entrance.

Ginger cupped her hands around her mouth. "Yes, all twelve, please."

Sherry watched the man hoist two wooden dining room chairs up with each arm and make his way to the truck. He was joined by Ginger's brother, Addison. "Those are the same chairs we had at the wedding party table at my reception. I remember admiring the intricate carving detail. Are you storing them offsite for some reason?"

"Unfortunately, I had to find a buyer for the set and the matching antique table. Got bills to pay, and business isn't what it used to be. Since two new inns have opened up closer to the water, we only get the spillover. More events like the cook-off would help, as long as there are no more murders." Ginger twisted her mouth into a frown.

"I'm sorry, Ginger. I didn't realize." Sherry paused. "Well, maybe I heard some rumblings of you closing the doors after the holidays. That can't be true, right?"

"Lady, this seat cover has a tear in it. I'll photograph it so we can discount the cost accordingly," Burly Man called out.

"Thanks for announcing that to the world," Ginger snapped at the man. "Addison, can you grab my phone for me?" Ginger backed away from Sherry's car. "I have to go. Thanks for stopping by."

Sherry watched Ginger make a beeline for the truck, and then she shifted the car into reverse. Her attention darted to the back-up camera sounding an ominous warning beep. Two people were crossing behind her car, one she recognized right away even from the grainy image on the camera's screen.

Ray tapped on her car's back window.

Sherry leaned back out her window. "Afternoon, Ray." She strained to get a better look at the young lady by Ray's side. "Hi."

The woman was dressed in a sweatshirt and blue jeans. She had a large purse slung over her shoulder.

"Hello, Sherry," Ray replied.

The woman beside him stayed silent, gaze fixed on her ankle-high sneakers.

Ray spoke to the woman, who then resumed walking toward the outer parking lot. She never looked back.

"I know you're going to ask, so I'll just save you the question. Oxana is the nights and weekend cleaner for the Augustin Inn and, unfortunately, she was the one who found Frye's body. She doesn't speak English fluently, so it's been difficult, to say the least, trying to get her side of the story. Not many Russian translators are available at short notice."

"How terrible. Traumatic for her."

"And yes, she has an alibi. She didn't do it. Oxana was making her rounds one room at a time. She took a full ninety minutes cleaning the party room after the ice sculpture was removed, during which time Frye met his end. She found the body when she went into the barn. She takes her breaks in a space set up for her in there. Frye had already been dead at least one hour, by the coroner's estimates. Oxana said she'd been in and out of the barn half a dozen times, before she saw the body in the water."

"Awful for the girl." Sherry checked the clock on the dashboard. "I'm sorry, I've got to get a move on. Meeting some new cook-off friends at the Taproom." She squared herself up to her car's steering wheel before one last look at the detective. "There's a Russian reporter named Vilma Pitney sniffing around. Normally, I'd say that's no big deal except, she seems very invested in the developing details of your investigation."

"Unless she's interfering and impeding the process, you just have to accept the fact there will always be interest in murder investigations. I wouldn't give her a second thought." He stepped back and tipped his hat before heading toward the parking lot.

Chapter 11

"We're meeting two people. Don Johnstone and Day Paulson. I hope they made a reservation under one of those names," Sherry told the hostess. "There may be five of us in total."

"Wait right here." The woman wore a dress printed with tiny lobsters.

"The décor is a bit overstated." Sherry scanned the fishing nets, lobster pots, and giant plastic lobsters that lined the dark wood walls. Party lights were strung throughout the display.

"I've seen worse," Amber laughed. "Once, I waitressed at a restaurant called The Unbridled Unicorn. Everything unicorn, pink, sparkly, overly lit. I would have worn sunglasses while working, if they let me. That's how bright it was. No accounting for people's taste. This place says coastal New England, and I like that."

The hostess returned with a frown. "Your party's not here yet, and you don't have a reservation, but I'm letting you take the table, despite." She collected some menus from her desk and marched away.

"I guess we're supposed to follow her," Amber suggested.

Sherry surveyed the dark restaurant. "It's five-thirty. I don't see crowds clamoring for the early-bird special. She should be happy we're filling an empty table."

Sherry followed Amber toward the back of the restaurant.

"Sherry? Is that you?"

Sherry jerked her head to the right. There, seated at a small table for four, were Vilma and two men. Sherry reached forward to stop Amber's progress by snagging her coattail, but her friend was out of reach. "Hi, Vilma. We keep bumping into each other."

"My good fortune. You remember Uri Veshlage and Roe Trembley?"

"Of course. Hi." Sherry nodded in the men's direction.

"We're grabbing an early bite to eat. We'd love for you to join us." If there was any sincerity in Vilma's voice, Sherry couldn't detect it.

"Thanks anyway, but—" Sherry began.

Amber tapped Sherry's arm. "Sherry, there you are. Turns out the table's not quite ready after all."

"Please, take the empty seat. Uri, would you mind pulling that extra chair over?" Vilma stood and extended her hand to Amber. "Vilma Pitney, journalist."

"Amber Sherman, friend and coworker of Sherry. Nice to meet you." Amber acknowledged the men with a smile.

"Please, don't stop eating." Sherry eyed Roe's

dinner plate. "It looks too good to let it get cold. Doesn't look like lobsta', which I assume is the specialty."

"Fish. Beer battered. Not sure what kind." Roe crunched down on a bite.

"Tilapia is often used as a generic white fish for fish sticks and fish fingers," Amber commented.

"Then, tilapia it is." Roe smiled and took another bite.

"Isn't Roe a fishing expert?" Sherry asked.

"Technically, a sustainable fishing expert. The lighting's dim in here. You can't expect him to see subtle varietal differences of the cooked fish on his plate when we can barely read the menu without a flashlight," Uri added. "Rest assured, my company counts on him to ensure we sell the finest local and sustainable product, and he does just that. You're putting that in the cook-off article, aren't you, my dear Vilma." The once-over Uri gave Vilma was intense enough to propel Sherry's eyebrows into a high arch.

Amber pulled her chair up beside Sherry's. "From what I've read about tilapia, you might want to be certain you're not eating it. Most tilapia comes from overseas, and it's grown in unregulated farms that put a premium on how quickly the fish can be raised and sent off to market. Forced growth involves sketchy practices."

Roe kept his sights on his plate and made no effort to prolong the conversation.

"We'll ask the waitress when she comes around." Vilma's smile could melt ice cream.

"I ran into Ginger on my way here," Sherry said.

"She's recovering from the ups and downs of last night's get-together."

"She's got rough seas ahead of her and her establishment, from what I've heard," Vilma added. "She should be thrilled to have had the party held at her inn. Despite the outcome."

Uri shifted in his chair. "Ginger is a lovely woman. Mr. Frye's death is a tragedy for his family and the Constable family." He poked at his baked potato with his fork. "I imagine the investigation into Fitz's murder will be ramping up very soon. Whoever's in charge should find that guy who was hawking spices."

Sherry softened her tone. "Any particular reason?"

Vilma dropped her forkful of kale with a clang. "Uri has a crazy notion Lyman had it out for Fitz and was stalking him."

Uri picked up his napkin and wiped a kale leaf from the tablecloth. "Me? Those are your words, not mine. But, Vilma's right. I saw the tail end of an argument between the two, and later, one ended up dead. Worth a second look, in my opinion." He set his napkin down and smoothed his wavy hair with his fingertips. He winked at Vilma. "We agree on that, don't we?"

"Lyman's not the only one who had words with Fitz. There seemed to be a line of people giving him the what for." Vilma cleared her throat. "I think you should tell Sherry what we discussed, Uri." She batted her unusually thick and lengthy eyelashes.

"I love the way you roll your *r*'s when you say my name," Uri commented.

Sherry winced when Amber kicked her leg under the table.

Uri leaned forward until his shirt scraped his plate. "Not many people know, Fitz got into this year's cook-off on a technicality rather than skill, like the rest of you cooks."

Vilma flashed a sly smile. "I'm trying to decide whether to include that fact in my article."

"Depends on how you spin it, my dear," Uri added. "I don't want Maine Course to suffer any repercussions backing a cook-off that bends the rules."

Amber leaned forward. "How did it come about that he got in on a technicality?"

"I'll tell her, Uri. I don't want to get you in trouble," Vilma answered. "Last year, Fitz did indeed make it into the Fall Fest Cook-off, which was not sponsored by Maine Course Foods or Shrimply Amazing, but by another seafood company. Do you remember, Sherry?"

"I didn't compete last year because the timing was off for me, so I really don't recall."

"I'll explain. Last year, Fitz made the cook-off finals. Unfortunately, he had to suddenly withdraw, stating personal reasons. The organizer offered him a spot in the following year's finals. As this year's cook-off neared, it took a while for Fitz to prove he was verbally extended the offer, but he persisted and was successful," Vilma explained. "The Hands-On category took on an extra cook as a result."

"That's unusual, but may explain why our similar recipes made it to the finals. That isn't usually the case," Sherry said. "Judges prefer a lot of variety amongst the finalist recipes. Shows the versatility of the sponsor's products."

"Be that as it may," Vilma continued, "as soon as Lyman had a dust-up with Fitz at the party, over who knows what, Lyman brought up Fitz's unusual circumstances. He spun it in such a way as to insinuate Fitz was given preferential treatment. A little underhanded by Lyman, in my opinion. Word circulated at the party that Fitz may have also stolen Sherry's idea for shrimp wraps. But, if you know the story, you'd know that wasn't the case."

Sherry raised both hands to her temples and rubbed. "No, no, no. People might think I believe he would steal a recipe idea from me. I certainly don't. I didn't invent the idea of shrimp wraps. Only my original take on them. There are plenty of other good ideas for serving shrimp in wraps."

"Don't worry," Vilma was quick to offer. "Pep came to your defense, stating you would never start such a rumor and that you welcomed the challenge."

"Pep didn't tell me he did that."

"Probably best he didn't tell you before the cook-off," Amber said.

"Lyman didn't mention any of that this afternoon when we talked," Sherry added.

"Ma'am, your table is ready. The rest of your party has arrived." The hostess waited, menus clutched to her chest.

Amber stood. "Enjoy your meals."

As they made their way to their table, Sherry said, "Vilma really has it out for Lyman. If it were up to her, he'd be on trial for Fitz's murder already. At the same time, I'm afraid she has it out for Pep, too. She just can't decide between the two."

"And does she have a thing for Uri?" Amber snickered.

"Hi, guys." Sherry waved to Day and Don as she approached the table. "I didn't see you come in."

Day waved back. "Hi. Long time no see. Pep's outside, sitting in his car. I tapped on his window. He signaled he was finishing up a phone call."

Don patted the seat cushion next to him, inviting Sherry to sit.

"Wonder what he's been up to for the last couple hours," Sherry added. "Or most any time he's not in sight, for that matter." She took the seat next to Don and smiled in his direction. He rewarded her with a warm grin.

Amber was left standing behind Sherry.

"I have a seat over here for you, Amber," Day announced.

Amber grinned at her friend as she sat. "Mother hens are necessary when the chicks are babies, Sher, but soon they leave the nest. Your bro might be testing his wings and needs a little space."

"You caught me." Sherry addressed Day and Don. "Amber practiced family therapy until recently." Then back to Amber. "Feel free to use the Oliveri example of dysfunctional family dynamics in your advice column. Problem is, your advice is easier heard than put into action. I regress to protective-older-sister mode when he's here." Sherry turned to face Day. "Before we knew you were here, we were chatting with Uri from Maine Course Foods, Roe Trembley, and a reporter named Vilma Pitney. Over there, sitting near the kitchen." Sherry pointed the way. "They have some theories about what may have happened to Fitz."

"Have you solved the case?" Day asked. "Amber was telling us what a great detective you are."

"It's a very intriguing quality," Don said in a soft voice.

"Amber! You're going to get me in big trouble with Detective Bease." Sherry turned back to Day. "As for solving the case, not even close. But to hear it from that group, the man at the party passing out spice samples should be locked up immediately."

"Hmmm. I'd never have guessed he was capable of murder," Don said. "But I'm no expert, and I'm kinda glad about that."

"Is anyone else having something to eat? I'd love to try the fish and chips," Day asked. "Should be good at a place like this, right?"

"I don't know," Amber weighed in. "We were just discussing that at the other table. I've read bad things about the mystery white fish used to make them."

"Ha, we should ask Roe," Don added.

"I did," Amber replied. "He wasn't an expert on tilapia. As a matter of fact, he had no information to offer about what kind of fish was in his fish and chips."

"Well, I'm throwing caution to the wind and ordering it," laughed Don.

"Proceed at your own risk." Amber peered behind Sherry. "Here comes the waitress."

"Hi, my name is Fuchsia. I'm your server today." The robust woman smiled. She was holding a tray balancing four full wineglasses. "The owner, who happens to be my husband, has sent the table a round of drinks." She set down a glass in front of each person.

"Attention, everyone," a man shouted as he approached the table. The restaurant went silent. "Let's raise a glass to our local star cook who just won the New England Fall Fest Cook-off." He heightened the volume of his announcement. "Sherry Oliveri."

Sherry's mouth dropped open as all heads rotated to face her. She raised her arm and waved a shaky hand. "Thank you," she said in the direction of Fuchsia's husband.

The restaurant applause died down, and the conversations at each table resumed.

"Now, may I take your orders?" Fuchsia asked.

"That was a shock," Sherry whispered to Don.

"I'm sure you get that wherever you go." He turned to the waitress. "Quick question about the fish and chips. Do you know what kind of fish is used?"

Fuchsia lowered her empty tray to her side. "Must be the topic of the day. That table asked the same question." She jerked her head toward Vilma's table. "Local cod, of course. We would sell nothing less than the best," Fuchsia boasted.

Don nodded. "We'll have two plates of fish and chips to share for the table, please."

"And please, thank your husband," Sherry added.

"Thank him for what?"

All heads pivoted toward Pep as he approached the table.

"Pep, you made it," Amber called out. "You missed a mini celebration for your sister. Have my wine in honor of your sous chef contribution. I haven't taken a sip yet."

Pep removed his jacket and extended a communal nod to everyone at the table. "Thanks, but wine's not my drink of choice. A cold brew suits me just fine. Thanks, anyway." He hijacked a chair from a neighboring table and pulled it next to Amber.

After a second round of drinks and a third plate of fish and chips, Sherry pushed back in her chair and yawned. "Guys, I've hit a wall. I think I'll call it quits and head home. I don't have to work at the store tomorrow, but I've got some editing to do for the town's newsletter. I need a good night's sleep to clear my head. So fun being with you both, Day and Don."

Pep pushed his chair back and stood. "I'll join you."

"How much longer are you here, Pep?" Don asked.

"Two more days, then I'm off," Pep replied as he avoided Sherry's glare.

Chapter
12

"Where'd you park?" Pep asked.

"There were loads of parking spots a while ago. Now that the lot's full, I'm having trouble remembering. I promise I only had one, maybe two glasses of wine." Sherry doubled back down a row of cars. "Here it is."

"Okay, see you later," Pep called out.

"Wait, Pep. Something terrible happened to my car!" Sherry cried out.

Pep sprinted back to his sister.

Sherry stood under a lamppost that shone a dull yellow light down on the line of cars. "My poor car."

Pep ran his hand down the side of Sherry's car, tracing the outline of a zigzagging, scratch that ran from the driver's side door back to the rear taillight. "It doesn't look like another car scraped the side, judging by the freestyle wave of the damage. The damage is from end to end."

Sherry surveyed the side of the car. "Some sort of tool, like an ice pick, would cause this damage."

"We need to call the police. Your insurance will want a full report."

Sherry whimpered and her shoulders drooped.

Pep stepped closer to his sister. "I know you don't want to, but your insurance does."

Sherry dialed the police and was instructed to wait by the car until a squad car arrived.

"The dispatcher said a car is in the area and—" Before Sherry could complete her thought, a police car pulled up. The driver rolled down the window.

Sherry approached the squad car. "Hi, Officer. I was the one who called you." Sherry studied the woman in uniform. "You're the officer who pulled me over for a missing taillight a couple of months ago. You also assisted me when I was being threatened by a deranged madman."

"Yes, ma'am. Just doing my job. What seems to be the problem this time?" The officer opened her car door and stepped out, hand on her holstered gun.

"My brother and I," Sherry tilted her head toward Pep, "were eating at the Taproom. When I came out, I found my car had been vandalized."

The officer held an unwavering stare into Sherry's eyes. "Let's take a look."

The trio approached Sherry's car. The police-woman shone her flashlight from one end of the car to the other. She circled the car before returning to Sherry and Pep. "Yup. That's a deliberate act of vandalism."

"I can't believe no one witnessed it," Sherry lamented.

"If anyone did, you'll be lucky if they step forward. If the act was random, it's bad luck your car was chosen." The officer turned her gaze to the car. "If it was deliberate and someone is targeting you, that needs to be evaluated. I assume you want to file a report?"

Sherry nodded.

"I'll need your information. I'll need your license, registration, and insurance information. Meet me at the squad car."

Sherry lifted her head slightly. "Be right there," she called to the officer. "I'll be okay, Pep. Why don't you head home. I'll be there in a while. Let me give you the house key." She pulled her key ring from her purse. She wrestled the house key off the ring and handed it to Pep. "See you soon, hopefully."

Sherry sorted through the papers in her car's glove compartment until she found the registration and insurance information. She brought the papers, along with her license, to the policewoman's squad car.

When the officer completed the report, she gave Sherry one last bit of advice. "If you have any idea who may have done this, I advise you not to take matters into your own hands. Could be a whole lot worse the next time."

Sherry watched the police car drive away. She peered around the parking lot and saw no one. She hugged her purse to her midsection and returned to her car.

As she waited for a clearing to pull her car out of the parking lot, Sherry dialed Ray. He answered in his familiar business tone.

"Bease here."

"Hi, Ray." Sherry pressed the gas pedal and

merged her car onto the main road. She relayed the events of the evening to him as she navigated the roads home. "I'm getting a feeling of déjà vu. Someone might be tracking me."

"Go with your gut." Ray's reply was blunt enough to sting. "Do you have a sense many people knew you in the restaurant?"

"Maybe not knew me, but the owner made a big hoopla about me being there. Free drinks for my table. He made a restaurant-wide announcement. So, unless someone arrived after that, like Pep, they knew I was there."

"Must be nice to be you," Ray commented in a soft monotone. "Drinks on the house."

"Not always nice to be me. Better to be the owner of the auto body shop I'll owe hundreds, maybe thousands, to. There go all my winnings."

"You realize what this most likely means. You're onto someone, and that someone isn't happy about you sniffing around."

Sherry steered the car into her driveway, she shifted it into park and stared through the windshield at her moonlit yard. Her car's headlights revealed two birds tussling over a worm on her lawn. In the rearview mirror, the high beams of a car pulling in behind hers caught her eye. A fleeting ripple of panic radiated through her core.

"Sherry, are you there?" Ray questioned.

"I need to mention, Pep's leaving in a couple of days." Sherry steeled herself for Ray's rebuttal. Her racing heart slowed as Pep exited his car, walked around her car, and tapped on her window.

She waved him off, and he continued onto the

house. Sherry listened hard but heard nothing through the phone. "Ray, are you there?"

"A couple of days cuts it close. Tomorrow I have a meeting about my mother's care. That's taking up most of my day."

"Okay."

"Use your best judgment and proceed with care," Ray added before the phone cut off.

When Sherry reached the front porch, Pep was talking to Chutney through the locked door. On the other side, Chutney was complaining about a lack of attention and outdoor time. Sherry thought of her neighbor, Eileen, who walked Chutney at lunchtime. The woman knew how to slather on the terrier love, so Chutney had no good reason to give Sherry an earful. A faint smile crossed her lips, knowing Chutney was always excited to greet her.

"Where have you been? I thought you were heading straight home."

Pep used the key to unlock the door. "I'm here now." He opened the door and bent down and stroked Chutney's head. "Everything go okay filing the car damage report? Tell me about it while we take this guy for a walk."

"Not much to tell. Got a clear warning from the policewoman and Detective Bease to keep a lookout for anyone with a vendetta against me. Easier said than done." Sherry set her purse on the front hall table and attached Chutney's collar to the leash. She grabbed a flashlight. "All set."

The trio headed back out the door.

Sherry allowed Chutney to sniff each shrub he deemed irresistible. One particularly interesting boxwood halted the walk's progress for an extended length of time.

"How well do you know Roe Trembley?"

"That's a funny question," Pep replied. "What made you ask that?"

"You're answering a question with a question. And you still haven't answered why you left the restaurant parking lot before me and got home after me. I'm beginning to think you work for the CIA or something."

Pep produced a burst of laughter that startled Chutney. The dog lifted his head to check on his people, then was quick to resume examining the bush.

"The answer is, not well. We crossed paths up in Portland. He works for Uri. Provides information on fishing practices. You know all that."

"He was in the group having some strong words with Fitz. You were part of the group. Do you know what the nature of the relationship is between Fitz and Roe?"

"Fitz is a property manager, and Roe works for Uri. Business dealings between them, most likely. Hard to say."

"If that's the case, I wouldn't think Fitz would be able to compete in a cook-off sponsored by a company he has dealings with."

"Let's get this pup inside. I'm tired." Pep did an about-face and Chutney followed, dragging Sherry's arm with him.

Once inside, Sherry gave Chutney his dinner. Any grudge the canine might have held against her about leaving him alone all afternoon evaporated as he gobbled up his kibble.

"Anything special you want to do tomorrow?" Sherry asked her brother. While she waited for his answer, she checked her phone. A text was waiting to be read.

"I'd like to spend some time with Dad. Got any plans?"

Sherry set her phone down on the table. "Ginger texted me. It's always hard to read emotions from texts, but she sounds a bit frantic. She'd like me to stop by the inn in the morning. Not sure what's going on."

Pep removed his shoes. "All I know is it's time to stretch out and read a good book."

"I'm going to read the Fall Fest contestant recipe booklet. Ruth said Fitz Frye's recipe was wonderful, and I'm curious what she liked about it."

Chapter
13

The next morning, after the coffeemaker had performed its duty, Pep poured himself a mugful of liquid energy. He and Sherry headed to the front hall, where he turned to her and said, "Are you sure you don't want to join us for brunch? It's only going to be the two Oliveri guys. No ladies, Dad said. Beverly's in the city, and Ruth's on a shopping excursion, looking for the perfect welcome home present for Frances." He chuckled. "You'd think she'd been gone for a year. I mean, where's my welcome home present?"

"I believe the custom is the visitor brings the present. And if it's not, it should be." Sherry joined in the laughter. "I'll take a pass on the brunch. I have a few things to get done on my day off, before I surrender my car to the body shop. Putting together the town newsletter is looming large, also. Text me later and we'll meet up. I'll probably be home before you."

Pep set his jacket and phone down on the front hall table. "I forgot to return the house key. Let me grab it upstairs." He proceeded to race up the stairs, skipping every other step in the process. On the front hall table, his phone began to vibrate.

Sherry cast a glance toward the phone. She blinked to make sure she was seeing the name broadcast in text with clear vision. "Could that be the same Oxana I saw at the Augustin Inn? Why's she texting Pep, and how do they even know each other?"

"Say something? I couldn't hear you." Pep descended the last step.

"Nothing. I was repeating my grocery list so I wouldn't forget anything. Heaven forbid I should write a list down one day." Sherry's words collided with each other as she spoke. She hoped Pep was oblivious to the apprehension creeping in.

"Funny, I'd peg you for a master list maker. I remember the chore charts you used to make for Marla and me. If that isn't the start of a habitual sticky note user, I don't know what is. Sticky notes are the early warning signs of a future list maker, you know."

"Okay, okay. Very funny."

"Guess I don't know you as well as I once did." Pep kissed Sherry's cheek. "Here's the house key." He set the key in the palm of Sherry's hand.

"I wish I knew you better, too." She put her hand up to her cheek and felt the warm area he had delivered his brotherly love to. "I'll put the key under the front doormat, in case you get back before me."

"I'm off. Catch you later." Pep gave Chutney a pat on the head and left the house.

"Maybe I'll go over to the inn a bit early and see if Oxana is working today," Sherry explained to Chutney. "I'll be back for a nice walk, boy."

Chutney employed his sad puppy dog eyes but

was still unable to change Sherry's plans. Sherry gathered a light jacket and her purse and left the house. She tucked the key under the doormat.

The Augustin Inn was bustling with activity when Sherry arrived. The parking lot was full of cars being loaded with suitcases and Sherry had a difficult time finding a parking spot within easy walking distance. She recognized many contestants and sous chefs hovering around cars, wedging their equipment and supplies inside their trunks.

Sherry was slated to meet up with Ginger in half an hour. She gathered her purse from the passenger seat and set out in search of Oxana. If the young lady were still at the inn, the barn in the back of the inn seemed the logical location to find her. The cleaning equipment was stored there. Sherry learned that nugget of information at her wedding reception, when she and Charlie had snuck off for some private time. They considered the rumored haunted barn a romantic setting for their stolen moments alone. She never dreamed the knowledge would come in handy years later and was thankful for her powers of observation.

Avoiding a walk through the main lobby, so as not to run into Ginger, Sherry followed the sign for the gardens and seasonal corn maze. The bluestone walkway led her through a lilac-lined veranda. She imagined the blooms' fragrance was intoxicating in the late spring, when the flowers were at their peak. On the other side of the veranda was the entrance to the red barn. Beyond the barn was the corn maze, a

Constable tradition started by Clarence, decades ago. She could see the edge of the popular attraction as she approached the barn.

Sherry pictured the sea of families who flocked to the inn on Apple Day to get lost in the maze. She imagined the idea was to have everyone develop an appetite for the many versions of baked and fresh apples offered for sale by local farms and bakeries. She was remorseful she hadn't attended the event since before her marriage, but, without children of her own, she avoided the boisterous celebration and bought her apples elsewhere. Still, her curiosity got the better of her. She considered heading to the maze for a better look until she checked her phone and realized time was getting away from her.

Sherry reached the huge sliding barn door which, to her relief, was partially open. She poked her head through the two-foot-wide gap. The cavernous space was dark, with the exception of the light the door let in. After a second look around, she discovered the back corner was lit with a single fixture. Her first step inside created a resounding creak that alarmed an orchestra of crickets. The tiny parade hopped across her path and sought refuge in ancient wall-board cracks.

"Hello?" Sherry heard a rustling from the far end of the barn. Pulling her second foot inside, her toe caught on the thick threshold. Next thing Sherry knew, she was flat out on the wood floor. She sat up and checked the conditions of her hands. They'd taken the brunt of the fall.

"You okay?"

Sherry looked up to find an arm extended in her

direction. She accepted the help and was pulled to her feet. The woman's grip was so strong, Sherry was lifted into the air for a split second.

"Thank you. I'm kind of clumsy."

The young woman's face screwed up tight as if she didn't understand what Sherry meant. "Clùmsy?" she questioned with a thick accent.

"I need to watch where I place my feet. My name is Sherry. Are you Oxana?"

The woman peered over her shoulder back at the lit corner of the barn. She returned her attention to Sherry. "Yes, Oxana. Nice to meet you." Her pronunciation was halting and almost painful. "I saw you talk to rabies."

"Rabies?" Sherry scrunched her forehead. "Oh! Ray Bease. Yes, the detective who met with you here at the inn. I know him. Just wishing him a good day. You and I didn't get a formal introduction. You seemed to be in a hurry to leave."

"Not a good day," Oxana lamented. "Finding a dead body not fun."

"That's an understatement." Sherry softened her tone. "I think you're a friend of my brother, Pep Oliveri. Is that right?" Sherry delivered her words slowly.

Oxana's line of sight darted around the barn interior before landing back on Sherry. "Pep is very nice. He help me, how you say, organize myself. I go to school. Need money. Need two jobs. School so expensive."

Sherry studied Oxana's expression. Her mouth was set in a pout, and the dark circles under her intense eyes told a story of determination and hard work. Sherry made a decision. "Yes, it is. Glad Pep is able to help you. He's a caring guy." Sherry paused. "It was nice to meet you. I should get over to my meeting in the library." She turned toward the door.

"Sherry?" Oxana beckoned. "My English is not so good, but I'm learning." She paused. "I don't want to get Pep in, how do you say, dagger?"

Sherry faced Oxana and willed her to come up with the word she was struggling for. "Dagger?"

"Dan. No. Daj. No." Oxana grabbed her throat with both hands and stuck her tongue out of her gaping mouth.

"Danger?" Sherry shouted. She covered her mouth with her hand when she realized she wasn't playing charades. "Danger," she repeated in a hushed tone.

"Where's the danger?" a voice called out.

Sherry turned toward the voice. "Vilma. What are you doing here?" Sherry regretted the urgent tone she used to address Vilma. "I mean, seems like we can't avoid each other wherever we go, right?"

"I think you know what's going on here." Vilma nodded as she approached.

"What's that?" Sherry's head swiveled from Vilma to Oxana and back again.

"You've found out I've been tutoring Oxana in English, and you wanted to know if I'm doing a good job." Vilma produced a startling laugh without cracking a smile.

"I was just introducing myself to the young lady Ginger speaks so highly of." Sherry's gaze darted toward Oxana, who returned a look of confusion.

"Do we have a session today?" Oxana asked

Vilma. "I hope I haven't, how you say, messed up the schedule."

"No, dear," Vilma replied. "I was summoned to the inn's library by Ginger to meet with her and Sherry. I thought I'd come say hi because Ginger's not ready yet." Vilma shifted her attention to Sherry. "Glad I did. I could use a moment alone with you, Sherry. That is, unless you're not done speaking with Oxana. It sounded like you were discussing danger?"

Oxana peered over her shoulder toward the back of the barn. She returned her gaze to Sherry. "We're done. Must get back to work. Nice to meet to you, Sherry."

"The proper way to say your sentence is 'nice to meet you,'" Vilma corrected.

Sherry detected the slightest eye roll from Oxana before the young lady walked away.

Vilma swung her arm forward. "Shall we step outside?" Vilma led Sherry out the barn door. She lowered her voice. "I wouldn't frighten Oxana with questions about the murder. She's like a deer in headlights right now. She happened to be in the wrong place at the wrong time when she found Fitz's body. She told me she's haunted by the fact she was in the room with his dead body for almost an hour before she discovered him. She couldn't even manage to tell me that in English, she was so distraught."

"Didn't ask her a thing about the murder," Sherry remarked with a nonchalance that chilled the air. "Did Ginger get our meeting times confused? Why would she set up a meeting with you and me at the same time?"

"Ginger wants to see both of us. She has a strong notion about the Fitz case, and she wants to run it by us."

Sherry scanned the surroundings for anyone within earshot. When she was satisfied she was alone with Vilma, she took a step closer to the woman. "Vilma, we aren't doing this together. My interest is in giving Pep relief from being on the suspect list in the investigation. I don't see how that's any concern of yours. I'm trying to be nice here, but you've bad-mouthed my friend Patti Mellitt, you've inserted yourself into my attempt to help my brother, you've sent me on a wild goose chase to find Lyman, only to get dunked in the Long Island Sound, and frankly, I'm almost getting the impression that you're following me." Sherry, so unused to taking a harsh tone with anyone, saw stars dance across her vision because she forgot to inhale in a timely manner.

Vilma's eyebrows lifted and her nostrils flared. "I, too, am trying to be nice." Vilma's accent surfaced with a vengeance. "I've got a job to do, and that means getting my story, whether you like it or not. Mark my words. It's going to be a blockbuster." She set her shoulders back and relaxed her facial muscles. "I don't want to see your brother charged with any crime he didn't commit, obviously. On the other hand, it's quite curious he's Oxana's friend. Convenient, some would say. Wouldn't you agree?"

Sherry wondered if her cheeks were betraying her attempt not to become rattled. She bit the inside of her cheek to hopefully cool any flush. "I don't like what you're suggesting. You don't know the first thing about my brother, so don't go making assumptions about his relationships. What makes you privy to what goes on at the inn concerning Oxana, anyway?"

"For your information, I got Oxana her job at the inn. I go way back with the Constable family. Clarence was the first person who took an interest in me when I came to this country many years ago. He let me stay at the inn when I barely had enough money to buy bread, let alone pay my room fee."

"The Constable family has always been very charitable."

"I wouldn't consider myself a charity case. Needed a minute to get on my feet, that's all." Vilma repositioned the glasses resting on top of her head.

"How do you know Oxana and Pep are friends?"

"Oxana has had me translate a few of your brother's text messages she's received. It would be a shame if that information got into the hands of anyone suspecting Pep. Seems like it would add fuel to the fire to have him connected to the woman who found the body of the man he'd had a dispute with. I'd be happy to keep that fact to myself in exchange for one small favor."

"What would that be?"

"I'm going to keep my nose to the ground and crack this case, and I'd like your full cooperation. No one will question Sherry Oliveri sniffing around her hometown of Augustin. As a matter of fact, the citizens of this fair town have come to expect that response from you when a murder happens here. What I need is for you to keep me in the loop. You could even call yourself my field reporter, if you like. That's an exciting way of labeling your sleuthing. Do we have a deal?"

"It's not so much a deal as a squeeze play by you, but I guess I have no choice."

"Perfect," Vilma said with a sweetness as artificial as saccharin. "Now, let's go find Ginger."

Chapter
14

Sherry and Vilma were seated in wingback chairs positioned beside the massive stone fireplace. Ginger paced across the inn's library floor. "Thanks for meeting with me."

"You're welcome," Sherry replied. "Compliments to the grounds and the gardener. Your gardens are lovely. I wish I'd seen them at their prime earlier in the summer. The lilacs must have been spectacular."

"Thanks. I'm the gardener, when I get time. The deer are tending the bushes right now and making an awful mess." Ginger let out a sigh. "If it's not one problem, it's another."

"I make my own deer repellent, and I think it does a good job, if I do say so myself. Water, vinegar, peppermint oil, canola oil, and hot sauce. I mix it in a spray bottle and spritz the plants after every rain. I'll bring you some next time I'm in the area."

"I'd appreciate that," Ginger said. "You're so multitalented. You should sell the stuff at the farmer's market."

Sherry saw Vilma check her wristwatch and

frown. "Can we discuss flora and fauna later. I'm on a tight schedule."

"I'll get right to the point," Ginger replied. "I have a theory about Fitz's death I want to run by you two."

"Why us two?" Sherry asked.

"Vilma has been extremely helpful providing me what little information there is about Fitz's death. I need this murder investigation to be solved ASAP, so the inn can get back on whatever shaky ground it has left. This is a black eye on the inn's reputation I needed like a hole in the head."

"That's one way to put it," Vilma agreed.

Ginger faced Vilma. "You've taken it upon yourself to help me keep the inn from being defamed by a prolonged scandal. I'm so lucky you're staying here, otherwise you may never have had any interest in pursuing the truth."

Sherry watched a grin wash over Vilma's face. The tall woman smoothed her hair, pulled tight in a bun.

"You're so kind, but I do have selfish reasons for seeing the murderer brought to justice," Vilma responded.

Sherry leaned in.

"I want the New England Fall Food Fest Cook-off to be held in the area every year. Covering the action has been the highlight of my journalism career. When the story's published, the game will be changed."

"I know you're right." Ginger focused on Sherry. "As for you, Sherry, from what Vilma tells me, it's no secret Pep is in some hot water because of the fight he had with Fitz. I know you'd like to find the killer for that reason."

Sherry side-eyed Vilma. "Pep had nothing to do

with Fitz's murder." Sherry spat the words out with renewed intensity. "Don't believe everything you hear."

"We know that, but it has to be proven. That's beside the point," Ginger stated.

"How could that be beside the point?" Vilma shook her head. "Enlighten me. What's the point?"

"I'm letting the cat out of the bag now. Uri and I have become fast friends"—Ginger winked and grinned a sly smile—"since he arrived last week to help coordinate the cook-off. He'd prefer I didn't talk about our relationship, but it's hard to keep the secret."

Sherry cringed as she recalled Vilma's adoring glances in Uri's direction the previous night at the Taproom. Vilma began bobbing her foot. If she bobbed it with any more vigor, her fashionable ankle boot was in danger of becoming a projectile.

"Doesn't he change his mind quickly," Vilma commented under her breath.

"Uri came into my life at a low point and has brightened my outlook beyond measure. Long story short, he's promised us a future together. He will use the only money I have left in my name, my retirement savings, to save his business and build us a nest egg. I wasn't going to touch that money until I'm old and gray anyway, so why not invest the funds with Uri. He promises growth. Saying good-bye to the inn will be hard, but he said everything will be fine."

Sherry straightened up and intertwined her hands. "Ginger, I can't tell you what to do with your life, but have you given this enough thought? How well do you know this man?"

"Sherry, I'm not a spring chicken. I may not get too many more, or any, opportunities to find someone I can spend the second half of my life with." Ginger faced Sherry. "Problem is, I'm not so sure Uri didn't have something to do with Fitz's death."

"What? No." Sherry shook her head. "Why would you think that?"

"Vilma told me Uri told her that Roe, his hire, was dead set on settling a score with Fitz. Right, Vilma?" Ginger nodded in Vilma's direction.

"That's right. The night of the contestant party, when Pep was finished giving Fitz the business about who knows what, Roe stepped in and picked up where Pep left off. I know because I'd taken a stroll with Uri to get some fresh air and talk some business. When we returned, Uri was the one who separated Roe and Fitz before fists could fly." Vilma glanced at Ginger.

"Don't worry, I'm not the jealous type," Ginger added. "Business is business."

"Nothing to be jealous about," Vilma muttered. She raised her voice. "Uri is strangely protective of Roe. When I interviewed the two, post cook-off, Uri answered every question for Roe, to the point where I stopped asking. I'm usually very good at getting answers, but every time Roe began to speak, Uri cut him off."

"You still haven't given reasons why Uri may have been in on Fitz's murder," Sherry insisted. "You should be careful planting seeds of guilt in people's minds without just cause. Especially if your boyfriend is involved."

"I'm not certain Uri was involved, but, Sherry, I

want you to prove he wasn't," Ginger stated. "My brother, Addison, told me Uri and Roe are hiding something. I think Addison, bless his heart, is protecting his big sister."

"You may want to listen to your brother," Sherry suggested. "I agree you may be in need of some level of protection."

"Did Addison elaborate?" Vilma asked. "I mean, everyone is hiding something, but a murder, now that's quite a secret."

"Can you think of a motive Uri may have for wanting Fitz dead?" Sherry asked.

"Maybe because Fitz didn't get into the cook-off through ordinary channels?" Ginger answered. "Bad reflection on Maine Course as a sponsor?"

"True, but, is that worthy of murder? I mean, Maine Course wasn't the cook-off's only sponsor," Sherry said.

"You're right," Ginger said. "Still, I can't shake the vibe I get from Uri. Like he's hiding something."

"Remind me, how long have you known him?" Vilma asked.

"Not long. When the attraction is real, time is meaningless." Ginger sighed.

"No offense, but there must be literally a lifetime of things you don't know about the man."

"I do know he doesn't like when I bring up Fitz's name in any context," Ginger added.

The corner of Vilma's mouth lifted. "Then he's not going to like the fact that I'm including Fitz's unique cook-off situation in my article. But to murder the guy because he was granted a spot in a cook-off at the last minute? I agree with Sherry. That's a stretch."

"Okay. A stretch." Ginger paused. "Consider this. Fitz owns the building Uri's processing plant is housed in—"

"How do you know that?" Vilma interrupted. "I made some calls, and I didn't find Maine Course or Shrimply Amazing housed in any of Frye's properties."

"Uri said the processing is done a step removed from the Maine Course corporate umbrella but is closely monitored by his company. People wouldn't necessarily know there was a relationship between the companies, unless they delved into the company books. Uri says he runs a tight ship, which I find so endearing." Ginger's eyes glazed over, and the corners of her mouth curled upward.

"Explains how it was legit for Fitz to enter a cook-off Maine Course was a sponsor of, without there being a conflict of interest. So, no problem there. No disputes between building owner, fish processor, and Uri's company that you know of?" Sherry asked.

Ginger shook her head. She offered no comment.

Sherry removed her phone from her purse. She glanced at the time. "So far, you haven't made a case for Uri being involved."

"I know, I know." Ginger began to pace again. She lowered her head. "The night of the party, before the guests arrived, I was visiting Uri in his room."

Sherry side-eyed Vilma, who was intently watching Ginger.

"Busy man," Vilma mouthed.

"When Uri let me in, I was passed by Roe leaving

the room, presumably going back to his own room. Not a big deal, except, once inside, I caught sight of a catalogue folded open on the bureau top. It was a fishing equipment catalogue, judging by what I saw on the page."

"And what did you see on the page?" Vilma asked with a chilly nonchalance.

"A full page of fishing hooks."

The room became so quiet, Sherry was certain the other two women could hear her heart pounding. She saw Ginger's eyes well up with tears. "Remember to never assume the worst. Roe is somehow connected to the fishing industry, so maybe they were doing research. Makes sense." The words Sherry uttered didn't alter the frown on Ginger's face or the stunned look on Vilma's.

"Just a coincidence a fishing hook was lodged in Fitz's neck when his body was found?" Vilma posed the question she appeared to know the answer to.

"Sherry, how quickly can you find the killer, so my Uri and your Pep are found innocent?" Ginger begged.

"That is unless you find one of them guilty, and I don't mean Pep," Vilma offered.

"Vilma," Ginger said, "I thought you were on my side."

Addison poked his head through the library doorway. "Excuse me. Ginger, we have a situation out in the corn maze."

Ginger halted her pacing and faced her brother. "What in the world could that be? It's not even finished yet."

Addison stayed outside the room but craned his

neck through the doorway. "Actually, I just finished it. Now, a guest's toddler is stuck in the maze."

"Stuck? How?"

"I was removing the *Do Not Enter* caution tape when somehow the little girl slipped inside, and no one can find her. Her mom says she knows she's in trouble and is staying silent. Seems whenever the little one gets into mischief, she won't answer her mother, so she's not responding to her name being called. I don't want to alarm the other guests. Would you mind lending a hand corralling the kid? If we close in together from different angles, she can't evade us."

"Sorry, ladies. I have to go," Ginger apologized.

"I'm coming, too. An extra hand will speed up the rescue. Coming, Vilma?" Sherry asked.

"Look at the time," Vilma remarked, even before she pulled her phone out to check it. "I'm already late."

"Come on, Sherry. Let's get over to the maze." Ginger tossed her hand up in a wave. "Thanks for your time, Vilma. I'll be in touch." Ginger pulled Sherry out of her chair with a tug of her arm.

Following Addison's lead, the two women took a shortcut through the red barn. Beyond the barn, they followed a pebbled path that led them to the giant banner hailing the entrance to the enormous corn maze. A woman, presumably the child's mother, stood vigil outside the labyrinth. Her arms were hugged tight around her waist.

"I didn't know the inn had this much land." Sherry contemplated the vast cornfield.

"It's amazing, right? This parcel of land is leased

to the neighboring farm, and every fall they give us
the right to construct a maze out of their harvested
cornfield. Dad made the arrangement the minute
he learned corn mazes were moneymakers during
fall festivals." Ginger turned to the woman positioned next to an empty stroller. "Stay right here,
Mrs. Alvarez, in case your daughter finds her way out
before we find her."

Sherry watched Addison enter the corn maze.
The dried stalks were at least seven feet tall, she estimated, and he was soon swallowed up and out of
sight. He called for Sherry and Ginger to take the
other pathway so as to corner the child from both
directions.

"Follow me," Ginger prompted. "Addison de-
signed the maze. I should've paid more attention to
the process. Right now, I'm regretting I didn't."

The two ladies were no more than ten steps inside
the maze before their first directional option was
presented.

"Dead end to the left." Ginger peered around a
cornstalk wall. She motioned Sherry forward. "Try
and keep up." She trotted the other way.

With the exception of the wood chips crunching
under foot, the maze was eerily quiet. The deeper
the women found themselves inside the maze, the
quieter their surroundings became.

"Is it my imagination or are the pathways getting
narrower with every turn we make? Addison's a
smart designer, if you like this sort of thing. Me? Not
so much," Sherry commented.

"It's normally an exciting experience when it's

packed with visitors. Kind of creepy when it's just you and me."

"Really claustrophobic." Sherry's heart was beating faster than she'd like, and her palms were beginning to perspire. "How will we know if Addison found the little girl before we get too deep inside?"

"Good question. There's no cell service back here, so we can't even text. That's what made this location extra attractive. Once inside the maze, it's impossible to cheat by calling someone to guide you out."

"Addison? Can you hear us?" Sherry's voice broke, despite her attempt to stay calm. Sherry extended her arms and touched both sides of the cornstalk corridor. The space was definitely getting tighter the farther in they navigated. "Didn't we just pass this way?"

Sherry blinked to get a clearer look at the pattern in front of them. Nothing but dried golden cornstalks in front, to the side, and behind them. The thick dusty air made catching her breath a chore. The stalk's height, and the narrowness of the passageways, pinched out most of the sky overhead. The shadows darkened the pathway. Sherry stopped to collect her bearings, and heard a series of distant crunches behind her. When she turned to ask Ginger if she heard the noises, she was alone.

"Ginger?" Sherry spoke barely above a whisper. No reply. She sucked in a deep breath and bellowed the woman's name in a voice she hadn't heard herself produce since the time Chutney took off after a squirrel, ending up on a street with a car heading straight for the unaware dog. "Ginger!"

Sherry advanced on uncooperative legs. A split second later, the cornstalk wall behind her crashed down and smothered the spot where she had previously been standing. A blanket of particles from the crushed stalk fibers rose up in Sherry's face. She struggled to clear the air with frantic hand waving.

"Sherry? Are you in there?" Addison's voice pierced the collapsed wall that lay in a haphazard pile separating them. "Stay put. I'll get you out."

Chapter
15

"Are you sure you're okay?" Ginger asked. "That scrape on your arm might have some splinters in it from the stalks."

"I'll check it out when I get back home. I'm just glad the little girl made it out safely."

Ginger and Addison held a stare between themselves.

Ginger broke the silence. "Turns out she was never in the maze. She had wandered away from her stroller when her mom wasn't paying close attention. She was found on the swinging bench on the veranda having a merry old time with Uri."

Sherry's mouth dropped open. "I would still do it all over again, if I thought she was in there." She inspected her scraped arm. "How in the world did that wall collapse inside the maze? The cornstalks are so rigid, I can't imagine they'd go down without a fight."

"Agreed," Addison said. "I can't let customers in until we figure that out. You're just lucky you were out of the way, because they came down with a force.

As if they were rammed down from the other side, judging by the damage to them."

"No good deed goes unpunished." Ginger forced a crooked smile. "I need to get inside. It's checkout day for eighty percent of my guests, unfortunately. Thanks for meeting with me, and I'll be in touch." Before Sherry could begin her response, Ginger had turned tail and was halfway to the inn.

"I better get to repairing our moneymaker." Addison frowned. "Glad you're okay."

Sherry acknowledged Addison with a nod and made her way to her car. As she passed the front entrance, she caught a glimpse of Vilma, Uri, and Roe in a close huddle. A fourth person in the circle, with her back to Sherry, was nodding enthusiastically. Oxana's jeans and oversized sweatshirt gave her identity away. The group turned their heads in unison toward the inn before dispersing. A moment later, Ginger walked through the inn's whitewashed doorway with a suitcase in each hand. A young family followed close behind.

"I guess that's the appointment Vilma was running late for," Sherry commented under her breath.

"Hey, Sherry! Over here."

Sherry strained to locate who, out of all the people gathered in front of the inn, had called her name. She couldn't make out any familiar faces.

"Sherry!"

A waving hand caught Sherry's eye. "Here I come!" she called.

Half the guests milling around the front entrance turned to see who was on the way over. When Sherry reached Don and Day, she fussed with her hair and found a cornhusk shred. She straightened her shirtsleeve, which was partially torn from the maze mishap. She wished she'd had a chance to glance in a mirror to check for more cornstalk debris. She gave up after a third swipe through her hair produced more remnants of the corn maze.

Don greeted Sherry with a welcoming grin. "Such a fun time last night at the Taproom. Although, did I hear something about your car getting sideswiped in the parking lot? That really stinks."

"That lady over there told us about the mishap this morning at breakfast." Day pointed to Vilma, who was walking out of the inn.

"Vilma. She says a lot of things." Before Sherry could turn her gaze away from Vilma, the woman tossed a look Sherry's way. "But it's true. My poor car needs to go to the body shop for repair."

The brother-sister duo gave Sherry the once-over.

"Looks like you were doing some yard work," Day commented. "Or possibly had a wrestling match with a bale of hay?"

"The bale of hay won," Sherry said. "What are your plans today?"

"We're heading home tomorrow. Today we thought of taking a hike along the Silty Pretzel River. The Hillsboro State Park seems like a good send-off point. That's where we're headed." Day peered from Don to Sherry. "If you don't have any dinner plans, want to meet up? Maybe your friend Amber would like to join, too."

"I like that plan. Text me later when you've chosen a spot. Have fun today." As Sherry turned to leave, another husk shred fell from her hair. She swatted the dry brown debris away.

Back home in her living room, Sherry set her phone on speaker, leaving her hands free to stroke her dog. She positioned the phone on a throw pillow. "Thanks for returning my phone call, Patti. I wanted to talk about Vilma Pitney."

Patti's groan brought a slight grin to Sherry's face.

"Vilma says she wants to work together to find the killer, but I have a sneaking suspicion she's more interested in sending me off in the wrong direction. I feel like I'm still in that corn maze wandering round and round. Who am I chasing? Not sure at this point. Who's chasing me? Also, not sure."

Sherry and Chutney watched her neighbor Eileen's leash lesson with her new cat, Elvis Purrsley. Chutney's rear legs and backside were on her lap, front legs propped up on the window ledge for prime viewing. Outside, the young American short-hair cat was tolerating the harness he was wedged into. Even from Sherry's distant vantage point across the street, she could see the potential of retaliation for the humiliation brewing behind the cat's eyes.

"I wouldn't trust that woman as far as I could throw her," Patti said. "Vilma has barged her way into the cook-off-coverage world without any credibility whatsoever. From what I see, she's cozied up to one of the sponsors and somehow has been granted access rights to interviews no one else is able to get."

"I may regret these words, but, at the moment, I believe she's harmless."

"As harmless as a bite of a habanero chili pepper," Patti huffed.

Outside the window, the cat was trying hard to wriggle free from Eileen's guidance. The more the woman tugged in an effort to steer the cat up her driveway, the limper the cat's body appeared. It was like she was dragging a boneless pelt. "I don't think cats were meant to walk on leashes."

"I once saw a leashed cat claw its owner's ankles every time they came to a stop. Finally, the owner just picked the cat up, which, obviously, was the feline's plan all along," Patti chuckled.

"So smart. I'll mention your story to my persistent neighbor. Back to Vilma. The reason I called was to ask you exactly that. What would you say are Vilma's intentions with the information she's gathering? It seems she's writing a book instead of an article. How much information does she need? Every time I turn around, she's there talking to someone connected to the cook-off, a second, even a third time."

"I wish I knew," Patti replied. "I handed in my article this morning so it would be timely. It'll be online by the end of the day, along with my review of The Hunger Dames. Old news is just that. No one's interested. Dragging her heels won't serve her well. Although, it served that cat well. He got what he was after—a free ride."

Sherry smiled to herself. "Since you've finished your article for the *Nutmeg State of Mind*, would you mind crafting a brief cook-off recap for the Augustin newsletter? We can't pay you much, but there's value in having the byline, right?"

"Of course. Anything for my favorite competitive cook. Do me one favor, though."

"If it's legal," Sherry joked.

"Be careful of Vilma. She's up to something. I just can't put my finger on it, but I will."

"She's harmless, just aggressive, but I'll do as you suggest."

"Anything new on Fitz's murder?" Patti asked. "Got anyone in your crosshairs?"

Sherry giggled as she watched Eileen pick up her cat. Elvis had won the battle of wills. Eileen peered across to Sherry's house. She waved to her onlookers. Chutney perked up and wagged his tail.

"Not laughing at your question. My neighbor's so entertaining. She and Elvis make Chutney's day." Sherry considered her answers to Patti's questions. "Not much is new. So far, the two who I keep coming back to are Lyman, the spice guy, and Roe, the fisherman. Oh, and Ginger is hesitantly throwing Uri into the mix. Lyman's argument with Fitz was so animated, a number of people have come forward to express concern. Lyman said the spat was about spice varieties, but things got really testy. Lyman was shoving papers into Fitz's hands, and they weren't well received. Fitz was found dead with papers in his hand. I'm guessing the same papers. How can I find out what those papers were?"

"And Roe?" Patti asked. "Why him? You know, I interviewed him for my article, because he was touted by the president of Maine Course Foods as being the fish expert. I have to say, I was underwhelmed by his depth of knowledge. Did you know the company almost pulled out of the contest that night because Uri thought Roe was mistreated by the organizers?"

"I had no idea things got that out of whack. Roe is swirling in my brain because both Pep and Addison feel he's a fake. Addison's the real fishing expert. Why would Uri give someone who's not qualified such a showcase position in his company? What was Roe and Fitz's argument about?"

"Hard to say. No obvious motive for murder there, though." Patti paused. "Unless Roe's a hired hit man. I'm half kidding and half serious."

While Sherry considered Patti's suggestion, she used the lull in the conversation to focus on Eileen's final steps before entering her house. The woman put her cat down on her porch landing. Elvis scooted up to the door, trailing the leash behind him.

"Did Fitz know something about Roe? Did Roe know he knew whatever he knew?" Patti asked.

"Sounds like I need to find out the connection between Fitz, Roe, and Uri. Add Lyman in there, too. And the papers. Plus, there's one small detail I've been putting on the back burner for two days."

"What's that?"

"Pep's been disappearing for hours on end. I'm getting the sneaking suspicion he's going over to the inn and meeting up with this young lady, Oxana. I don't have any more proof other than seeing her name come up on his phone. Wouldn't be an issue, except for the fact she was the person who found

Fitz's body. I'm certainly not going to ask Vilma Pitney if she knows anything about them getting together."

"Why would you ask Vilma?" Patti asked.

"Vilma is helping Oxana improve her English. I just hope that, if Vilma does know something, she comes to me and not anyone else. I don't want Pep's name connected with multiple visits to the inn, especially right now."

"That makes sense." Patti paused. "Even if he made them."

"You've given me an idea. I need to go. Oh, and would you mind emailing me that cook-off recap in the next twenty-four hours?" Sherry bit her lip. "I forgot to mention the deadline."

Patti huffed. "Wow, I better get to work. Last thing before you go. That Lyman fellow with Spice Attitude. You had some concerns about him and what went down at the contestant party, right?"

"That's right."

"He gave me his business card."

"He handed me one, also. I put it with Fitz's card and later found them in my car."

"Well, I called the number listed and was told he's given his two-week notice. The person who answered said he wasn't expected to return to the office, except to pick up his things. Not only that, I learned he was only a part-time employee. I was given the name of a full-time rep who could answer my spice questions."

"That's very interesting." Sherry thought for a moment. "Did you, by any chance, ask what he might be up to after he leaves Spice Attitude?"

"The woman I spoke with wasn't excited to engage

in a conversation. She couldn't get me off the phone fast enough."

"Maybe I'll pay him a visit at the Augustin Motor Lodge."

"Are you sure about that?"

"No, you're right. That doesn't seem safe. He said he was sticking around a few days for business. I need to think about how to get a hold of him. You said the number on the card isn't his direct line?"

"Doesn't seem to be. Sherry, be careful."

"It's usually Detective Bease cautioning me. We'll talk later. Thanks in advance for the recap."

Sherry ended the call with the push of a button. Sherry took a last look out the window. Eileen wasn't outside anymore. A few cardinals and blue jays were perusing the lawn, keeping Chutney entertained for the time being. Sherry went to the kitchen, where she found her purse. She collected Lyman's business card from the side pocket. She returned to the couch and nestled in with Chutney.

"Yes, hello. May I speak with Lyman St. Pierre, please." Sherry was greeted with a sharp exhale.

"He cannot be reached at this number anymore."

"He left his business card with me. I saw him this past week, and, after our meeting, he left behind what looks like a very important item. By the time I discovered it, he was long gone. Do you have a for-warding number I could contact him at?"

"Sure. He was a nice guy. I'll do him this favor. We're told not to provide that information, but if you think it's important, I'll take you at your word. I once left my wallet and cell phone in a taxi, and, two weeks later, a Good Samaritan went above and beyond and found me. Contacted me through our local police department. Not a dollar was missing! Pay it forward, I say."

"Thank you so much. I'm sure he'll be very appreciative."

When Sherry ended her call with the woman, she dialed the number she was provided.

"You have reached Lyman. Please leave a brief message."

Disappointed, but undeterred, Sherry left her name and number, only to get a callback within two minutes.

"Hi, Ms. Oliveri. What a surprise to hear from you. I don't remember leaving you this phone number." Lyman's tone was cautious.

"It took some work, but I tracked you down," Sherry said, with a light-hearted voice. "I'm interested in some spices, and since you said you would be in town for a few days, I wondered if I could pick some up from you."

The length of silence that followed Sherry's question left her checking her phone for a lost connection.

"I don't work for Spice Attitude any longer, with the exception of filling a few last orders placed before I gave notice. It was only a part-time job, and I decided to move on. But, the number on the business card is valid. You could place an order with whoever answers the phone."

"I'll do that. Thanks anyway. Good luck in your next endeavor. Hope it's something exciting." She disconnected the call. Sherry sighed and ruffled Chutney's neck fur. "What next?"

And then it came to her.

Oxana.

Chapter 16

"I hope Oxana's still at the inn. I bet she puts in extra hours on Sundays." Sherry parked her car on the edge of the inn's lot closest to the red barn. She lowered all the windows a few inches to let the cool breezes keep Chutney comfortable while he waited for Sherry's return. "Be back soon," she told Chutney, after unstrapping his safety harness.

As Sherry skirted the lot, a familiar car was pulling out of the far corner. Sherry lifted her sunglasses to confirm it was Pep's car. He had a memorable sequence of numbers, 911, after the three letters on his car's license plates. The sun's glaring rays reflected off the metal, obscuring the last number, but the first two were definitely a 9 and a 1. Close enough.

The crowd of people milling around the front of the inn, waiting to check out, pack their cars, or otherwise hang out, had diminished since her visit not long ago. Sherry made her way around the edge of the lawn where she picked up the path to the barn.

She poked her head inside the barn door. "Oxana?"

"Yes, coming." Oxana trotted from the back of the

barn toward Sherry. Her sweatshirt was tied around her waist. She peeled off her rubber gloves. "You, again. Sherry. Pep's sister."

"Yes, me again." Sherry imagined her cheeks bloomed a rosy hue. "I forgot to ask you a question." Sherry moved to within an arm's length of Oxana and lowered her voice to a breathy whisper. "I threw something in the garbage the night of the Fall Fest Cook-off party. I was in the main gathering room next to the ice sculpture. There was a small trash receptacle to the side of the sculpture."

Oxana pinched her forehead into a tight row of lines. "Receptacle?"

"Garbage can, a small one. Maybe for used napkins and such."

"Yes, yes." Oxana nodded vigorously. She repeated the word, receptacle, as if she was committing it to memory.

"Do you think there would be a way of finding the envelope I threw away?"

"I know words for that—Dumpster diving." Oxana threw back her head and let out a burst of laughter. "Some of the first words I learned. Many people lose things at the inn. Somehow, I'm head of Dumpster diving."

"So you think it's possible?"

"I have system." Oxana beckoned Sherry with a sweep of her hand. "Follow me outside."

They left the barn and circled to the back of the building, where two massive lidded garbage bins stood side by side. Oxana pried open one lid, revealing eight garbage cans. Sherry peeked inside the huge container. The prospect of searching the eight garbage cans, filled with who knew what, turned her stomach. She imagined gooey, sticky, oozy, slimy, smelly contents. She should have thought to bring rubber gloves.

"This could take all day," Sherry whined.

Oxana pointed to the green plastic garbage can second from the back right. "Can number six."

"How in the world do you know that?" Sherry was incredulous.

"My system. So I know which garbage cans go back where, after I put out for pickup day. See red dot on the handle? Means first floor, reception room, main building. Only one day and night's trash in it. Today's is in other container, can seven." Oxana pointed to the adjacent massive container. "Pickup is every other day. No weekends." She lifted the desired canister's lid and removed the black plastic bag. "If you'd used the inn's recycle container, even easier."

Sherry pushed the corners of her mouth upward, hoping for mercy. "Next time, I promise. Thank you so much. That's all I needed. If you need to go, I'll put the bag back where it belongs."

"If Miss Constable sees you Dumpster diving, I'll be fired." Oxana's tone was suddenly urgent.

"Right. Gotcha. Here I go." Sherry held her breath and plunged both hands in the bag. She pushed past the shrimp tails, cocktail sauce-doused napkins, and lemon and lime wedges until she struck gold. A brown envelope with the name Fitz Frye typed across the center of the front. "Bingo." She handed Oxana the bag. Without any other option, Sherry wiped her hands on the grass beside the refuse storage.

"You've done this before," Oxana remarked. "You're good."

"Sadly, yes. Too many times to count. Thank you." Sherry watched Oxana pull the garbage bag drawstring closed and replace it in the garbage can. The can went back in its designated canister. Together, they started their return to the barn.

After a few steps, Oxana came to a stop. "Sherry? Can you teach me to cook a meal?"

Sherry studied the young lady's face. Oxana's eyes were a brilliant green and sparkled in the sunlight. She had a smudge of something yellowish orange on her cheek.

"That's a good idea." Sherry bounced a glance off the blue sky before returning her attention to Oxana. "I have just the recipe for you. I'm thinking of entering it in the Pacific Salmon Run Recipe Contest next month. Only has a few ingredients. It'll wow whoever you're making it for. Pecan Salmon with Sweet Red Pepper Mayo. Promise me you won't give out the recipe."

"Ah! I promise. Don't know what is mayo but sounds delicious."

"Mayo. Mayonnaise. Anyway, if you like salmon, you'll love this." Sherry softened her tone. "Do you have a boyfriend?" She braced herself in case her brother's name was mentioned.

"Too busy. School. Work. Lessons. But one day, maybe." Oxana stared off into the distance for a moment. "Mamma says learn to cook and love will find you."

"Wise woman," Sherry laughed. "I'll keep cooking and there's hope for me. I'll text you, and we'll set up a cooking-lesson date."

Oxana recited her cell number as Sherry entered it into her phone's contacts. Sherry reciprocated with her phone number, then walked Oxana back to the barn. She thanked her and they said their good-byes. Back at her car, Sherry retrieved her favorite water bottle, the one she received at the Mushroom Festival Cook-off two years ago. Instead of taking a drink, she splashed water on her soiled hands. She picked up the emergency all-purpose towel she kept on the floor of the car. She dried her hands on it and draped the towel across her car seat. She positioned herself on the towel in hopes that her car seat would be protected from any trash residue she might have picked up from the garbage rescue operation.

Even after a good hand rinse, Chutney was very interested in the new scent Sherry brought into the car. Eau de Garbage. With twitching nostrils, he paid his owner extra close attention as she examined the recovered envelope. She ran her finger under the words in the top left corner that read, "Service of Process."

"Fitz Frye was served. For what, and by whom? I know who physically served him. Lyman. Spice sales-man by day, process server by night. Who was Lyman representing?" Sherry reached back and set the cocktail sauce–stained envelope down on the unused portion of dog seat cover beside Chutney, which pleased him to no end.

He not only made sure that the delicious-smelling

envelope never moved from under his guard, he gave it a good washing with his tongue for good measure.

"Okay, that's enough," Sherry scolded. Chutney resigned himself to noncontact sentry duty.

"Whew, it really stinks in here." Sherry lowered the windows all the way. "Glad you're buckled in, boy. Gonna be a windy ride home. At least we can breathe fresh air." She reached back and retrieved the envelope. "Don't want you flying away after all the work it took to find you." She nestled the envelope under her leg and drove home.

Sherry parked behind Pep's car. She unbuckled Chutney, and he followed her and the towel-wrapped envelope to the front porch. She set the towel bundle down on the porch. "You can stay right here for now."

She found Pep seated on the couch in the living room. "How was brunch with Dad?"

He stood and collected an empty glass off the side table. "Fun. I hope we can do it one more time before I leave."

"About that," Sherry began.

"Sher, I need to get back to Maine. I can't hang here forever." Pep's tone was defensive.

"Message received."

"Do you know you have splinters in your hair? Or is it straw?" Pep reached up and pulled a sample from over Sherry's ear. "You don't smell great, either. No offense, but I recommend a shower. What have you been up to?"

Sherry ran her fingers through her hair, dislodging a cornstalk shard. "Nothing good. You're right.

I need a long shower. What do you know about the company Maine Course Foods?"

"Not much more than that they specialize in seafood."

"Do you know of any reason Fitz would have been served?"

"You're a bundle of questions. Slow down, you're changing subjects so quickly. What do you mean served?"

"Served, as in by a process server. Maybe divorce papers, maybe a subpoena to appear in court for a lawsuit?"

"I know you're trying to help, but I didn't know Fitz very well."

Sherry widened her eyes. "I'm trying to help because I don't think you're taking this whole mess seriously enough. Listen to someone who's been at the top of a murder suspect list. The investigation can't go fast enough for my peace of mind. If you're not going to jump in and look for the murderer, then I have to."

"Okay, okay. I really appreciate your efforts. Let me think. Fitz is divorced, and he was seeing his girlfriend, Kelly. So, not divorce papers from a disgruntled spouse." Pep paused. "Your phone is ringing."

Sherry grumbled an inaudible phrase before rummaging through her purse. "Hi, Day. Yes, I'd love to grab some dinner. I have to check with Pep. Never know what he's up to. How about The Hunger Dames? It's a new restaurant in town. Or maybe I should first check out the review my friend wrote on the place. She said it would be online today. I'll go read it, right after I take a much-needed shower. Call you back in a few."

After Sherry showered and changed her clothes, she brought her laptop over to the couch and wedged herself next to Pep and Chutney. She searched for the *Nutmeg State of Mind* online edition restaurant reviews. She read Patti's review of The Hunger Dames to Pep, who approved the choice of restaurants. Three stars was high praise for the new establishment. They both agreed, "American classics with a modern twist" sounded perfect. She texted Day and set the time for six-thirty.

"Speaking of classics with a twist, I was going to make a kimchi turkey burger for lunch. Care to join me?" she asked her brother.

"At brunch, Dad and I shared pancakes, an omelet, bacon, and the best French toast I've ever eaten, besides yours, of course. Oh, and I had a vanilla-strawberry smoothie. I don't think I need to eat until tomorrow."

"Sounds fantastic. I'll be in the kitchen, if you'd like another crack at being my sous chef," Sherry laughed. She made her way to the kitchen counter. She pulled out a mixing bowl from the storage below. "I think this burger could be a winner at my next grilling contest."

She pulled ground turkey, fish and soy sauces, ginger, and sesame oil from her fridge. She combined the ingredients and formed burger patties from the blend. In a small bowl, she stirred together mayonnaise, chili-garlic sauce, honey, soy sauce, and scallions. She fried up a burger, along with an over-easy fried egg.

With a toasted, sesame seed burger bun as the

base on her plate, she topped the bottom bun with the burger. Next, chili-mayo and chopped kimchi were piled on. Finally, she laid the fried egg and bun lid on top. The enticing aroma swirled around her nose, and a smile crossed her lips.

Pep entered the kitchen. "What in the world is that? Smells awesome. Now, I'm starving."

"See? You should never turn down an offer of a classic with a twist," Sherry teased. "While my masterpiece was cooking, I texted Patti and thanked her for the recommendation of The Hunger Dames."

"I bet she's happy about that. If the place gets your stamp of approval, it's well on its way."

Sherry took a bite of her saucy, tangy, exotic burger. She sang a tune of pure satisfaction. She savored the combination of flavors with each chew. Earthy fish sauce, spicy crunchy kimchi, and salty soy sauce rocked her taste buds. The red pepper punch lingered only to be replaced with the luscious gingered turkey as the dominant flavor.

After swallowing, Sherry glanced at her vibrating phone. "Interesting. Patti texted she forgot to tell me she saw Vilma sharing a table with Fitz the day she wrote her review of The Hunger Dames."

Pep cocked his head toward Sherry's phone. "I know why. Check your emails. I got a request the day before the cook-off asking for an interview with that woman. I bet you did, too. I blew it off. We were too busy wine shopping. Didn't even mention it to you. Figured you'd make up your own mind to do it or not."

"Vilma told me she never interviewed Fitz and wished she had. Why would she lie about that? Did he tell her something she wasn't willing to share?"

"Didn't your friend Patti warn you about that woman?" Pep kept his sights on the burger. "Mind if I try a bite?"

"She did, and I told her Vilma was harmless." Sherry pushed her plate closer to her brother. "Save me some." He went in with two hands. He jammed the edge of the thick burger concoction into his gaping mouth. He rolled his eyes back.

Sherry rescued the remainder of the burger. "Looks like you're enjoying it."

"Has anyone ever told you, you're too nice? That Pitney woman may not be as harmless as you think. You might regret cutting her so much slack."

Chapter 17

"I'll meet you guys for dessert," Pep said. "I'm still full from the massive brunch Dad and I had. Maybe also from the kimchi megaburger I begged you to make me an hour ago, too." Pep handed Sherry her car keys.

"That's fine. See you later." Sherry knelt and ruffled Chutney's neck fur. "And would you mind giving this guy his dinner in about a half hour? Thanks." Sherry shut the door behind her before Pep had a chance to answer. As soon as she was outside, she caught a whiff of the towel-wrapped envelope. She pinched the corner of the bundle between two fingers and walked it to the outdoor garbage can around the side of the house. "Good riddance, you smelly thing. It was time to replace that old towel anyway."

As she returned to the front of the house, Sherry caught sight of Eileen, across the street, attempting another leash lesson with her cat.

"He's doing well, wouldn't you say?" Eileen called out.

Elvis Purrsley was lying down on the sidewalk, tail lashing back and forth furiously.

"He's taking a little rest."

Sherry swallowed a giggle. "You're the cat whisperer, for sure."

"Heard about the cook-off contestant's murder. Do you think the hobby's safe? I mean, people can take competition to the extreme when big money's on the line. Not everyone is as talented as you. Killing the competition may be the only solution. You know, last man standing wins?"

"I hope it's just a coincidence the deceased man was in the cook-off." Sherry was unwilling to muster the energy to refute Eileen's assertions. "Who knows? You might be on to something, Eileen. Thanks."

"My pleasure, dear. Glad to help. Have a nice evening." Eileen tugged on the leash. The cat replied with a yawn.

When Sherry arrived at The Hunger Dames, she considered parking on the street, but the sign along the curb was ambiguous as to whether she'd be ticketed after 6 PM. What came to mind was last week's mayoral editorial in the town newsletter. The subject was revamping parking restrictions. Would a stricter set of regulations give Leila, the meter maid, increased ticketing potential or aggravate potential local shop customers to the point of shopping elsewhere? Augustin's constituent response was strongly in favor of relaxing parking regulations.

As a result, new signage was issued in multiple locations. The problem was, the hours the signs listed as no parking and short-term parking, versus off-hours parking, overlapped and cancelled each other out. Sherry had worked with the mayor long enough to recognize the ambiguity was his way of leaving the decision making to Leila, parking meter monarch for many decades. Small towns had their own way of governing, and Sherry was resigned to accepting what others might see as an annoyance.

Not wanting to risk a ticket, the cost of which was also notoriously open to fluctuation, Sherry made her decision. Headlights glaring through her rear-view mirror urged her to act quickly. A U-turn later, she steered the car into the parking lot. The head-lights followed closely behind.

"I wonder if that's Day and Don."

The car moved at a snail's pace. She darted her hand out the window and waved the car forward. "Follow me, guys." Sherry parked her car on the far edge of the lot, leaving plenty of space for the in-coming car. She gathered her purse and exited her car. One glance through the other car's driver's side window led to a surprise discovery. She waited until the person exited the vehicle. "Lyman. What a coin-cidence seeing you here."

The man was dressed in a windbreaker and cargo pants combo.

She shuddered when the word "coincidence" left her lips. The saying, "there are no coincidences," tip-toed across her brain.

"Not a coincidence at all. I've been looking for you." Lyman squared himself up to Sherry.

"Me?" Sherry squeaked. "Why?"

"A reporter, last name Pitney, tells me you think I had something to do with Fitz's murder." Lyman's words were timed slowly and deliberately. "I did an interview with her the day before the cook-off, and she was kind enough to text me today with that news. I'm not happy." The scowl on his face made the hair on Sherry's arm rise to attention.

"She said you've told the investigator in charge, a Detective Bease, I was in a two-way confrontation with Fitz the night of the party at the Augustin Inn. Now he's after me with questions." Lyman paused and stared into Sherry's eyes. "I admit, that night Frye and I weren't toasting to a possible win on his behalf, but you're only half right."

"Better than usual."

Vilma's name swirled in her head. The woman had riled Lyman up. The slack she considered cutting Vilma was growing taut. Sherry glanced in all directions. Empty cars as far as she could see. No one else in sight, except Lyman.

Lyman's jaw muscle was visibly pulsating. "He and I weren't arguing. I was doing my job, and he didn't hold back his sentiment. He wasn't having it."

Sherry softened her words. "He was upset you were a spice distributor? That doesn't make much sense." She waited for what seemed like minutes for his reply.

Lyman's face relaxed enough for Sherry to exhale the breath she'd been holding far too long.

"Not that job. My second job. Besides my former employment at Spice Attitude, I am an independent process server. A challenging job serving legal papers. You like cook-offs, I like the law process." He cracked a sly smile.

"You served Fitz the night of the party."

"You've done your homework. People saw me hand him documents. They wouldn't necessarily know what the documents were all about, unless he was willing to share that information. You, obviously, made it your business to find out."

"You served him in such a public place. He became agitated. As if it was bad news you'd delivered." Sherry searched Lyman's face for a clue to the degree of bad news. If he were in a poker game that very moment, judging whether he was holding a winning hand or a dud would have been impossible.

Lyman shrugged. "Safe to say, good news doesn't usually need to be forced on the recipient."

"So, it can be deduced as being bad news you delivered."

"Good deduction, Sherlock. I delivered papers to Fitz, but I'd have thought he'd keep the details of the papers to himself. At least until he'd read through all the documents. My job is to record when he receives the papers. When he reads them is up to him."

"You don't feel bad about where and how you served him?"

"My job is about moving the judicial process forward, and that's what I did. Not my fault he's been hard to track down. I found him where I could find him. May I ask how you knew I served him legal papers?"

"I've been known to get to the bottom of a mystery a time or two."

"I'm impressed."

Sherry let her shoulders relax when Lyman paid somewhat of a compliment. "Okay then, you admit you were in an argument with Fitz because he wasn't happy with you for doing your job during what should've been a celebratory night for all the cook-off contestants. So, I'm not wrong."

"You're wrong about our confrontation being two-way. I served Frye a subpoena to testify under oath. Getting those papers in his hands wasn't easy. He's a slippery devil when he doesn't want to be found."

"How did you know he'd be involved in the cook-off and that you'd find him there?"

Lyman softened his tone. "That's why I'm good at my job. Research, timing, and location are the keys to success. I have to file a report on all my attempts to serve papers. In the case of Fitz Frye, I was getting a bit worried about completing my task. I'm motivated to get the job done in a timely fashion. The guy doesn't sit still. I learned he was a cook-offer, or whatever you people call yourselves. I got Spice Attitude to get onboard with a sponsorship to get a foot in the door. That alone wasn't easy, as I wasn't a full-time employee and had hoped to leave Spice Attitude by the end of the month."

"Once he'd been served, what was the point in him arguing? From what you're saying, Fitz wasn't in any legal trouble. Rather, he was possibly getting rid of a tenant that was trouble."

"Agreed. No point. He was venting, I suppose. My job never comes with roses from the served. Fitz may have been upset, but I wasn't, and certainly, I've never been upset enough to murder someone I've served. That's what doesn't make sense. Ironically, he had reason to kill me, not vice versa."

"Was any of this associated with Maine Course Foods?"

"You're persistent. But I'm not comfortable giving names. Let's just say it's a company headquartered in Connecticut. That's all I'm willing to say. That's the reason I had to serve him in Connecticut." Lyman's windbreaker billowed as the breeze picked up. "Listen. I didn't kill Fitz Frye. I did my job, returned to the Augustin Motor Lodge by nine PM and ordered my favorite surfer movie, *The Endless Summer* on Netflix. I can show you the charge on my hotel bill. Date and time listed. I would imagine the hotel surveillance videos can't come up with an image of me leaving any time that night after nine, because I didn't."

"Putting two and two together, you have an alibi. Detective Bease shouldn't waste his time looking any further into your comings and goings." Sherry managed a gentle smile.

"I'd appreciate you spreading that word around. Shouldn't be hard. Word spreads like wildfire around this neck of the woods."

"Part of our small-town charm. I like to think it makes people think twice before doing something crazy."

Lyman grunted.

"Sherry. Hope I'm not late." Don appeared from behind a row of cars. He parked himself alongside Sherry, keeping his gaze fixated on Lyman. "Hi, I'm Don. It's pretty dark out here. Even so, you look familiar."

"Don, you remember Lyman from the cook-off and kitesurfing. He was representing Spice Attitude," Sherry said. "We ran into each other out here."

"That's quite a coincidence," Don commented.

"I'm on my way out. Decided not to eat here after all." Lyman averted his gaze away from Sherry.

"Glad we ran into each other. Take care," Sherry said with a hastened tone.

Lyman got inside his car and the engine hummed to life.

"He's leaving Spice Attitude. His was a part-time position."

Don laughed. "Might have been a good decision. Those spices were lacking, compared to others I've used. Let's get inside. It's getting chilly out here."

Sherry scanned the parking lot. "Where did Day park? Should we wait for her inside?"

"Day has a migraine. She sends her regrets. She went to lie down, back at the inn. We're leaving in the morning, and she was sad to miss a fun night out, but she was hurting."

"I'm so sorry. Please send my best wishes for a speedy recovery. Those things can be nasty."

"Hopefully Pep's joining us?" Don peered over his shoulder. "You didn't come together?"

"He'll be here by dessert time. I know what to order for him. If there's apple pie on the menu, a la mode, of course, that's what he wants. No Amber, either. She has tennis."

"We'll have to make the best of it, just you and me."

Once inside the restaurant, the hostess showed Sherry and Don to a corner table sized to fit four diners. They placed their drink orders with the waitress and browsed the menu.

Sherry peeked over top of her menu and saw Don's eyes shifting from side to side as he mulled over the choices. "My friend, Patti Mellitt, who you were probably interviewed by at the cook-off, reviewed this place. She recommended the seafood chowder, the ranch skirt-steak tacos, and the oyster pancakes with rainbow-cabbage slaw."

"I was interviewed by her. I'm sure she was bored to tears with my lack of cook-off experience. The requirements for a sous chef are nil, except maybe nepotism. I was perfect for the job. Another reporter, Vilma Pitney, wanted me to meet her here the day before the cook-off for an interview. No time. Too busy helping you pick the perfect merlot for your winning sauce." Don winked.

Sherry checked the room for their waitress. *Why is the Pinot Grigio taking so long?*

"Glad I waited to come here with you. Thank you, Patti Mellitt, for your recommendations. One of each, please. I was getting overwhelmed with how good everything looks. The name 'The Hunger Dames' is very appropriate if the food delivers on its promise. I'm starving."

Sherry set her menu down and laughed. "Agreed. I'm going out on a limb and ordering the free-range roast game hen. Kind of a gamble, because those little suckers are really easy to overcook."

Don closed his menu. "You probably can't help yourself, judging other people's cooking. Admit it."

"Maybe a little bit." Sherry shrugged. "I try to hold my tongue. Everyone thinks their cooking is the best. I don't want to hurt feelings. When I first stumbled into cooking contests, I had the thinnest skin ever. I took not winning as a slap in the face for all my efforts trying to create the perfect recipe. Being judged is tough. It was a big step for me when I was able to learn from my losses."

The waitress approached and took their orders.

"People say they learn from their losses, but do you really mean it?" Don asked.

Don has such gentle green eyes. An unusual color. On second thought, his eyes are blue with yellow flecks, lending the appearance of green. And those lashes. The long curly ones that some people are lucky enough to be born with.

"Sherry?"

Sherry cleared her throat. "Lashes, I mean, losses. Learning." She blinked with conviction. "Yes. Cooking is so subjective. You have no control over so many unforeseen variables. What the judges' personal preferences are, what the contestant next to you is preparing, your choice of serving utensils. On and on."

Don narrowed his eyes and their color deepened.

"When you submit a recipe in August for the perfect peach tart and the contest isn't until February, you better come to grips with the fact there are no local fresh peaches in February."

"Sounds like what you learn at cook-offs is, there's no tried and true formula to success."

The waitress made an appearance. She set down a beer in front of Don and a glass of Pinot Grigio in front of Sherry. They clanked their glasses together.

Don announced, "Here's to a new friendship. Back to your cook-off formula for success. You say there really isn't one?"

"Exactly. And that's what keeps me coming back for more. I can't crack the code, but I can make a mean shrimp lettuce wrap."

"I like your attitude. Mind if I ask about your personal life? A lady like you must be beating guys off with a stick." He peeked around the table at Sherry's purse. "You don't have a stick with you, do you?"

"Ha. I should look into purchasing one." Sherry mentally prepared the summary of her social life. A few beats later she was ready to continue. "I was married for about seven years. We divorced, and I've been single since. A sad and boring tale."

"No, no. Not at all. I was asking in case I could persuade you to go on a proper date with me when the time is right. I don't want to infringe on anyone else's territory. That's why I'm asking. Do I have a chance?"

"You do have a chance. I can use a spatula to beat off any other guys in the meantime. I have plenty of those."

"Another great thing about you. You're adaptable."

"No one who knows me well would agree, but here's to the hope of progress. The new me." Sherry lifted her glass.

Don held up his glass of beer. "Cheers to the old and new Sherry. I can't wait to discover both versions of you."

After the last morsel of dinner was eaten and the dinner plates were collected, Sherry and Don were handed the dessert menu.

"I'll have the apple pie a la mode, please," Pep announced as he approached the table. His head pivoted from Sherry to Don and back again. "Oh, no. Three's a crowd. Where are Day and Amber?"

"Now, it's a party," Don said. "Have a seat. We've been waiting for you."

Pep passed a glance from Don to Sherry. Sherry nodded her head, and Pep took a seat.

"Did you come from home?" Sherry asked.

"No." Pep's answer was snippy.

"The mystery continues. Two apple pies, a la mode, please," Sherry told the waitress who arrived while Pep took a seat. "Don and I will share."

"I guess I have no choice. The lady has made up my mind," Don chuckled.

Chapter
18

"Sherry, did you hear me?" Pep pushed his empty breakfast plate to the center of the table.

Sherry peered up from her phone. "No, sorry. What?"

Pep shoved his chair backwards. He stood and refilled his coffee mug. "Don's nice."

"Yes. Don. Nice." Sherry returned her attention to her phone. She switched between her text messages and her calendar.

"Now who's the one attached to her phone?" Pep teased.

"Got a text from Oxana. She's interested in learning how to cook and yours truly volunteered to teach her a recipe. She doesn't have much free time between school courses and two cleaning jobs. Next Tuesday might work." Sherry texted, Tuesday's the day. I've got you on my calendar.

"I'm heading out tomorrow," Pep said, with an unemotional insistence that brought a tear to Sherry's eye.

"You've only been here for a few days. Can't you spare a little more time to keep your big sis company?

Plus, Ray's not going to be happy if you leave town." Sherry pleaded. Silence. She switched gears to a gentler approach. "At least sit back down and tell me what your life plans are."

"You know, I see someone like Oxana, how hard she's working to get to a better place in her life. I've come to realize that, as much fun as I've had traveling the world, it's time to settle down."

"Any chance you'd settle down back here in Augustin?" Sherry dredged her question in love.

"You never know. I'm asking for some space right now until my plans come together. You don't have to understand, but I wouldn't mind if you'd trust me." Pep stirred sugar into his coffee.

"So hard for me to be calm about this, having you right here to try and convince, face to face." She brought her mug to the kitchen sink and rinsed it out with water. "How is it you know Oxana?"

Pep cocked his head to the side and cracked a sly smile. "Sort of a funny story. I have a friend staying at the inn, and she locked herself out of her room the night of the cocktail party. Nothing unusual about that, except I was hiding in the room to surprise her. She found Oxana in the hallway with her set of master keys. When Oxana unlocked the door, I jumped out and welcomed the wrong person in, shall we say, an intimate way."

"I have so many questions. I'll start with a logistical one before I move on to the really juicy ones. How did you get in the room without a key?"

"Can we save the juicy ones for a little later, please?"

"You're torturing me, but I'll respect your privacy, at least for right now."

Back to your question about the room and the key. I did have a key. The front desk offered my friend a second key at check-in and, well . . ." Pep's explanation trailed off to silence.

"Okay, go on," Sherry prompted. In front of her was her baby brother, who had done some questionable things as a teenager, but always managed to maintain an innocence Sherry found so endearing. Or was she projecting that innocence onto him, merely to keep her role of older sister relevant? Sherry blinked the image of a pimply, gawky, preteen brother out of her head and looked with clear eyes at the man in front of her.

"I feel like you're looking directly through me. It's making me nervous," Pep said.

"Sorry. Continue."

"Needless to say, I didn't know she had misplaced her key and that Oxana would be opening the door instead of her. Anyway, after the awkward first moments, we invited Oxana to stay for a chat to diffuse the situation. We got to be friends real quick. Even with the communication barrier."

"And does your friend like her as well?" Sherry framed the word "friend" with air quotes and drew out the word in two syllables for emphasis.

"Absolutely. Charlotte admires her work ethic so much. That coming from a marine biologist, so you know she understands hard work."

Sherry's mouth dropped open as a thought occurred. "If you were with Charlotte at the time of the murder, you're set. She's your alibi. Tell the detective."

"Nope. Not happening. She cannot be involved."

"I guess I can figure out where you've been the

times you've been unaccounted for. Why so secretive? Especially when it's so important to give Detective Bease your alibi?" Sherry shrugged. "You're making it seem like you're hiding something about this girl-friend of yours. I'm assuming she's your girlfriend. Any chance of meeting Charlotte? Maybe at dinner tonight, your last night?"

"Sher, please, don't press," Pep implored.

"Not pressing. Merely extending a kind invite."

Pep managed a brotherly smile. "I'll see if dinner tonight works for her."

The phone in Sherry's hand buzzed.

"I'm jumping in the shower." Pep sprang up the stairs.

"Ray. How's everything? How's your mother? I've been thinking about you."

"It is what it is." His voice dragged as the words stumbled out of the phone. "Thanks for thinking of me."

"While I have you on the line, I have a question for you."

"Sherry, I called you. I'm the one with the ques-tion."

"There's the Ray I recognize. Prickly as an arti-choke. Don't ever lose that edge. What's your question?"

"Vilma Pitney."

Sherry groaned. A thick bitter taste swathed her tongue.

"The woman interviewed the cook-off contestants," Ray continued. "Did she mention the publication she writes for? The last record of employment states she was on staff at a regional paper in North Caro-lina. Her employment was terminated."

"Freelance. She said she was freelance and hoped to get a good price for her article."

"She has a book out. Under the pen name Stella Granger. Self-published, two years ago. Titled, *How to Solve a Murder or Die Trying.*"

"Bet she regrets that title right about now. It's beginning to make sense why she's so interested in the Fitz Frye investigation."

"How interested is she?" Ray asked. "You told me she asked questions, but has her intensity changed?"

Sherry paused while she considered her answer. "Her interest is growing. I've run into her at every turn for the last forty-eight hours. She's always with the people who were involved with Fitz the night of his murder."

"Oxana told me about a request Vilma made of her to check something out in Uri's room at the Augustin Inn. She might be asking Oxana to do her dirty work in exchange for English lessons."

"Oxana is a sweet girl trying to eke out a living. I doubt she'd throw it all away for that woman. Unless Vilma was holding something over Oxana's head, and she wasn't able to refuse. What was she looking for in Uri's room?"

"Believe me, it wasn't easy to get the English translation from Oxana. Fishhooks. Vilma asked Oxana to check for any evidence of fishhooks in Uri's room the day after the murder. Vilma was told by Ginger she saw a catalogue in his room open to a page of fishing hooks."

"Does Vilma think Uri may be the killer? That he keeps a fishhook supply in his room?" Sherry asked.

"Not necessarily. Don't jump to conclusions. And you said Roe was leaving Uri's room the night

Ginger visited Uri's room. That makes three people who may have left a fishhook catalogue open to that particular page."

Sherry sucked in a breath. "Would you mind if I had a word with Oxana? I have a feeling she's leaving out a detail or two of Vilma's request. And Vilma's leaving out a detail or two about her relationship with Oxana."

"I wouldn't be able to stop you now, would I? When I spoke to Oxana, she said she didn't find any actual hooks when she went to Uri's room to clean. She told me she checked the trash can in the room, too, on Vilma's recommendation." A moment of silence passed. Ray's voice wavered a bit. "I'm out, dealing with mother issues, this afternoon. I'd appreciate any news you have to offer after you talk with the girl. And your brother? What's he up to?"

"He's leaving soon," Sherry stated, in no uncertain terms.

"Hmmm. Get back to me today then." Ray ended the call.

Sherry scrolled through her phone contact list. "I don't even know Oxana's last name." She reached the *O*'s. She clicked on Oxana's cell number, labeled *Oxana, Augustin Inn*.

"Sherry?" Oxana's voice was scratchy.

"Hi, Oxana. I was hoping I could meet with you for a few minutes this morning. Are you at the inn? Can I stop by? It's concerning something I'd rather not ask you on the phone."

There was a shuffling, a crackle, and muffled voices dribbling through the phone. "I'm downtown at Crunchtime Coffeehouse doing schoolwork. I should be here one hour, then class."

"I'll pop by very soon, if that's okay."

"Pop by?" Oxana asked.

"I'll be there soon."

When Pep came downstairs, Sherry had her corduroy barn coat on and Chutney's leash in hand. "If you could just give this guy a walk, I'd be eternally grateful." She handed Pep the leash.

"Guess I have no choice. Eternity is a long time. Hard to pass up that offer. Where are you going and when will you be back?"

"You know, I can be as mysterious as you." She waited for Pep to beg her for details.

Instead, he shrugged.

"Okay, fine. You've worn me down with your endless interrogation." Sherry's words dripped with sarcasm.

"I actually didn't ask you one question." Pep's sly expression gave Sherry little satisfaction.

"I'll be back in forty-five minutes to an hour. Maybe we can meet Dad for lunch somewhere." She tossed Pep a wave and left the house.

The short drive to Augustin's popular coffeehouse gave Sherry ample time to consider the approach to use. She didn't want to alienate Oxana with a hard line of questioning, but something wasn't adding up. Sherry recited a few scenarios as she drove, waving her hand for emphasis. At the four-way stop intersection, labeled, year after year, as the most dangerous in Augustin, Sherry practiced her delivery. Her misconstrued hand gestures were returned in an angry unspeakable tirade from an oncoming driver as he vented about the traffic backup.

"The mayor needs to do something about this intersection and put the parking meters on the back burner." Sherry watched the angry driver speed away out of turn.

Sherry couldn't remember the last time she had been in the Crunchtime Coffeehouse. Spending six to eight dollars for a cup of coffee was such an extravagance, she didn't enjoy the taste the few times she partook. Too much guilt brewed in each cup for her liking. The fact that Augustin might be pricing out locals, in favor of big-spending visitors, irked her to no end.

Inside the coffeehouse, the lighting was bright. Sifting through the small crowd was easy. She didn't recognize anyone waiting in line at the sales counter, so she moved to the rear of the shop. Sherry neared the corner sectional sofa filled with readers and laptop users enjoying scones and cups of coffee. Wedged in the cushions at right angles to one another, knees nearly touching, were two familiar women. Oxana lowered her gaze as Sherry approached.

Sherry waited until Oxana lifted her head. "Hi, Oxana."

The woman next to Oxana flashed a toothy grin.

"Vilma. I had no idea you'd be here with Oxana."

"I'm on my way out. Stopped by for a moment with my favorite student." Vilma reached forward and patted Oxana's knee. "See you soon, dear. And, Sherry, let's talk later."

Vilma gathered up a large bag and hoisted it across her shoulders. With a commanding strut, she left the coffee shop.

Sherry took the seat Vilma had vacated. "You two appear to spend a lot of time together."

"When she's in town on business. She's my . . ." Oxana glanced skyward.

Sherry jerked her head back when she digested Oxana's partial reply. "Your mother?"

"No, no, no. Mama's brother. Wife. What's the English word?"

"Aunt. Vilma's your aunt?"

"Married my uncle. She was married to Mama's brother. He died. Vilma doesn't have any kids of her own. She likes to spend time with me. Mama says she's lonely. That I should let her teach me better English. Family is important where I come from." Oxana massaged the charm bracelet on her left wrist between her fingers.

"I understand. Family's very important to me, too. I'll make this quick. I'm trying to help my brother, Pep, get off Detective Bease's suspect list. He didn't kill Fitz Frye. If I can find out who did, that will secure Pep's innocence. Pep was at the inn at the time of the murder, but it was a case of being in the wrong place at the wrong time."

"I did not kill Mr. Frye," Oxana stated.

"Not saying you did. I'm gathering information to speed the investigation along." Sherry shifted her body to face Oxana squarely. She leaned in and lowered her voice to a near whisper. "Did your aunt tell you to check Uri's room at the Augustin Inn for anything that might incriminate him in Mr. Frye's murder?"

Silence.

"Incriminate. Did Uri have a supply of fishhooks in his room when you went in to clean it? Or a gun or knife? A murder weapon?"

Oxana's eyes widened. "*Da.* Yes. Aunt Vilma tells me to look carefully around the room. Didn't say why."

"Do you know what incriminate means?"

"*Da.*"

Sherry held an unblinking gaze into Oxana's eyes. "Do you think Uri murdered Fitz from what you saw in his room?"

"*Nyet.* No."

"How can you be so sure?" Sherry asked.

"I told her I found nothing. When I clean his room, I see nothing except man's body things— deodorant, razor, and hair hat. She was not happy."

"Hair hat?"

Oxana flicked her finger through her hair. "Hair, wig, on chest of drawers."

"Oh! A toupee." Sherry smiled. She envisioned Uri's magnificent head of hair before picturing the same head as a shiny dome of hairlessness. "I've never seen him hairless, so he must keep a toupee for emergencies. A hair and a spare."

"She gave me a box to put in his room. In his drawer. She says he needs his box back." The smile disappeared. "I have the box with me. Vilma's not family anymore. I don't have to do what she says, even if Mama says she's an elder."

"Elder? I'd guess she's about my age."

"Sorry. Older, right word?"

"I know what you meant." Sherry peered around Oxana toward her backpack. "Can I take a look at the box?"

"I understand what she asks was wrong. I have the box right here."

Instead of reaching into her backpack, Oxana pulled a small gold box from her jacket pocket.

"Do you know what's inside?" Sherry asked.

"I do not care. Miss Constable is my boss, not Vilma. I need my job. I do not break rules for anyone. You take. I have to go to class." Oxana thrust the box toward Sherry. The contents rattled with the force of the motion. Oxana stood and slung her backpack over her shoulder. "We cook Tuesday. Thank you."

Sherry watched the young lady strut to the door with the same no-regrets conviction her aunt displayed.

Chapter
19

"How about lunch at my house today, Dad?" Sherry asked.

"Are you in the car? The reception's not very good. You sound like you're in a tunnel," Erno yelled into the phone.

"I can hear you perfectly well. No need to shout. Yes, I'm in the car. I'm making a trip to the Augustin Inn. Lunch? My house?"

"Ruth, too?"

"Sure, the more the merrier. You, me, Ruth, and Pep. Since The Ruggery isn't open Mondays, Amber may be busy. I'll ask her, though."

"We'll be there around twelve-thirty. See you soon."

Before Sherry could respond, the call dropped. She double-checked the time. "Two hours 'till lunch." She texted Pep the logistics of the lunch plans, and he gave the plan a thumbs-up emoji. She copied and pasted the same message to Amber, who preferred the applauding emoji as her acceptance of the invitation.

Sherry scrolled through her phone contacts. *Ginger Constable.* She picked up her purse and exited the car. As she walked toward the inn, she clicked on Ginger's phone number. The call went directly to voice mail. When Sherry reached the bottom step of the inn's columned entrance, she paused to calculate her next move.

"Anything I can help you with, Sherry?"

Sherry rotated her head in the direction of the deep voice. The day-old, gray-flecked scruff was a welcome sight. "Addison. I was hoping I'd find you here."

"Me? What can I do for you?"

"I'm planning a surprise for a friend who's taking up fishing." Sherry plunged her hand into her purse. She pulled out the box Oxana had given her. "Is this hook proper? Should he start with something smaller? It's for whatever kind of fish can be caught in the Long Island Sound." She handed the box to Addison.

He lifted the lid and took a long look at the steel, double-barbed hook attached to a colorful lure. "I do think you've gone for the Maserati rather than the Kia. Plus, I'm not sure the fish in the Long Island Sound are big enough to latch onto this sucker."

"I should have asked your opinion before I sent away for this monstrosity. Do you know anyone who might be interested in buying it from me at a nice discount? I overheard Uri and Roe discussing an upcoming fishing excursion. Maybe one of them?"

Addison raised his gaze from the box. "I could ask, or you could. I believe they're checking out tomorrow. Technically, I'm a contract fisherman, and my hope is to do more work for Maine Course. I don't want to spoil my chances by bothering Uri with questions that aren't work related."

"A fishhook is work related." Sherry made no attempt to take the box back, even though Addison moved his hand closer to hers.

"Where'd you say you got this beauty?" Addison held the open box up to eye level and rotated the box in a full circle, admiring it from all angles.

"A catalogue. What did I know? If it's not food, gardening or Ruggery related, I'm no expert. I should just make my friend a casserole and stick to what I know best." Sherry laughed. She tucked her hair behind her ears and gave Addison one more pleading look. "You don't want to ask Uri or Roe if they're interested in buying it?"

"I really don't." The tone of his voice left no room for negotiation. He closed the box and tucked it in Sherry's palm. "Anything else I can do for you?"

"Have you run into Uri or Roe this morning?" Sherry replaced the box in her purse.

"Saw them at breakfast. On the early side."

"Thanks. Maybe I'll take a quick look for them in the library." Sherry headed up the stairs and through the massive white doors framed in thick dental molding. The library opposite the front desk was bustling with activity. She stepped inside the open French doors, where she joined a group gathered around a table of cookies and pastries. Reaching for what looked like a lemon Danish was Vilma. As Vilma backed away from the table, Sherry reached in and their arms collided.

"Pardon me." Vilma recoiled her arm, dropping

crumbs on Sherry's slip-ons. "Well, well. Sherry. We can't seem to avoid one another."

Sherry lowered her chin and stepped a few paces away from the table. Vilma followed close behind.

Sherry clenched her jaw. "Vilma, what you're doing is very wrong. Patti was right about you. You're a fraud."

"I'm a guest here, and the Danish are for the inn's guests," Vilma pointed out. "No need for name calling."

"That's not what I mean, and you know it."

Vilma placed the Danish in her mouth and bit off a hefty portion. She chewed for such a long time Sherry was prompted to stare her down. When Vilma swallowed, she dabbed the corners of her mouth with her napkin.

She turned her back and gathered a handful of cookies before addressing Sherry. "Can't resist gingersnaps. Sherry, how's your brother? I saw him here when I returned from the coffee shop. You know what they say about the perpetrator always returning to the scene of the crime."

"That's impossible. He's at home walking my dog. Anyway, I'm not here to talk about Pep. I'm here to see why you asked Oxana to plant evidence in Uri's room. She didn't do your bidding, by the way. She has morals and obeys the law." Sherry tried to steady her voice as she spoke, but nerves crept in and she hit some unsteady notes in her delivery.

"The investigation needs to move along faster. The story needs to keep pace with my deadline. A properly placed piece of evidence may spark some action," Vilma whispered. "How about you try a little harder to find the murderer if you don't like my methods."

"Take this back and stay out of the way. Detective Bease knows what he's doing. Stop interfering." Sherry jammed the gold box into Vilma's Danish.

Vilma huffed.

Sherry spun on her heels and left the room. As she headed toward the car, her temples were pounding. A new sensation, one she could only label as abandon, was pulsing through her body, and, like any new acquaintance, it would take some time to become familiar with.

Sherry returned home and, with Amber's help, prepared lunch. Ruth and Erno showed up on the dot of twelve-thirty. Familiar with her father's punctuality at mealtime, she was ready with the platters of food by twelve twenty-five. For her father, a lunch invitation at his daughter's house meant eating nearly the moment he entered the house, or he grew impatient. She took that as a compliment.

The round wooden table in Sherry's screened-in porch was the perfect size for ten diners or less. One empty chair and place setting sat unused.

"I thought Pep was eating here, so now there's more than enough." Sherry sighed and checked her phone for the time. She carried the sandwich platter in one hand and a bowl of fruit salad in the other from the kitchen and passed both to Ruth.

"Can I have the secret recipe for these *bánh mì* minis, Amber?" Ruth asked as she scooped one onto her plate. "They look fabulous."

"No secret. I marinated thinly sliced pork tenderloin

in ginger, and added pickled veggies, like radishes, cukes, scallions, mint, Thai basil, fish sauce, rice vinegar . . ."

"Stop, stop, too much already," whined Ruth. "Instead of the recipe, can I get you to cater my next luncheon? I can plan for Sundays or Mondays, when The Ruggery's closed."

"If I add catering to my résumé, along with The Ruggery manager and advice columnist, I'll be encroaching on Sherry's trifecta of holding down three jobs."

"Only two right now. Lost my pickle business when Frances Dumont came out of retirement."

"Right. Truth is, I learned this recipe from Sherry. Between the two of us, we'll get a minute to teach you someday."

Sherry passed around the lemonade. When the pitcher neared empty, she left her lunch guests and returned to the kitchen. She refilled the pitcher and turned her attention to dessert. "I wish Pep had come. This very well may be his good-bye lunch. Without the guest of honor," she told Chutney.

He wagged his tail in response or possibly because Sherry knocked a brioche bun crumb onto the floor.

When everyone had had their fill of sandwiches and fruit salad, Sherry cleared the plates with Amber's help. In the kitchen, Sherry placed coconut-macadamia blondies on a blue dessert plate in a graduated circular pattern. She placed mint sprigs on the peak of the dessert pyramid for a pop of color.

"Gorgeous. We got here in a nick of time," Pep announced as he entered the kitchen.

Sherry's hand lurched forward, knocking the top blondie from its perch. "You scared the bleep out of me," Sherry laughed. "Chutney, what good are you if you let people wander in off the street unannounced?"

"That's the closest to cursing I've heard you come in a long time," Pep remarked. "Sorry we're late. I know how Dad likes to eat the minute he gets here. We ran into a problem."

Sherry put down the plate and found Pep standing under the arched doorway leading from the front hall to the kitchen. "We?" Sherry checked the area behind Pep. His imposing frame blocked any sighting of a companion.

Behind Pep a hand lifted and waved. "Hi." A dark-haired beauty peered around Pep.

"Is that your friend, Charlotte?" Sherry's excitement prompted Chutney to raise up on his back legs with a greeting for the couple.

"Ta, da!" Pep sang out. His hand was clasped in Charlotte's.

She skirted around him and wiggled through the doorframe. She was draped in a flowy green shirt. Her side ponytail sprouted curls escaping from the lime scrunchie gathering the majority of her shoulder-length hair.

Sherry's mouth fell open as her gaze dropped to Charlotte's midsection. She reached for Charlotte's free hand and guided her forward. "Come in. You need to sit. Pep didn't mention you were, I mean, are you, I mean, you know what I mean." Sherry turned to Pep. "You gonna help a sister out here?"

"You're doing a great job all by yourself," Pep laughed.

Sherry threw her hands up in the air. "Pep hasn't told us a thing about you, to be perfectly honest."

Charlotte and Pep shared a look only intimate partners dared to exchange.

"No ganging up on me, you two. I had my reasons. One being, we didn't want to rain on your cook-off parade by sharing the news too early. Charlotte's been holed up at the Augustin Inn. Then, with the small matter of the suspicion of murder hovering over me, I didn't want to stress her out by introducing her to our crazy family too soon. We've been working through this surprise for a time now. Our decision to go public had to be on our terms. Sorry."

Sherry put her hand on Charlotte's belly. "I'd say it's not too soon. What a surprise!"

"I think you're right, Sherry. That's what I've been telling Pep," Charlotte added. "Can I give you a hug?"

"Of course," Sherry answered before they embraced. "Just to be sure. Congratulations to *both* of you?" Sherry posed the question in a near whisper. Her sight darted from Charlotte to Pep and back again.

"No doubt about it. You're going to be an auntie to the sweetest niece in history," Pep proclaimed.

"A girl." Sherry clapped. "Fantastic."

Pep raised his arms as if he'd just kicked the winning field goal at the Super Bowl. "Baby has the best parents ever. Mommy's a marine biologist and Daddy's a, well, that has yet to be determined."

Sherry wrapped her arm around Charlotte. "Now,

let's go meet Dad. I mean Grandpa. He's going to flip his lid with joy." Prepare yourself to meet some of Augustin's finest." Sherry led Charlotte to the porch.

"What's all the commotion?" Erno asked.

All heads turned toward the trio entering the room.

"Everyone, I'd like you to meet Pep's special friend. Is that term accurate?"

The air in the room was thick with silence. Sherry scanned each face, from her father's to Ruth's to Amber's. The ticking of Chutney's nails on the floor broke the quiet. Charlotte's hands rested on her bundle of joy.

Pep added, "The perfect term. She is special. And baby makes three."

"Baby?" Ruth asked.

Pep nodded. "We're expecting."

"You mean we all are," Erno hailed.

A united greeting filled the room and flooded out through the screened windows.

"Isn't this the most wonderful surprise? You have filled my heart with joy. Come right over here, young lady." Erno held his arms open wide. "Welcome to the family. What's your name?"

Laughter filled the room.

"Charlotte Knight." Her reply was nearly smothered by Erno's bear hug.

Erno guided Charlotte toward Ruth. She greeted the expectant mother with another hug.

"Meet my special friend, Ruth." Erno puffed out his chest. "We don't have anything to announce like you two, though."

Pep groaned. "Ugh, Dad, please. I hope not."

"I second that," Sherry added.

Ruth adjusted the silk scarf fashionably knotted around her neck. "That ship has sailed, but we still know how to have fun. Congratulations, you two." She eyed Sherry. "Listen, dear. Just because Pep may have beaten you to the punch doesn't mean you should give up trying to find that special someone."

Sherry cringed. "I'll give that thorough consideration, Ruth. Right now, I can hardly find five free minutes, even on my days off, let alone start a full-blown relationship with Mr. Right, if he's out there."

Pep cleared his throat. "Charlotte, this is our good friend Amber."

Amber stood and Charlotte took her hand. "So nice to meet you. You must be the gorgeous gal Sherry was trying to fix my fiancé up with? If this doesn't work out, he's all yours."

Amber's mouth dropped open. "Sherry? You're in big trouble. I swear I knew nothing about any of this."

Sherry covered her face with a napkin. "No good deed goes unpunished," her muffled voice whimpered.

Charlotte laughed. "Please continue eating. Sorry to interrupt."

"Are you kidding? You're the guests of honor. I'm assuming you guys haven't eaten lunch? We have plenty," Sherry offered. "Charlotte, take this seat."

Charlotte waddled to the empty seat and sank down in the chair.

"Take my seat, Pep. I'm done," Sherry said. "I'll get you a clean fork. How hungry are you two?"

"Starving. Haven't eaten for hours," Pep replied. "We're late because we were looking for Oxana. She was supposed to meet us at the inn after her class but never showed up. It's very unlike her to be late for anything. I've never met a more punctual person, other than Charlotte, in my life."

Sherry cleared her throat.

"And you, Sher. Oh, and you, Dad."

"Did you try calling her? I saw her at Crunchtime this morning. She was going to a class right afterward."

"We did, but her phone was off. It was kind of an important meeting. Since we're leaving tomorrow, we told her we'd help her sort out the documents she needed to remain in the country. Finishing her degree is her top priority, and her country is very restrictive with students studying abroad for lengthy amounts of time. It's a complicated process, hard to navigate on your own."

"Class probably ran long." Sherry went to the kitchen and prepared two lunch plates for her brother and Charlotte. She delivered the overflowing plates to the eager diners. Returning to the kitchen, she picked up her phone from the counter. "I bet Vilma knows where she is. I'll shoot her a text."

No sooner had Sherry delivered the text to Vilma than her phone buzzed. Sherry read the words on the screen. Sherry returned to the porch with the remaining sandwiches and fruit salad. "Hey, guys. Vilma says she's been looking for Oxana, too. The community college called her because she's listed as Oxana's emergency contact. Her backpack was left on the town bus. Her school ID was found inside, and a Good Samaritan brought the backpack to the college admin building."

Pep grabbed Charlotte's arm "She's in trouble. She told us if she disappeared, we should suspect the worst. That's why we felt the need to check in with her as often as we could."

Chapter 20

Sherry considered the options. "Oxana may have just decided enough is enough. She finds a dead body at work. It's difficult enough to not speak the language. Her aunt is a tough cookie. Maybe the circumstances got to her, and she took off."

"Her aunt?" Pep asked.

"Vilma Pitney is her aunt," Sherry explained. "Oxana's mother's brother was married to Vilma. He passed away."

Charlotte frowned. "I hope that's all it is and not something nefarious."

"Sherry, it's obvious now that Charlotte's the reason I haven't been a willing participant in the murder investigation, right? If I admit where I really was at the time of the murder, Charlotte might be in danger. And you. Strange things are happening. Your car is vandalized, and you're nearly squashed in the corn maze. Someone, obviously, knows you're sniffing around to help me out of a pickle. He or she isn't happy about your snooping. I can't risk putting Charlotte and the baby in the crosshairs, too."

"Pep's right," Ruth added. "In the girl's condition, she doesn't need undo stress."

Pep patted Charlotte's knee. "She's my alibi, but I want her out of the spotlight."

"Don't worry about me. I'm a big girl." Charlotte smiled. "I've heard stories about your sleuthing, Sherry. Who would actually count on becoming involved in an investigation on their first visit to Augustin? Kind of exciting, if you look at it a certain way. We can help find the murderer, possibly." Charlotte sat up as straight as her stomach bulge would allow.

"Now that things are out in the open, I have some intel to share," Pep announced between bites.

"Related to Fitz's murder?" Amber asked.

"Yep. I knew him a bit longer than I've been letting on."

Sherry tsk-tsked. "Lying to your sister? That's grounds for culinary punishment. I may have to withhold sharing my best recipes with you from now on, until I see remorse."

"I'd call it an error of omission rather than lying, your honor. Let me plead my case. Charlotte and I met in Portland, Maine. She was finishing up research on one of her remarkable projects that will one day save the planet."

"Makes sense why you stayed up there so long," Erno said. "I thought you had a thing for moose."

Ruth gently slapped Erno's arm and warned him to behave.

Pep chuckled. "Knowing we weren't going to make Portland our forever home, we bounced from residence to residence, not wanting to sign a long-term lease."

"We were basically living out of our suitcases for

about six months. Not the ideal arrangement," Charlotte added.

"You'll never guess who came to our rescue," Pep teased.

"I can," Ruth volunteered. "That Fitz fellow you mentioned. The dead one."

"Bingo. I was on a panel at our local library about the geology of New England. Fitz and his girlfriend, Kelly, were in the audience."

"That's surprising," Erno said.

Pep shrugged. "There were lots of people in the audience. Many people find geology fascinating."

"No, I mean, that's surprising you're finally putting your college degree to good use. Studying rocks for four years seemed like an expensive hobby I was funding for no good reason."

"I bet you don't call Sherry's cooking-competition hobby a waste of time," Pep countered.

"Because it's not. Her hobby didn't cost me a dime. As a matter of fact, she makes pretty good money crushing the competition in the kitchen," Erno said.

"Is this because you want me to settle back here in Augustin and help you run The Ruggery?"

Sherry eyed her father. Erno seemed to be holding his breath for a moment before he produced a weak squeak.

"I thought so. Things will happen as they should. Give us time, Dad."

"Getting off track here, guys. Although, I do appreciate the kind words about my cooking contesting, Dad." Sherry broadcast a sunny grin in Erno's direction. "Can we get back to Fitz rescuing you and Charlotte?"

"See, you are Dad's favorite. Anyway, Fitz sought me out after the presentation and asked me if I was related to you. We chatted about his business dealings, and I picked his brain about commercial real estate. He told me how much he admired Sherry's cooking and how much he'd enjoyed competing against you in a cook-off. He made extra sure I knew he beat you."

Sherry let loose a long exhale. She opened her mouth to respond but reconsidered.

"He asked for my business card. A day or two later he emailed me. He and I had discussed mine and Charlotte's haphazard living arrangement. He offered us short-term lodging for as long or short as we needed. I took him up on his offer, sight unseen. We only needed a place until Charlotte finished her research. How bad could it be?"

Charlotte dropped her fork with a clatter. All heads turned toward the pregnant woman.

"Is it time?" Ruth called out. "Pep, get the car."

Pep handed Charlotte her fork. "I think she's being polite by not stabbing me with her fork. I forgot to check with Charlotte when I made the arrangement with Fitz."

"Never heard the saying, 'wife first or it won't last'?" Erno asked.

"We're not married, Dad, but point taken. Anyway, we moved in the very next day. We were given a giant room, which served as a kitchen, living room, and bedroom. At first we were pleasantly surprised."

"The feeling of euphoria didn't last long," Charlotte added. "Imagine living above a seafood-processing facility. As nice as it was for Fitz to let us stay there, the minute I got morning sickness, we had to move. Ugh. I can still smell the acrid fish odor to this day. I couldn't possibly have set foot in the Lobsta' Taproom, when Pep invited me to join you all." Charlotte stuck her tongue out and clutched her throat.

"I like this girl. She lets it all hang out," Ruth said.

"Phew. I came very close to serving shrimp salad today. Credit intuition for changing my mind," Sherry admitted. "You answered how you met Fitz, but what about Uri and Roe? I'm guessing Maine Course uses the seafood processing facility that Fitz was the landlord of? What was your beef with those guys at the contestant party?"

"Whoa, whoa, whoa. One question at a time. Back to our Portland living arrangement. The situation quickly became a nightmare. Night deliveries were the worst. One night I couldn't sleep, with the trucks coming and going below the apartment, so I took a walk. That's when I met Uri and Roe. The men were coordinating the trucks that night and thought I was an intruder when I came out of the building. I almost ended up in jail. I persuaded them to call Fitz, our shared landlord, who cleared my name and explained my presence."

Sherry kept her sights on Charlotte's plate as she ate the last remaining chunk of fruit salad. "What a small world. Maine Course becomes a sponsor of the cook-off, Roe becomes the fisherman ambassador, and Fitz is a contestant who ends up murdered at said cook-off. The missing piece of the puzzle is, who had a major problem with Fitz? One that only murder could resolve."

"What was the argument with Fitz all about? The

guy did you a solid, even though it smelled fishy," Erno asked.

"He said we owed him money for some damage to the floor. We didn't agree. Usual landlord stuff." Pep lowered his gaze to Chutney, who was scavenging for crumbs at the feet of the newest diners.

"Landlord stuff," Sherry repeated softly.

"You didn't tell me that," Charlotte said. "Probably the heels of my boots scratched the floors."

"Do you think Oxana's disappearance is directly related to the murder?" Amber asked.

"Oxana told us she was fearful Vilma might be the missing puzzle piece. Not that Vilma committed the murder. More likely, she knows more than she's letting on," Pep said.

"Not just Vilma. Others know more than they're letting on." Sherry put a blondie on Charlotte's plate. "Pep, any chance you'd come over to the Augustin Inn with me after lunch? I have a few questions for some of the guests and Ginger. You'd be a big help, and we could get things done twice as fast."

"Charlotte, can I show you around The Ruggery while they're gone? It's closed, but I know the owner, and he can give you a private showing," Erno offered.

"Love to. I've heard so much about the store." Charlotte broke off a piece of the blondie and popped it in her mouth.

"I'll come along with you two," Ruth added. "We can discuss baby names."

"Speaking of old businesses, Dad, did you know

the Augustin Inn was in financial straits?" Sherry placed a blondie in her father's hand,

"I did know. Very sad." Erno spoke, despite chewing a bite of the buttery, crunchy, chewy dessert bar. "Clarence Constable is rolling over in his grave, as we speak. The right investor could bail Ginger out of trouble. Not to mention, one less murder would help, too."

Sherry presented the dessert plate of blondies to each guest for one more round. Everyone put up his or her hand as a refusal except Erno, who plucked the largest remaining one off the plate.

After the last plate was stacked in the dishwasher, Sherry and Pep loaded into the car. Sherry side-eyed her passenger. "Very exciting news about you and Charlotte and baby onboard. Now that the cat's out of the bag, can you tell me what your plans are? Settling down comes with the territory. At least for the immediate future. Why not make your home in Augustin?"

"Charlotte's finishing up her research in the twelfth hour. She's a hero, balancing everything. Problem is, babies can't read timetables. They come when they come. That's why we need to get back to Maine. The debate's ongoing for our next move. Right now, let's focus on the business at hand. Time's running out."

"I'm betting on the fact Uri has a lot of information he's not sharing. What's your opinion of Roe, besides the fact he's not fully versed in what he should be an expert at?"

"Roe and Uri are a package deal. Roe does what Uri asks of him."

Sherry parked the car in the service entrance lot at the inn. The spacious lot was empty. Sherry considered that Ginger was most likely cutting down on expensive repairs and deliveries to save money.

"I want to find Uri," Pep said. The severity of his tone gave Sherry goose bumps. She recognized the tone from the night of the party, when he was deep in discussion with Fitz. "Do you want to wait here for me?"

"I'm going to track down Ginger. She might have some idea where Oxana's gone. Text me when you're heading back to the car."

Pep flipped a wave as he exited the car and headed across the lawn to the inn. Sherry turned in the opposite direction, toward the corn maze. She skirted the perimeter and made her way to the weathered wood barn.

Once she entered the barn, harsh shafts of light, bleeding through the door and windows, made for difficult viewing. Particles of dust shimmered as each of her steps stirred them up. She squinted to get a clearer picture of what she was heading into. To her left was the spot previously cordoned off with crime scene tape to mark the location where Fitz's body was discovered. The floor where the ice sculpture had been was cleaner than its surroundings. A shiver ran through Sherry's scalp when the image of the submerged body crossed her mind.

Sherry made her way to the back of the barn. There she found Oxana's chair and tiny table. The single bulb, dangling from a low-hanging wire, was off. Sherry pulled the attached drawstring, hoping the makeshift contraption wouldn't collapse on her.

The harsh glare of the bulb illuminated the small table and the two items resting on it. A white envelope caught her attention first. She blinked to be sure what she read on it was correct.

For Sherry

She reached for the envelope at the same time she heard footsteps by the door. With a shaky hand, she snatched the envelope and filed it in her back pocket.

"Sherry? This is a surprise. What are you doing in here?" Ginger made her way in and out of the shafts of light to reach Sherry.

"Ginger? You in here?" A voice called out from outside the far door. "Did you find it?"

Ginger eyed the object on Oxana's table. "That's what we're looking for."

Sherry stepped back, and Ginger grabbed the garden clippers from off the table.

"Don't know why Oxana would be using these. She doesn't do any of our garden work." Ginger shrugged. "Found 'em," she called out.

"I'll meet you back at the maze," the male voice responded.

"Addison and I are securing that darn maze. Better be a popular attraction this year. Right now, the labor alone doesn't seem worth any profit." Ginger faced Sherry. "What did you say you're doing in here?"

"I didn't, actually." Sherry reached back with one hand and patted the pocket with the envelope. "I'm trying to get ahold of Oxana. She's not answering her phone, and I don't leave messages. No one listens to voice mail these days. I texted her but no reply. We have a cooking lesson on Tuesday, and I'd like to adjust the time a bit. Have you seen her today?"

"I gave her some extra time today, knowing she had to make up a class this morning. She's not due in until closer to dinner. If you want to leave a note, she has a mailbox. Hardly ever gets mail, but she checks it for her pay envelope, once a week at the very least."

"That's okay. Hopefully, she'll answer her phone soon."

Ginger wiped her garden-gloved hand across the dust on Oxana's desk, leaving a streak of clean wood. "I'm not very good at keeping secrets."

Sherry studied the woman under the sunhat. Her hair was spilling out across her neck in various shades of grays and blonds. The glaring light she stood under emphasized the creases the years had etched around her mouth and neck. "Something you want to tell me?"

"Pep. He's been here every day for the last few days. With a girl. A pregnant girl. She's checked in as Charlotte Knight. Did you know any of this?"

"He shared the news about two hours ago. I'm sure he appreciates your discretion in the matter."

"Thank goodness. You know, I've been privy to some wacky information as a hotel manager. I learned early on to keep my nose out of my guests' business. But, your family is different, and I wasn't sure how to handle the situation. Especially since Detective Bease was asking me so many questions about Pep. I was afraid he thought Pep was Fitz's killer." Ginger broadcast a brilliant smile. "Listen, how about the Oliveris come for dinner tonight? We have so much leftover food from the weekend, I don't know how we'll ever get through it all. You, Erno, his gal pal Ruth, Pep, Charlotte Knight, and be sure to bring a special someone for yourself. Everyone's welcome. Six o'clock. What do you say?"

Try as she might, Sherry couldn't come up with a valid reason why the family, which was set to dine together anyway, couldn't dine at the Augustin Inn. "Sure. Sounds nice."

Chapter
21

Ginger clutched the garden clippers with her gloved hands. "I wouldn't give the notion of Pep being the murderer another thought. Roe is guilty. He killed Fitz."

"Can you be one hundred percent certain? What did Roe have against Fitz that would lead to murder?"

"If Uri says he's certain, so am I. He needs a bit more time to prove his theory."

"That's quite an about-face from Uri. And from you. He and Roe seem awfully tight. You seldom see one without the other. You're probably one of the few who's seen Uri without Roe."

"Not as much as I'd like. But you're right. They appear joined at the hip sometimes. Hard to wedge between the two of them."

"There must be some physical proof of Uri's claim?"

Ginger peered over her shoulder. "Oxana saw something in one of the rooms and informed Vilma, who, in turn, confronted Uri, who admitted he suspected Roe."

"I'm skeptical of anything Vilma says. I'm having a hard time trusting her motives." Again, Sherry's hand traveled to her back pocket. "Why doesn't Oxana go to the investigators with whatever she discovered?" As soon as she finished her question, there was a commotion in the far corner. "What was that?'

"A mouse. We have to get pest control in here. What am I saying? Addison and I are our pest controllers. Maybe a barn cat is the answer."

The dark corner yielded a scratching noise followed by the sound of something heavy hitting the floor. "I don't think we're alone."

"Oxana's treading lightly, trying to stay in the country. The girl doesn't want any undue attention, especially from investigators. Finding the body was about all she could handle."

"Vilma, on the other hand, doesn't seem to have any problem throwing Oxana to the wolves."

Ginger lowered her voice. "What do you mean?"

"Afternoon, ladies," a voice sang out. "Addison said I could find Ginger in here. Bonus, I also found you, Sherry." The hazy lighting of the barn was bright enough to showcase the silhouette of the large-framed woman heading in Sherry's direction. When she could make out the purple swath painted above the approaching woman's eyes and the reading glasses poised to slide down her forehead, Sherry sighed.

"Afternoon, Vilma. Did you make it to the lunch service in time?" Ginger seemed to add an extra dash of sweetness in her voice.

"Just iced tea for me. I've packed on a few pounds the last couple of days. Time to take control." Vilma cackled. "Ginger, I'd like to extend my stay one extra night. I'm sure you have room. I've seen so many people check out this morning."

"No problem. You can stay put in the room you're in," Ginger responded with a hint of sour tempering the prior sweetness.

"Vilma, I have a question for you," Sherry said.

Ginger cleared her throat. "Look at the time. Are we done here, Sherry? I'd like to turn off the lights in the barn. Might deter the mice."

"Rats thrive in darkness," Vilma said.

"Vilma," Sherry spoke through a clenched jaw. "Do you know where I can find Oxana? And do you have any information on Roe being the guilty party in Fitz's murder?"

Vilma sneered at Ginger. "Oxana doesn't want to be found. As for our friend, Uri, he certainly didn't pass the confidentiality test. Seems he couldn't wait to share with his new girlfriend what I told him about Roe." She lowered her voice. "That's going to be a nice twist in my story."

"Well, Vilma?" Sherry urged. "Any new info?"

"Our dear Oxana let me know that, while tidying up Roe's room, she straightened up a pile of papers that the open window had strewn about the room. It was a report with page numbers, so she was able to organize the pile in proper numeric order. She said the front page was titled 'Maine Course Foods Inspection Report.' The kicker is, the inspector was listed as Albert Roe Trembley."

Sherry let the information sink in as she watched a daddy longlegs scurry down an elaborate web.

"There is something else." Vilma's purple lids swallowed her beady eyes as her eyebrows caved in.

"When the time was right, I asked Uri if Roe worked for him under any other capacity besides being his go-to fishing expert, which no one believed in the first place. Before he could answer, I told him I knew Roe was a food inspector and found it interesting he could inspect the very company he is contracted for in another position. A conflict of interest, no?"

"Aren't you concerned that if Uri put two and two together, he and Roe would figure out Oxana was the one who told you she found the report, and you might be putting her in danger? Is that why she's suddenly gone AWOL?" Sherry's words tumbled out with increased intensity.

"I don't like what you're insinuating." The words echoed throughout the cavernous space from a different direction.

Sherry's head jerked in the direction of the voice. A wave of panic washed over her.

Vilma gasped. "Uri, you scared the life out of me."

"Didn't mean to interrupt your very interesting conversation. Roe's not answering his phone. I don't pay him the big bucks to not be at my beck and call. He's mentioned so often how he'd like to check out this barn, I thought he might be in here."

Uri stepped closer to the women. His hair was disheveled, as if he had rolled out of bed and couldn't locate his toupee's hairbrush. The collar of his polo shirt was crumpled under. One of his pant legs was cuffed higher than the other. Sherry lifted her gaze from his askew pants alignment and met his stare.

"Obviously not in here, so I'll leave you cackling hens to your party." He turned, but not before sending Ginger a wink. "This place makes my skin crawl."

Sherry sucked in a deep breath. "Uri?"

Uri ran his hand through his hair before facing the women. His hand slipped down to his shirt collar. He unfolded the fabric and set it straight as if he were standing in front of a mirror with a perfect view of himself. "Yes?"

"Is Roe a food inspector who reports on the quality of Maine Course Foods and also works for you as a sustainable fishing expert?" Sherry's voice trembled as she posed the question.

"You're very inquisitive, Ms. Oliveri. I'd hate to think you went into someone's room and snooped through their personal items to satisfy your lust for amateur sleuthing. Don't cook-offs give you enough satisfaction? Some might agree you've broken the law."

"Sherry didn't go in Roe's room, Uri. Oxana was cleaning the room and had to pick up a report that had scattered around from the open window breeze," Ginger said. "It's her job to keep the rooms tidy."

"To answer your question, yes, Roe is contracted by me to share his knowledge. He's an independent inspector, who I hired to report on our high-quality products." Uri plunged his hand into his pants pocket, pulled out a phone, then raised it high overhead. "Speaking of conflict of interest, is it one of Oxana's jobs to snap a photo of something that doesn't belong to her and text it all around like headline news?" He put the phone screen up to his face. "Wait, not that picture." He blushed before swiping the screen. "This one." He held up an image of the title page of Roe's Maine Course quality report.

"I'm sure I don't have to tell you, stealing Oxana's

phone is breaking the law." Sherry reached her hand forward, toward the phone.

Uri put the phone gently in Vilma's hand. "Stealing? Hardly. Tell the young lady, in order to succeed in her future life of crime, she needs to be more mindful of leaving hard evidence at the scene. Roe did the right thing when he gave me this phone he found in his room. You and Vilma can quit calling. Oxana's not answering. There are a total of six missed calls on her phone between the two of you."

"Not the best way to do business, Uri," Ginger said. "You know we're in it together now."

"Sweetie, trust me. I know what I'm doing. It's short-term. Saving a business takes some creative measures." Uri eyed Ginger, who lowered her chin. "I'm going to continue my search for Roe." He produced an outburst of laughter. "He may have taken his loyalty to Maine Course a bit too far. I better put the brakes on his enthusiasm before someone else gets killed."

"What does that mean?" Ginger called after Uri.

He left the building without responding.

"Roe killed Fitz. No doubt about it." Vilma dusted her hands together.

"Not so fast, Vilma," Sherry said. "There's evidence Roe's on the shady side of the law, but where's the evidence he's a killer?"

Vilma shrugged. "Time will tell. Mark my words. Even if there's no smoking gun so far, there's one out there, and Roe pulled the trigger, so to speak."

Rustling in the far corner assaulted Sherry's ears. "I need to go find Pep. This barn is haunted, for sure." Sherry headed across the wide plank floor, each step announced by rising dust and creaks.

"You dropped this." Vilma trotted up behind Sherry and delivered an envelope. "If I didn't know any better, I'd swear that's Oxana's handwriting." She glared at Sherry's name on the front.

Sherry whisked the envelope from Vilma's hand and, without an acknowledgment, walked out into the sunshine.

"Pep. Over here." Sherry held the envelope tight and raced over to her brother, who was leaning on the car. "Did you get a chance to talk to Uri? He was in the barn, and he had some interesting tidbits to say."

"I ran into him. He's such a smooth operator."

"Did you know that, besides working for Uri, Roe is a food inspector? He wrote a report on Maine Course and gave it a very good grade. Doesn't seem completely above board."

"Might be the tip of the unethical iceberg."

"Unethical business practices. What did Fitz have to do with any of that?"

Pep eyed Sherry's hand. "What've you got in your hand?"

Sherry tucked the envelope under her arm. "Let's get in the car. I feel like there are eyes and ears all over the place. Did you ever hear the barn might be haunted?"

Pep poo-pooed Sherry's suggestion as he got in the passenger seat. "Rumors. What's in the envelope? Hopefully not another hotel bill."

Sherry wrestled with the seal of the envelope, attempting not to rip the paper. "This was on Oxana's little desk in the barn. How in the world did she know I would come looking for her?" She slid a card out. Her eyes darted across the handwriting. "I was wrong. If this is from Oxana, I'll eat my hat."

"What does it say? Don't keep me in suspense."

"*Sherry. I know how hard you're working to clear Pep.*"

Pep huffed, and the card waved in the midst of his breath storm. Sherry tried to steady the paper. She read on.

"*Check the box.*"

"Let me see that." Pep guided Sherry's hand closer to his face. "Oxana didn't write that. She's a pawn in this game, and it's not going to work out in her favor. I hope she's okay, wherever she is."

"More like a puppet, and I know Vilma is pulling the strings, but how far is she willing to go? She's creating a story here, and the worst offense is Vilma's crafting the ending because it's not happening fast enough for her in real time." Sherry stuffed the note back in the envelope. "Let's get home. I need to call Ray."

"You won't have to wait until then to talk to him." Pep pointed out the windshield. "Over there."

A man in a blue-gray windbreaker, rumpled hat, and khakis was heading up the path leading to the maze.

"Come on. Let's catch him." Sherry slid out of her car. She slammed the door behind her, muffling Pep's response. She didn't wait for him to join in her jog toward the detective.

"Ray! Ray!" Sherry called out. When Ray turned her way, Sherry saw glistening eyes and a mouth twisted into a frown. "You okay?"

"One of my favorite memories of my mother was visiting corn mazes with her every fall. And I mean every fall for twenty years. Now, she can't remember my name."

"I'm so sorry, Ray. But what great memories you have. You have to look at it that way, at least."

"Hey, Detective Bease," Pep said as he approached.

Ray tipped the brim of his hat. "Figuring out these mazes helped inspire me to become an investigator." He touched the side of the impenetrable cornstalk wall. "How far inside the maze were you when the wall collapsed?"

"Hard to say. I lost my bearings pretty quickly. Only about three to four minutes in. I'm pretty sure I'd made at least three turns and maybe two semi-loops, hit a few dead ends, and made a couple U-turns."

Ray nodded. "Got it. No idea where you were." Ray focused on Pep. "And you're expecting a baby?"

"How can you be so matter-of-fact, Ray? The news is so exciting," Sherry gushed. "How in the world did you know? I just learned a few hours ago."

"I'm a detective. Gathering information is what I do."

"Sorry 'bout that," was all Pep said to Sherry.

"Congratulations. Circle of life and all that. Some are nearing the end of their life while the lucky ones are only beginning theirs," Ray added.

Pep cracked a guarded smile. "Thanks. We're excited. Sorry about your mother. Sherry told me you're doing an amazing job looking after her."

"Thanks. And thanks, Sherry." Ray cleared his throat and brought forth his on-the-case detective inflection Sherry had come to recognize, which meant no emotions allowed. "Back to business." Ray pulled a notepad from his jacket's inside pocket, along with a pen. "Oxana was advised not to leave the area. Now she's gone. Any idea where?"

"My fiancée and I have known Oxana for a few days and that's it. She helped me sneak into Charlotte's room when I didn't want anyone to know what I was doing, including the night of Fitz's murder. We offered to help the girl with navigating the red tape her country wraps around every citizen who leaves the country for an extended length of time. I know she had a class to make up this morning. Turns out she never made it there."

"Any chance your fiancée is ready to answer a few questions?" Ray asked.

"I told you, she's off limits. I can't risk involving her and the baby."

Ray poked at his notepad with the pen tip. "I'm a patient guy up to a certain point. If the investigation doesn't keep moving forward, I'll have no choice but to force the issue. Now, Oxana's gone. She could have been helpful for your cause."

Sherry's stomach settled back down after a wave of nausea. "Fiancée? You didn't tell me that, either. Your exact words describing Charlotte were, 'special friend.' I need to launch an investigation to learn what else I don't know about you, dear brother."

Chapter 22

"We were getting to that detail," Pep said. "I can hardly remember who I've told what."

"Well, your family should be the first you tell," Sherry said.

"Noted," Pep replied.

Ray blinked hard and softened his tone. "Can we stay on track, Oliveri family? You can talk about these issues when I'm done. Oxana?"

"Vilma tried calling Oxana, around midmorning," Sherry said. "Oxana didn't have her phone with her. She'd left it in Roe's guest room at the inn when she cleaned it. I don't know what could have happened to her, and I'm worried."

"Why was Ms. Pitney calling her?" Ray asked.

"She's her aunt. I imagine she calls her often. Oxana had some information that could possibly be of use in the murder investigation."

"Continue," Ray prompted.

"I had a conversation with Uri a few minutes ago." Sherry looked to Pep for any sign she should or should not continue providing details of the meeting. His disengaged expression left her on her own.

"Uri took it upon himself to browse Oxana's photo library. He found she'd snapped a shot of a Maine Course Foods inspection report prepared by none other than Shrimply Amazing's fishing expert slash food inspector, Roe Trembley. Uri told Vilma. Nice to have someone on the inside authoring a report that could make or break the company's success."

"It's interesting that Oxana knew to capture the moment."

"No doubt at Vilma's urging. Her hand seems to be in every pot. The woman's out of bounds and should be penalized for interference," said Pep, his voice dripping with sarcasm. "There was more to the argument between Fitz and Lyman than anyone has let on. I was hoping not to be the one to have to provide details."

"Go on," Ray gently encouraged.

"Fitz was being served by Lyman as part of an investigation into false product representation."

"What was Fitz falsely representing? His buildings?" Sherry asked.

"Fitz wasn't at fault. He was being served to provide any knowledge he may have about one of his tenants," Pep replied.

"Maine Course," Ray mumbled.

"Actually, Shrimply Amazing. A Connecticut State Consumer Bureau investigation is getting underway. Shrimply Amazing sells their fish under the guise of local and sustainable. No chemicals, no GMOs, etcetera. Unfortunately, for the buying public, folks aren't getting what they're paying for," Pep explained.

"And you know that, how?" Ray said.

"One night, while Charlotte and I were staying in

the apartment in Fitz's building, I couldn't sleep because of all the truck noise outside. Apparently, pregnant women can sleep through anything because she didn't even stir. After wallowing in my insomnia for an hour, I got up and went outside. I met Uri and Roe on the loading dock. When I say they were shocked to see me, I mean more shocked than my family was today when I gave them the baby news."

Sherry met Ray's judgmental gaze. "Don't look at me that way. You don't know Pep like I do. I was shocked to learn he's going to be a father so soon. I didn't even know he had a girlfriend. A girl needs a little warning for news of that caliber."

Ray shrugged his shoulders. "Can't relate. Continue, Pep."

"After introductions, the men couldn't get rid of me fast enough. Not fast enough to keep me from taking note of what was printed on the trucks— PRODUCT OF THAILAND. Thailand's not local, last I checked."

"Why didn't you get served if you had that information?" Sherry asked.

"Uri and Fitz knew I knew what was up. Even though I wasn't interested in using the info about where their product truly came from, I needed help finding our next residence, and I figured they could be useful. I made a deal with Fitz. We'd move out the next day to a townhouse Uri rents to visiting clients, and he'd handle Shrimply Amazing his way. I'd keep their secret. Even from Charlotte."

"You didn't tell Charlotte?" Sherry's mouth remained open.

"Wanted to keep her out of the loop. Even so, I

didn't think we'd ever see Uri and Roe again. Well, small world of small worlds, they show up at your cook-off. Another shocking turn of events. Needless to say, Fitz and I had words at the contestant party."

"You told Charlotte you had an argument with Fitz over apartment damage."

"Another bad attempt to keep Charlotte safe."

"The argument was really about . . . ?" Ray asked.

"I warned Fitz to be very careful. I didn't know he'd be served that evening, or at all, for that matter, but I knew he was playing with fire, housing Shrimply Amazing in his building."

"Veshlage and Trembley are in cahoots to flim-flam the fish-loving public." Ray jotted down notes on his pad.

The corners of Sherry's mouth curled up. "They're up to some shenanigans."

Ray glared at Sherry from under the brim of his hat. "You know what I'm saying."

"Fitz promised the scheme was ending and Shrimply Amazing was back in financial good standing, back to selling products as advertised," Pep said.

She turned to Ray. "If someone killed Fitz to keep him quiet, why didn't whoever it is kill"—her voice broke—"Pep?" Sherry shivered.

"Hard to say. Most likely, Pep was considered the average Joe, living in a warehouse with his girlfriend, and no threat to their scam," Ray said.

"Way to make my life sound utterly unromantic," Pep scoffed.

Sherry's expression sobered up. "If Fitz knew Shrimply Amazing was selling fishy products, pardon the pun, would they kill him to silence him? What do you think, Pep?"

Pep squeezed his eyes shut and lowered his chin. "I've been hoping that's not the case." His eyes popped open.

"What does that mean?" Sherry asked. "What are you not telling us?"

"I'm the one who made sure Fitz understood what was going on in his building. I had to, knowing Charlotte would, despite my efforts to protect her, find out. She would say it was the right thing to do." Pep paused.

"Go on," Ray urged.

"Fitz was livid at the party because Maine Course was a last-minute addition as a sponsor at the cook-off. He claimed the company's participation in the cook-off was Uri's attempt to save face with consumers. Uri, in turn, was livid Fitz was also a last-minute addition. Uri chided Roe for not controlling the situation. The blame game was in full force that night."

"I'm beginning to think the coincidence of Maine Course Foods personnel and Fitz being at the same event wasn't a coincidence. Could Vilma have had a hand at setting up the chance meeting?" Sherry's gaze traveled over Ray's shoulder and stalled on the maze.

"Need proof." Ray turned his head in the direction of Sherry's gaze. "So tempting."

"Never too old for fun."

Ray jerked his head in Sherry's direction. "No time for fun. Too much to do."

"Who took it to the next level, murder? Fitz had a reason to kill Lyman, I suppose, but not vice versa. Uri had a vendetta against Fitz for spilling his company's secret. Definitely. But, Uri's just secured an investor in Ginger. She told me she was giving Uri her retirement savings. I highly doubt he'd commit a murder and spoil his sweet deal. What if Roe, Uri's henchman, did the dirty work as payback for Fitz's double-cross?" Sherry smiled at Ray. "A fifties reference in your honor."

"Appreciated."

Ray tipped his wrist toward his face and glanced at his watch. "Late. I gotta hit the road. Thanks for the chat. I'll be in touch."

"Do you ever get the impression he's not even listening?" Pep asked when Ray had walked away.

"He's a man of few words," Sherry explained.

"We need to get going." Pep motioned Sherry forward with urgency. "Charlotte texted she's not feeling well. She's sitting in The Ruggery, and Amber's out finding her a cup of chamomile tea with honey and cream. One of the odd foods she's craving right now. I told her we'd swing by and bring her a sandwich. If she doesn't eat every hour, she gets a terrible sour stomach."

Sherry and Pep arrived at The Ruggery to find Charlotte resting in a chair at the sales counter. Charlotte lifted her teacup and toasted their arrival.

Sherry raised an imaginary cup in response. "Glad you're feeling better. Hope you got through the tour of the store. We brought you this." Sherry handed Charlotte a sandwich loosely wrapped in foil.

"Thank you so much." From the seat Charlotte was resting in, she scanned The Ruggery showroom. "The store is beautiful. I was so honored to have a private tour."

"How does everyone feel about eating Pep and Charlotte's farewell dinner at the Augustin Inn, courtesy of Ginger? She extended the invite this afternoon. Says there is tons of leftover party food that will otherwise go to waste." Sherry watched her father defer to Pep and Charlotte. "Amber, you are, of course, invited."

Charlotte massaged her belly gently and stood. She rested her hand on a sample rug strewn across a display railing. "That sounds glorious. I'm feeling a lot better after a bite of that bacon avocado turkey sandwich. Eat, rest, pee, repeat. That's my life now."

"Thanks for sharing, Char," Pep laughed. "Sounds like we have a dinner plan. Then we need to pack up so we can get an early start in the morning."

Sherry watched Erno's gaze drop to the floor. "Should we call Ruth and invite her to dinner, Dad? Why isn't she here with you guys?"

"She was invited to dinner with the Van Ardans. We both were, so we're splitting the good fortune between two dinner parties. You'll have my full attention, Pep."

Outside The Ruggery's front door, the CLOSED sign rattled against the glass windowpane as someone twisted the door handle.

"I was afraid that would happen if we put on too many lights. Someone thinks the store's open." Sherry approached the door.

Through the glass, she made out a figure dressed in sweatpants and a T-shirt. The face was obscured by the interior light's reflection and a hat. Sherry waved her hand in an attempt to signal the store was closed, but it only served to draw the person closer to the windowpane. A sun-kissed face peered in. The man tapped on the door.

"Is anyone going to do something about the gentleman peeking in the window, or are we pretending he doesn't see us all in here? What's the matter with you all?" Erno passed the frozen bodies and made his way to the door. He opened it a crack and wedged his face in the opening. "So sorry. We're closed now. Can you please come back tomorrow?"

Before Erno could close the door, Sherry shimmied between her father and the door opening.

"I've got this, Dad." She pulled the door open. "Lyman. What can I do for you?"

As the fresh air wafted through the doorway, Sherry's sense of smell was overwhelmed with the memory of childhood afternoons at the beach. The salty brine of the ocean baked onto skin combined with coconut-scented sunblock tantalized her nose. "Coming from the beach?"

"I worried I needed a shower. Sorry if I offend. Couldn't resist one last sail before I leave town. The wind is perfect today."

Behind Sherry, a manly throat clearing broke the small talk. "Lyman, this is my father, Erno, my friend Amber, and Pep's friend Charlotte. I think you know Pep."

"Hi, everyone," Lyman offered. "I took a shot you'd be here, Sherry. Can I come in for a sec?"

Sherry made no attempt to move out of Lyman's way. "This is our day off. If you'd like to come back when we're open, we can help you then. We were about to leave."

Lyman strained to get a better look over Sherry's

shoulder. "Beautiful rugs. I'll definitely be back. For now, I need a quick word. Will only take a sec."

Sherry nodded. Lyman walked forward in flip-flopped feet. He glanced at the group assembled around him. No one relinquished their spot to give him room to pass. He was forced to park himself just inside the door.

"I have some information to share about Fitz. It's been bugging me since I found out he was murdered. I didn't mention it to the detective at the time he interviewed me. I don't know how important it is, but I need to get it off my chest. I called the number the detective left me in case I remembered a detail. He didn't answer, and I didn't leave a message. I know you've done some investigating in the past. Everyone knows that."

Sherry shifted her weight from one leg to the other. "Only to get my name off the suspect list in a murder investigation."

"And another time to clear my name from the suspect list," Erno added.

"And a third time to keep the legacy of an Augustin family from being tarnished with a false murder wrap," Amber said.

Lyman removed his hat. His hair was plastered flat on his head. His forehead sported an upside-down half-moon sunburn where the opening in the backward cap didn't shield his skin from the sun. "See? Good results prove you're a natural. What's nagging at me is what Fitz told me about his reason for participating in the Fall Fest cook-off, despite the fact he was fully aware he didn't qualify in the traditional way."

"It's not unusual he'd be in it. I've run into him at

other cook-offs," Sherry suggested. "He is, I mean, was, a fantastic cook."

"I know. He told everyone how he beat you the last time you two cooked off."

Pep grumbled something she couldn't make out. All heads turned his way.

"Lyman's right. He had other reasons."

"The night of the contestant party, I knew I had a job to do. But I'm not heartless. I engaged in a pleasant conversation with Fitz before serving him his papers," Lyman said.

"You get more bees with honey than with vinegar." Erno's eyes twinkled. "You get a bear that way, too."

Lyman nodded in agreement. "Things took a turn when I asked him how he picks the cooking contests he enters. He told me normally he's inspired by the theme of the cook-off, but, in this case, he wanted to beat Sherry Oliveri one more time."

Pep sucked in a deep breath. "That wasn't all Fitz said. Right, Lyman?"

Lyman wiped his brow with the back of his hand. "He'd had a few cocktails by the time I caught up to him. His tongue was kinda loose. He asked me if I knew you, Sherry. Since I didn't, it gave him license to speak freely. He said he'd done some legwork. He found out what recipe you were making at the cook-off. Said he went out of his way to create a dish similar to yours."

"That's why he should have never been let in, based on last year's withdrawal. They must have let him prepare any recipe at the cook-off since he was so last minute. Normally, cooks qualify with a current recipe, so the judges know what they're dealing with." Sherry lowered her head and sighed. "I don't begrudge him trying to beat me. We'll never know who had the better recipe."

"Thing is, he wasn't trying to beat you. He was trying to get your attention," Lyman said.

"Huh?" Sherry studied Lyman's face for any hints of meaning.

"His girlfriend, Kelly, I think her name is, joined us midconversation that night. When I say joined, I really mean she took over the conversation. She has a big presence for a petite gal, and Fitz couldn't get a word in edgewise. It was almost like she was trying to prevent him from saying too much."

"What did she say?"

"The pint-sized powerhouse said the reason Fitz found himself at the Fall Fest, even though he had no intention of being there, was pressure from a journalist named Vilma Pitney. She convinced him to pursue whether he was eligible to enter the cook-off, due to last year's circumstances. She felt strongly he was eligible, because she had spoken to a cook-off official regarding his situation. She told him if he entered, she'd provide him with the recipes the other finalists were preparing. She recommended he specifically take on Sherry's recipe for shrimp lettuce wraps, because the judges would love to see two cooks with competition history face off against one another."

Sherry shook her head. "What is that woman up to? She's inserted herself into every aspect of the cook-off. Now I see why she cozied up to Uri, one of the largest sponsors. It's almost as if she were trying to shape the outcome of the contest, but that's not how it works. The best cook wins. Period. No funny business."

Chapter 23

"I'm just telling you what I know," Lyman replied.
"Don't shoot the messenger."

"I still don't get why a seasoned cook-off competitor, lucky enough to choose the recipe he
prepares without having it go through the rigorous
vetting process the rest of us go through, would
choose a recipe so similar to mine or one of the
other finalists? There's no advantage there," Sherry
pointed out.

"What's the chance Fitz knew someone was trying
to kill him?" Amber asked. "The old saying 'keep
your friends close but your enemies closer' might
apply here."

"Enemy? Did he think I was his enemy?" Sherry
asked.

"No, no," Pep said. "Amber means if Fitz was
being threatened, he might consider jumping into
the snake pit with the vipers. Not the cooks, in this
case. Peripheral vipers outside the kitchen. A sponsor, perhaps? A sponsor with a secret? That way,
there might be a better chance of survival. Like
hiding in plain sight."

"Kelly said something very interesting to me on behalf of Fitz," Lyman continued. "At the time, I didn't think much of it. Now it makes perfect sense. She said Sherry would welcome the challenge of figuring out why Fitz chose the shrimp wrap recipe. That's why I think he set out to get her attention rather than win the contest."

"And then he was murdered," Erno said.

"I feel awful I served him in such a public way." Lyman shook his head slowly. "That may have given the green light to the killer—time to act."

Sherry's thoughts began to race. The facts and theories were colliding, but none were willing to rise to the surface, leaving her thinking harder. "The timing is interesting. Fitz entered the cook-off in the eleventh hour. Every cook I spoke to didn't know there was an added contestant until the day of the cook-off, including myself. How did you know where to find Fitz, Lyman?"

"I've been tracking Fitz for almost a month. I had to wait until he was in Connecticut, since the inquiry is taking place here. He has properties in many states, so pinning him down wasn't easy."

Sherry paused to reframe her question. "But exactly how did you know he was in the cook-off?"

"Okay. I admit I was getting desperate. He has a residence in Maine he's at often, so I staked out his townhouse. That meant hours and hours in a parked car or strolling down his building's sidewalks. I was getting sick and tired of the miserable bleak weather people have to put up with there. I caught a month-long cold and was close to handing off the assignment to someone else when, one day, an overnight delivery envelope landed on his doorstep.

The return address was the cook-off. I googled the contest information, took a chance he'd be one of the contestants, and showed up. I figured the contestant cocktail party would be the best place to catch him."

"Speaking of feeling awful, I feel awful I was the one who provided the initial information on Maine Course Foods that got the investigation started and put Fitz in harm's way," Pep added.

"Who would imagine murder would be the outcome?" Erno asked. "People are going to start avoiding the cook-offs you're in, Sherry."

"I need to take a close look at Fitz's recipe in the contest booklet at home. If Kelly told you I'd welcome the challenge of beating his similar recipe, you're right. What he really may have wanted was to get my attention. If he was aware of my occasional sleuthing, his recipe could contain the clue as to who was after him. He knew me as a competitor. I always read the other finalists' recipes from start to finish at some point, especially if I've lost to them."

"Just when I thought cook-offs were safe again," Amber said.

"That's what I say," Erno added.

"Cook-offs are safe," Sherry said. "It's the cooks that aren't."

"I have an idea," Pep said in a near whisper. "What if we plant a seed of doubt in Vilma's head? She's so insistent on forcing the investigation forward on her time and in her preferred direction. She needs a nudge to knock her off balance. Give her someone else to think about besides Roe."

"Honey, dare I ask what that seed might be?" Charlotte rubbed her belly, which, in return, produced a growl so loud everyone laughed. "The baby wants to know, too."

"Sherry, can you text Vilma and tell her you and Charlotte are beginning to worry about my suspicious behavior? That Detective Bease is going to lock me up if I don't start answering questions."

"I don't know if that's a good idea." Sherry glanced at Charlotte's chatty stomach. "You're out of the crosshairs. Why would you want to have her think you're possibly guilty again?"

"Vilma's so close to pinning Roe for the murder, she's unwilling to change her mind. She's written the ending. There's no going back. She'll ramp up her evidence and either present a cut-and-dry charge against him or uncover another truth as to who the murderer is."

Sherry brought her phone up to face level. "Couldn't hurt." She tapped out a message and hit the send key.

"Good luck in your search, Sherry." Lyman headed out the door. "I'd like to see whoever did this behind bars ASAP. For my peace of mind."

When Sherry stepped out The Ruggery's front door, she was struck by how quickly the afternoon was cooling off. Across the street, the sun lowered behind the Wine One One lounge. Traffic was light. Only a few pedestrians were out window shopping.

As she headed toward her car parked along the curb, her mind drifted to her admiration of Augustin's adherence to cleanliness, while being such a dog-loving community. Every other block provided a doggie pickup bag dispenser for owners to keep sidewalks unsoiled. The fastest way to draw a crowd, while walking around town, was to ignore your pet's mess. There was no shortage of enforcers ready to call an owner out if immediate action wasn't taken. Sherry should know. She had once, and only once, put convenience over her duty to pick up. She received a summons in the mail, along with her name listed in the town's police blotter. In the very same newsletter she would years later edit.

Sherry's cell phone rang, bursting the bubble of shame she found herself in as she recalled her misdeed.

"Sherry," the solemn voice on the other end of the phone began. "You texted Vilma."

Sherry peered around her, not expecting to see anyone but still wanting to be sure no one was approaching. "Ray? How did you know that? Are you with her?"

"I'm with her. She's dead."

"Dead? Vilma? Dead?"

"Yes, yes, and yes."

Sherry took a moment to track a single seagull flying across the darkening horizon. The squawking bird's piercing cry reminded Sherry of the gull flock that had circled the Fall Fest Cook-off judging table before the awards ceremony. One had landed on the table and stolen a potato off Heidi's presentation platter. If only gull annoyance was the most unusual occurrence of the cook-off weekend.

"I was with her a few hours ago at the inn. Well, not really with her. She inserted herself into a conversation I was having with Ginger. In the barn. What happened to her?"

"She was found slumped over the steering wheel in her car. The motor was running, but she never left the inn's parking lot," Ray explained. "When I checked her phone, she had a new text from you. The phone was locked, so I couldn't get past the notification. Care to share what you were texting her about?"

Sherry mulled over the thought that her text from Vilma may have been the last text the woman was ever to send. Sherry shut her eyes. How to present this to the detective. He wasn't going to buy Pep's idea without a convincing sales pitch. It seemed a good idea at the time. In an instant, the timing went from good to horrendous. "Uh, well. Okay. Hear this with an open mind, Ray. Since Vilma was so set on butting into the investigation, Pep and I came up with a plan."

"Continue."

Sherry cloaked her tone in a creamy softness. "Let me say again, it seemed like a good idea at the time. We were going to give her a specific clue path to follow and see what she could come up with. She doesn't seem to mind sending me on wild goose chases, so we were reciprocating, shall we say. If she came up with the murderer, all the better. The point is mute now, of course." Sherry paused. "Did she suffer a heart attack? Stroke? She was always running this way and that, I could see how either could've happened." Despite her insistence, she didn't believe the scenario she tried to convince Ray of.

"Nope. She was strangled while sitting in the driver's seat of her car. Apron strings tied tight around her neck. Her car was idling, and her phone was at her feet with your text notification on the screen."

"Oh, no. Was the apron red, by any chance?"

"If you're asking whether it was a cook-off apron, I'd have to say, yes. New England Fall Fest was embroidered on the front. The good news, if I can call it that, is her car had a dashboard camera. Possibly the killer walked across the front of the car at some point and the camera caught the image. I'll check."

"Any sign of Oxana?"

"I was gonna ask you the same question. It's in Pep's interest she gives a sworn statement stating exactly where she saw your brother the night of Fitz's murder, if you want to keep his pregnant fiancée out of it. Hear me?"

"Loud and clear." Sherry caught her toe on a crack in the curbstone and almost regained her balance before she went down. She swallowed an expletive she seldom uttered, except in times of extreme duress. "My feeling is, she may just reappear now that Vilma isn't looming over her every move."

"The sooner the better." Ray left no room for misinterpretation. "Gotta go. My mother took a bad turn this morning, and I had to hire full-time care. Another situation to keep my eye on. The department is insisting I either crack this case in record time or hand over the reins to one of the young bucks. Once the reins are out of my hands, I won't ever get another assignment. I'm certain of . . ." His voice faded away.

"Get going. I'll contact you when . . ." Sherry realized it wasn't the time to hand out promises she wasn't sure she could keep. The phone call ended without a good-bye. "Vilma, what did you get yourself into?"

* * *

Even after her initial prep was complete, Sherry paced around her kitchen counter, opening and shutting drawers. "Ginger's got another mess to clean up. Poor gal." She pulled open another drawer. "I can't remember what I'm looking for."

"The microplane for the lemon peel," Amber said. "You're refreshing the lemonade. Why don't you add a little vodka? That might take the edge off."

"That's right. Thanks. Too much on my mind." Sherry resumed her search. "And good idea about the vodka. I wonder if Addison likes hard alcohol or beer or what. I'm surprised he's coming without Ginger. The last thing the Augustin Inn needed was another murder. But how could I not be thrilled Addison's bringing the party leftovers with him?"

"Let's rewind back to Vilma." Amber handed Sherry a lemon. "Did she text you back before she died?"

"Yes, she did. I didn't mention that to Ray. If the phone was locked, I know he hasn't read it yet."

"Share, please."

"Vilma wrote back in no time. She said not to worry about Pep. He wouldn't be under suspicion as soon as R—she didn't write out the entire name, but I assume she means Roe—trips up. He was very close to, in her words, taking the bait."

"Interesting. She was fully invested in pinning Roe. Why? What's in it for her?"

Sherry opened her mouth to speculate but was interrupted by Chutney and Bean's eruption of barking.

Chutney and Bean scampered through Sherry's kitchen. Sherry followed the canine alarmists to the front door. She peered out the sidelights and saw no one. The dogs continued leaping and strutting in a show of full terrier bravado.

"What is it, guys? I don't see anyone." Sherry squatted to get a better perspective on what the dogs saw. "We have a visitor. It's not a someone, it's a something."

Seated on the bristled porch doormat Sherry used to scrape the grass and mulch off her shoes was Elvis Purrsley. Attached to the cat's body harness was the feline leash, covered in garden debris.

"I bet Eileen is worried sick. I'll be right back, Amber. Need to run across the street for a minute." Sherry stepped into the rain boots she'd parked by the door for early morning Chutney walks. She used her leg to barricade the dogs inside long enough to slip out the door and then stepped gingerly over to Elvis Purrsley. She picked up the leash loop. "Okay, Elvis, it's back home for you."

Sherry made her most persuasive kissing noise to urge Elvis forward. When that didn't work, she coaxed, meowed, cooed, and cajoled, all to no avail. "Guess I'm not the cat whisperer, either." She bent over and scooped the cat up into her arms. "I'm not opposed to a hand delivery."

Sherry crossed the street and knocked on Eileen's door. After some time spent staring at the red paneled door, Sherry gave up. "Hope you like little feisty dogs because that's your company tonight. Got no other choice."

Elvis was perfectly relaxed in Sherry's arms until she opened her front door. Chutney and Bean expressed their displeasure at the visitor by leaping up Sherry's legs and nipping at the cat's tail. The scolding they received sent them pouting to the dog bed in the corner of the living room. Sherry unclipped Elvis's leash. He began an inspection of the house.

"Who have we here?" Amber asked as the cat pranced past her.

"Elvis Purrsley. Eileen's cat. I'll text her. Not sure how he got out, but Eileen's not home, so he's visiting us for a while." Sherry picked up her phone. Her posture stiffened when she noticed a text had come in. A breathy gasp escaped her lips. "Ginger texted me. Says time is running out. What does that mean?"

Before Amber could respond, there was a knock at the door. Chutney and Bean slinked quietly to the front hall, staying behind Sherry in a show of obedience. As soon as she praised their calmness, they let loose with full terrier abandon. "Guests are here."

Sherry opened the door to Erno, Pep, and Charlotte. They filtered through the doorway and inside the house. Strolling down the path toward the door, a few steps behind, was Addison. He was balancing two large sacks.

"Guys, Addison could use a hand." When no one returned to offer assistance, Sherry stepped out in her dog-walking boots and greeted Addison as he approached the door.

"Thank you for your flexibility, Sherry. I brought some great fish, shrimp, and a bunch of veggies from the party. As you can imagine, Ginger wishes circumstances were different and that you all were coming to the inn for dinner. She sends her best."

"Thank you for coming and bringing all these goodies. I'm so sorry about Vilma. What an awful situation for the inn again." Sherry reached out for one of the sacks of food.

Addison clung tightly to his bundles. "I've got it. I might tip over if I hand one off. Show me where to set these down. My arms are about to give out. It's been a long day."

Once inside, Sherry unpacked the food on the kitchen counter. She was thrilled to see bottles of merlot among the seafood and produce. Gorgeous green butter lettuce was a featured item in one of the bags. The produce gave Sherry an idea.

Before she began cooking, she made sure her guests were settled in with a drink in hand. As soon as she placed chips, salsa, and guacamole within reach of the guests, she set out in search of the Fall Fest Contestant Cookbook.

"Anything I can help you with?" Amber entered the kitchen. "What's on the menu for Pep's last supper?"

Sherry heard Amber, but the words registered no meaning as she was lost in the cookbook.

Amber asked again, adding, "What are you reading?"

"I'm going to make my lettuce wraps and Fitz's lettuce wraps from the cook-off. I'm reading his recipe. Snappy Shrimp Lettuce Wraps with Thai Basil Avocado Aioli."

"You have all those ingredients for his recipe?" Amber asked in amazement.

Sherry circled her arms around a collection of ingredients on the counter. "Since he didn't cook off, none of his ingredients were used. They're all right here. Addison brought everything listed in Fitz's recipe."

A smirk crossed Amber's lips. "This is your chance to see if his recipe could've beaten yours."

"True. More important, I have a nagging feeling his recipe might contain a clue as to who was threatening him. If I'm way off base, then yes, it's my chance to go head to head with him one last time. I'll dedicate dinner to his memory. Since you asked, here's a bowl of shrimp to peel." Sherry slid the plump crustaceans toward her friend. "I'll pop my head in the living room and tell everyone dinner is in thirty minutes. Keep peeling."

"Wait. How did I go from guest to sous chef in a span of one minute?"

"Be careful what you volunteer for."

Chapter
24

"Attention, everyone."

All heads turned in Sherry's direction.

"If you know me at all, you know I can't let too many days go by without partaking in a food competition. So, tonight I'm making my winning lettuce wraps from the Fall Fest Cook-off. Inspiring me to raise the bar was a recipe also in the contest for another version of lettuce wraps."

Pep nodded. "Fitz Frye's," he said to Charlotte in a not-so-subtle whisper.

"Fitz didn't get a chance to compete, so I thought I'd make his recipe and have you all decide whose is better." Sherry presented her idea with caution.

Around her, the faces in the room returned a blank stare.

"Come on. Don't give me that look. It's not always about the competition for me. Fitz's recipe was also a wrap, and I'm intrigued. Play along. It'll be fun."

Erno shifted in his seat. "A little morbid, but let's humor her."

"I can hear you, Dad." Sherry turned her attention to Pep. "Pep, you're in charge of drink and appetizer orders and refills, while Amber and I get to work in the kitchen. Make sure Addison is well taken care of. Dinner's in thirty minutes."

"Yes, ma'am," Pep answered. "Once again, no rest for the weary. Thought I was the guest of honor."

Sherry returned to the kitchen. She propped the recipe booklet up against her food processor and went to work re-creating Fitz's wrap recipe. Her own recipe was committed to her short-term memory. She was confident she'd be able to pull off her Savory Shrimp Lettuce Wraps with Balsamic Merlot Reduction in less than twenty minutes, while simultaneously preparing Fitz's wraps. With Amber's help, that was.

"Shrimp's all naked," Amber announced. "Now what?"

"If you wouldn't mind making the merlot reduction, that's the lengthiest part of my recipe." Sherry gathered a stained and splotched paper from the corner of her work desk. "Here you go. Reduce away." She thrust the recipe into Amber's hand.

"Are you sure you trust me with your baby? What if your award winner becomes the big loser in my incapable hands?"

"I'm hoping you'll be inspired to enter another contest when you remember how fun cooking is."

Amber took the paper to the cupboard in search of ingredients. "I have no problem with how fun cooking is. My issue is cooking for cash and valuable prizes under extreme pressure, with time limits, and in a strange kitchen. Let alone murderous undertones that creep in when least expected. You're a different breed than the rest of us."

Sherry puffed out her cheeks. "Is the reduction ready yet?"

Amber let out a shriek. "No! See? The pressure is intense."

When the wraps were complete and assembled in presentable perfection on two distinct platters, Sherry and Amber set them down on the dining room table. The evening had cooled off below a comfortable outdoor dining temperature, so Sherry felt it best to eat indoors rather than al fresco. As she opened her mouth to announce dinner, Elvis Purrsley scampered under the table with Chutney and Bean in hot pursuit.

"I forgot to call Eileen. With the news of Vilma clogging my brain, it completely slipped my mind. She's probably sick with worry about Elvis."

On cue, there was a pounding at the front door. "Sherry! Sherry!" A muffled voice bellowed through the wooden door. "Elvis Purrsley is gone!"

Sherry raced to open the door. On the other side was her neighbor. Eileen's hair was tossed about her head, and her cheeks, usually a ghostly pale from avid sunscreen use, were deep red. She could barely catch her breath to form a sentence.

"I was carrying Elvis a few blocks away during another leash lesson and he jumped out of my arms after a chipmunk. I've been searching for two hours. I went about a mile up the street and trespassed in everyone's backyards. No Elvis. I'm sick about it." Eileen lowered her voice. "I did learn, from what I saw, that I'm the best weeder in the neighborhood, besides you, of course. People should take more pride in their landscaping."

Sherry motioned Eileen into the house. The cat approached his owner fully invested in a keep-calm-and-carry-on strut.

Eileen's mouth dropped open. "My baby!" She scooped the cat up into her arms and was greeted with the cool nonchalance of a pet that took more than he gave.

"He appeared at my door. I was about to call you." Sherry cringed when she heard the footsteps behind her.

She shot a glance to her friends and family, pleading for solidarity in keeping her little white lie under wraps. No one said a word.

"I'm giving up on his leash training. I'm not the cat whisperer after all."

Addison stepped forward. "Don't give up. If you have a minute, we can try something. Let's go outside. Sherry, we'll be back in a few minutes. Please start without me."

Eileen kissed Elvis on his forehead and cheered. Sherry could have sworn the cat rolled his eyes. Eileen pulled a folded paper from her back pants pocket. Elvis wriggled around in an awkward pretzel posture when Eileen's second hand came off his underside. Sherry collected the cat's leash and handed it to Eileen.

"Oh, and I've been meaning to drop this article off from today's paper. I know you don't subscribe to the *Sun* and the *Snow Daily*." Eileen clutched the cat tight. "In today's edition is an article about the cook-off, although mostly about the murder of the contestant, written by a woman named Vilma Pitney. Thanks again for saving my little furry man." Eileen followed Addison out the door.

Sherry put the paper on the counter and gave it a penetrating glare.

"Aren't you going to read it?" Pep asked.

"No, not now. Let's eat. I want to hear everyone's reviews of the two wraps. Now, more than ever." Sherry shoved a plate in each of her guest's hands. "Make sure you take one of each."

Erno, Pep, Charlotte, and Amber filled their plates with two wraps, cornbread, and asparagus. When everyone except Addison was seated at the table, the feasting began.

"I realize you all know whose wrap is whose, but do your best to be honest and forthright with the truth." Sherry saw multiple glances exchanged. "Yes, the old Sherry would have never been able to stomach your criticism, but my skin has thickened."

"No criticism here. Your wrap screams American cuisine at its finest. Comfort food with a flare," Charlotte offered. "The other wrap is very different and quite wonderful. Crunchy ginger coating on the shrimp, Asian spices, and the Thai aioli is to die for." Charlotte bit her lower lip. "Shouldn't have phrased it like that."

"You said it perfectly," Amber said. "American elevated, Asian fusion."

Erno smacked his lips. "If I was a judge at the cook-off, these two would need to go to sudden death overtime to decide the winner."

"You shouldn't put it that way either, Dad," Sherry scolded.

"Knock, knock. Sorry to bother. I want to show you all what Addison taught Elvis in five minutes." Eileen slipped into the dining room.

All heads swiveled to face the woman. She was

holding the leash in one hand and a metal rod with a shrimp tied to it in the other.

"Watch." Eileen lowered the rod with the shrimp lure, a paw's length in front of Elvis Purrsley. The cat trotted forward as Eileen guided him in a circle around the table. Heads pivoted to follow the action like the audience at a tennis match.

"Wow, you are the cat whisperer after all." Sherry started a round of applause. "That handy tool looks like it's been through the ringer."

"All thanks to Addison. Have a good night everyone. I'm emotionally drained."

"Good night, Eileen," Sherry called after her neighbor. "Take a seat, Addison. I'll bring you a plate."

Addison joined the group at the table. "My folding fishing rod came in handy. Lucky, I had it in the car."

"I think she walked out with it," laughed Pep.

"No problem. I don't need it anymore. I don't need any of my fishing equipment." Addison's voice hit a forlorn note. "A second death in a week is definitely someone trying to tell Ginger and me it's time to change careers. The fishing industry is dead in the water, literally, and so is the Augustin Inn."

"Maybe cat training is the way to go," Erno suggested.

Addison eked out a half-smile. "Easy for you to say, sir. Everyone wants a beautiful hand-loomed rug. Your business is secure for generations to come. Got any openings?"

"Isn't there any way the inn can be saved?" Charlotte wiped a dollop of aioli from the corner of her mouth.

"At the rate Ginger's falling for Uri, any chance of saving the inn is evaporating quickly. Her heart isn't in the business anymore." Addison studied the wrap in his hands. "Am I tasting ginger snaps coating the shrimp? The flavor is amazing. Very unusual."

Sherry watched Addison handle each of his lettuce wraps. He alternated between the featured recipes, not seeming to prefer one over the other. He didn't take his gaze off his plate until his hands were empty. Sherry preferred a more expressive diner when it came to judging her food.

"Okay, guys. Is there one wrap you prefer?" Sherry turned her attention to Addison. "Sorry to drag you into this, but I've made dinner into a mini cook-off between my wrap recipe and the one Fitz would've made."

"Pep told me you were competitive. Now I believe it. I've never been to a dinner that became a cook-off and the guests were the judges."

Sherry's face warmed. "I forget that what I consider normal, most people consider odd. You can abstain if you'd like."

"I wouldn't dream of it," Addison laughed. "It's been such a crummy day. This may be exactly the kind of fun I need. I'll even go first."

"Phew. A willing participant. How refreshing," Erno stated. "You can't imagine the pressure Sherry's family is constantly under."

"Okay, Dad. Take it easy. You're scaring our gracious guest," Sherry scolded. "I appreciate your honest opinion, Addison."

Addison put his hand over his stomach. "Maybe there's an opening for a taste tester somewhere. I'm liking this job. Sherry, I know yours is the one with the wine sauce. Honestly, it's the one I like best. Blue ribbon for you."

"What do you think of Fitz's?" Sherry asked.

"Everyone loves gingersnaps. My sister was named after the cookie. They are my family's favorite, and growing up, we always had them in the cookie jar. The inn has them every day on the snack table. We used to make them fresh, but now Ginger buys the boxed variety. But as a coating for shrimp, I can't wrap my taste buds around that. A touch too sweet for a main course."

"Why do gingersnaps as a coating sound familiar? Didn't you have a recipe with lamb meatballs and gingersnaps in a cook-off once?" Erno asked Sherry.

"Dad, I'm amazed you remember my recipes that well. Yes, I did. Wonder if Fitz got his idea from me?" Sherry studied the wraps and considered the idea. *What is Fitz trying to say with his over-the-top recipe?*

"Ginger and lamb sounds like a better combo than gingersnaps and shrimp, but I have no clue how way-out you contest cooks like to go," Addison added. "Mark me down in favor of your wraps, Sherry."

"I'm for yours, too," Amber agreed. "Fitz's are good, but I'm not used to the flavor combination he used. I do love Asian flavors and shrimp, though. He lost me with the abundance of sweetness."

Pep and Charlotte sat up straighter. They raised their hands together. "It was close, because Charlotte's craving sweets at the moment, but we swung over to Sherry's wraps at the last minute. By the way, Charlotte didn't try the shrimp. She pulled them out."

"I still have no stomach for seafood. But I got all the flavors in Fitz's wrap contents. Delicious."

Sherry watched Pep rub his palms together. "Sherry, I have something to confess."

"Not sure I'm ready." Her shoulders rose toward her ears. "What is it?"

"Detective Bease said I was observed sticking my hand in the water below the ice sculpture, presumably to measure the depth in preparation for drowning my victim."

"Yes, I know."

"What I couldn't say was I used the water to rid my hands of the shrimp smell. I knew Charlotte couldn't tolerate seafood yet, and I made a snap decision to dip my hand in for a quick cleanup. I couldn't say my reasoning at the time. There, more truth."

"You're so romantic to do that for me," Charlotte said.

"Speaking of Fitz, does anyone think whoever is responsible for killing Fitz was behind Vilma's murder?" Amber asked.

Sherry nodded. "I think there's a good chance the same person killed twice."

"How worried should Sherry be?" Charlotte threw the question out to the table. "I mean, someone tracked her to that restaurant, trashed her car, and nearly crushed her and Ginger in the corn maze."

"Plenty worried," Erno said. "You need to find the killer, Sherry, before he finds you."

"I'm trying, Dad," Sherry said. "What's your vote? You're last up. Sweet ginger or savory American."

"Your wraps, of course, sweetie." Erno pointed his finger toward the last bite of lettuce wrap on his plate. "This one's a winner."

Sherry sighed. "That's Fitz's, Dad. There's no merlot sauce on top. That's aioli."

Erno popped the last bite in his mouth. Despite his mouth being full, he faced Pep. "We're having a daughter, prepare yourself for always being wrong."

Chapter 25

"Thank you so much for bringing everything we needed for dinner." Sherry patted Addison on the back and held the door open for him. "Amber, I'll see you tomorrow afternoon at the store. Thank you so much for all your help tonight. You're the best. In the morning, I have a few loose ends to tie up, including closing out the latest edition of the newsletter as soon as I receive Patti's cook-off recap. I'm aiming for one o'clock."

Amber blew a kiss to Pep and Charlotte. "Hope to see you both very soon with a plus one. Thanks again, Sherry." She lifted Bean off the floor and left the house.

"Remember, Amber. Pep's all yours if this doesn't work out," Charlotte called after her.

Sherry shut the door and looked at her three remaining guests. "Do you guys have time to take a look at the article Eileen dropped off?"

"Of course. Do you have a few more minutes in you, Dad?" Pep asked.

"Barely," Erno replied. "I'm at your mercy, since you're my ride home."

Erno, Pep, and Charlotte each took a seat on the living room couch.

Sherry retrieved the article from the kitchen and sat across from her family in the comfy armchair. She unfolded the paper. "Vilma titled the article, 'Murder Well Done—Cook Offed.' Very clever." Sherry browsed the article, mumbling words aloud every so often. When she reached the end, she looked up. Not until then did she realize everyone was staring at her, patiently waiting for any word of the content.

"Well?" Pep prompted. "We're holding our collective breath. What does it say?"

"Vilma told the tale from soup to nuts. She starts with the contestants prepping for their entry into the contest. Recipe trials and errors. How the entrants came up with their recipe creations. Nothing out of the norm for cook-off articles. She goes on to describe Fitz's dish in detail. I remember Patti said Vilma had interviewed Fitz at The Hunger Dames."

"Interesting," Pep commented. "Did she give any detail about Frye's inspiration for his shrimp wraps?"

Sherry referred back to the paper. "Her exact words are, 'going into the cook-off with the sole purpose of maintaining dominance over his worthiest rival, Fitz Frye came up with a shrimp wrap he felt would best represent his talents in the kitchen. He took a chance on a unique flavor combination for his crunchy shrimp coating, hoping to catch the eye of his opponent. He couldn't wait to see how the judges would receive the sweet and briny blend.'"

"Ironically, it probably would have been the coating that did him in. If *we* didn't think highly of it, would the judges have been dramatically different in their opinions?" Charlotte asked.

"Interesting way of putting that. The coating did him in." Sherry glanced at the ceiling while she pondered Charlotte's remark. "The coating was certainly what made his recipe unique."

"What else did the article say?" Erno put his hand up to his mouth to mask a yawn.

Sherry brought her focus back down to the paper. "She described the cook-off fairly accurately. She was harsh on the Shrimply Amazing seafood provided. Called it low quality. Ouch! A dig aimed solely at Uri, no doubt. She couldn't get the fishhook planted in his room. Maybe her words were plan B. I don't think she considered him a suspect. She may have been a scorned lover, though. Vilma did a good job of highlighting the empty station where Fitz would have cooked and emphasized how no contestant realized he was missing because they were fixated on their own work for two straight hours. She's right about that fact. Even if he was murdered up on the boardwalk during the cook-off, I'm not sure I would have noticed."

"Laser focused," Pep said.

"Yep." Sherry nodded.

"Beyond the cook-off, what did she say about the murder? Does she reveal her choice of suspect?"

"Not only does she reveal the suspect, she goes a step further."

"Don't keep us in suspense any longer," Erno cried out.

"Remember Vilma had me chasing Lyman, Roe, and Uri? What was she having me do all that chasing for, when, it turns out, none of them was her actual suspect? In a surprise twist, she writes in this article, 'the killer is the brother of one of the best cooks in the county. This was the killer's chance to serve up a warm helping of vengeance because he didn't want to see his sister's reputation get burned.'"

"That's an intriguing storyline. You have to admit." Erno nodded.

Sherry side-eyed her father. "Dad. How can you say that? She's talking about Pep. How can she put that story out there when it's not the truth?"

"Did she specifically name names?" Erno asked.

"No, but you'd have to be an idiot to not know who she means. If she were still alive, our plan to have her think I feared Pep might be guilty would have backfired, because she had already submitted the article. She had some nerve telling me not to worry about Pep." Sherry threw up her hands. The paper went airborne before floating back down to the floor. "She's fabricated the ending. The thing is, there's no real ending. Not yet, anyway. She can't do this. It sheds a terrible light on Pep, cook-offs, the Augustin Inn, and all the dedication that goes into the hobby I love so much."

"Have you watched the news or read the headlines recently?" Pep asked. "News is served up with sides of inaccuracy, speculation, and mistruths all day long. Vilma got her story sold, didn't she? That's what she was after, I suppose, minus the professional integrity."

"And isn't it ironic there's a good chance whoever did Fitz in did her in as well? If she'd been correct—" Charlotte began.

"And stayed alive," Erno added.

"—she'd have caught her own potential murderer," Charlotte said.

"Too little too late," Erno said.

Sherry collected the papers off the floor. "Unfortunately, the mystery she crafted makes you look guilty, Pep. You'd have every reason to make her pay, too, for exposing you as the killer, had you actually done the killing. Anyone who reads her words has every reason to go there."

"This might put a crimp in my plans to leave to-morrow," Pep told Charlotte. "If I leave town, that's one more strike against me." He studied his pregnant partner. "Can we stay one more day?"

"Please stay here, you two," Sherry insisted. "I have plenty of room. No more secret trips between here and the inn."

"I was hoping you'd suggest that," Charlotte admitted. "But would you mind picking up my clothes and bathroom items, Pep? I'd go, but I'm getting so sleepy after all that good food."

Erno raised his hand. "Me, too."

"Come in here, Charlotte, and take a seat. Put your feet up." Sherry led the way into the living room. She swept her arm across the sofa and fluffed up the pillows. "Pep, I'll take you. I think we should have a word with Ginger."

Erno raised his hand. "Can someone give me a ride home?"

"Of course," Sherry laughed.

Pep put his arm around Charlotte and helped her settle into the puffy cushions.

"Time's running out. If whoever did it has struck

twice, what's to stop him or her from striking again? If the killer's seen this article, he or she may feel safe, and that's a recipe for a slipup," Charlotte pointed out.

"You're beginning to think like a real investigator, baby," Pep said.

"Thanks, I think." Charlotte smiled slyly. She patted the cushion next to her. Chutney jumped up and curled into a ball. "I'll hang here with Chutney."

"Just to be safe, don't answer the door under any circumstances," Pep said. "The key's under the doormat, so no need to wait up for us if you fall asleep."

"Not *if*, when. I'm exhausted." Charlotte's tone was as sweet as honey. "See you soon."

"Let's go, Dad," Sherry said.

Sherry considered the majority of the cook-off guests and sponsors had departed the inn. She scanned the deserted property. Inns and hotels were sad places when they weren't full of visitors. The upcoming apple season might draw the crowds Ginger needed to spark cash growth and get the inn back on its feet, but too many days like this and Ginger's retirement would be right around the corner.

"First, let's gather Charlotte's stuff. Then we'll find Ginger. I'll check Charlotte out and pay her bill," Pep said.

Solar lights guided Sherry and Pep down the pathway toward the inn. As they entered the inn's majestic colonial entrance, Sherry noticed, for the first time, the flakes of paint chipping off the columns. The ornate trim framing the porch was littered with cracks and splits. The floor leading to the oversized wooden doors was in desperate need of refinishing. The whitewashing was nearly all worn away, and the exposed wood was turning green from weather exposure.

Once inside, the wide, red-carpeted hallway led them to the back of the first floor.

"How did you sneak in here without being seen these last few days?" Sherry asked.

Pep smiled a cat-with-a-bird-in-its-mouth grin. "Mum's the word. What if I need to sneak in again? I don't want to give away any secrets."

"I thought you were done with secrets," Sherry said.

They came to rest in front of room 119.

"You're right. No more secrets. I went unnoticed the old-fashioned way. After we met Oxana, she lent me a bellhop uniform and a cap. Ginger's had to let nearly all the bellmen go anyway. I carried Charlotte's suitcase back and forth about twenty times in the guise of working at the inn and helping my guest to her room. The things you do for love. My goal was not to get recognized, at least until after the cook-off, so the baby news didn't distract. Mission accomplished, thanks in large part to Oxana."

Pep reached in his jeans pocket and pulled out the room key. "One of the last hotels not to use a keycard, I bet. Probably too expensive to modernize." He inserted the key. Before he applied any pressure, the door swung open. "Uh-oh. Someone's been in here."

Sherry shivered. "Or is still in there." A second

later she heard a crash. "Pep," she hissed. "Don't go in."

She might as well have said, "get in that room as quick as you can so whoever's in there can bop you on the head and add you to the body count."

Pep flung the door wide open. "What are you doing in here? This isn't your room." Pep shouted with as much ferocity as Sherry had ever heard him generate.

Sherry put one shaky foot in front of the other and scanned the room for intruders. A few feet inside the bedroom, Pep was holding a block of a man by his squirming shoulders.

"Look who I found in Charlotte's room. What the hell are you doing in here?"

Roe choked on his reply.

"Speak up," Pep said. "What's in your hand?"

Roe wriggled free of Pep's grip. He opened his clenched hand. In his palm was a small gold box.

"Not that it's any of your business." Roe lifted the box to eye level.

Sherry studied the soiled box.

"I believe you were planting evidence in this room," Pep shouted.

"Slow down with your accusations. This isn't even your room. You're trespassing. At least I got permission to enter. See?" Roe held up a room key. "Maybe I'll just go find Ms. Constable and discuss the situation with her."

"Why are you still in Augustin, Roe?" Sherry asked.

"Maine Course has a few details to clean up." Roe puffed out his chest. "Uri and I work closely together on a number of projects, and what goes on behind the scenes is as important as the quality we bring to the consumer." Roe's words became robotic and scripted.

"Like break-ins and falsified reports?" Sherry added.

"I hear shouting. I see three people in here, none of whom the room is registered to," Ginger announced in a harsh monotone as she entered the room. "There's been enough foul play going on at the inn, and I don't need any more, please."

"We have Charlotte's full permission to be in here. We came to collect her stuff and check her out. She's staying with Sherry tonight," Pep said. "No idea what Roe's doing here."

The heat of the looks exchanged between Roe and Ginger could ignite a charcoal grill.

"Roe, my error. You're in the wrong room. I found Roe in the lobby and asked if he'd do me a favor. I sent him to return a box to a guest, since Addison is already in bed after your nice dinner." Ginger lowered her gaze before making eye contact with Sherry again.

"If you gave him the key, wouldn't you know this was Charlotte's room? One nineteen?" Pep asked Ginger.

"I have dyslexia. It's a little known fact I keep under wraps. Doesn't help that my livelihood is centered around room numbers and spelling names, but I do the best I can. Roe, I meant to give you the key for room one ninety-one." Ginger manufactured the smile Sherry had seen her welcome guests with many times over the last few days. "Follow me. I'll take you down to the room. I'll see you two at the front desk in a few minutes for checkout."

Ginger strutted out of the room before Sherry could respond. Roe tucked his chin to his chest and followed closely behind.

"Same box Oxana had and gave to me and I rammed into Vilma's Danish. There was even a yellow smear on the box from the lemon curd. There's a fishhook inside, or at least there was when I opened it," Sherry said. "Fitz gets a fishing hook calling card in his neck. Common thread. Roe was sent to return the box with a fishing hook. The same box I returned to Vilma. How'd Roe get it?"

She and Pep came up with one name simultaneously. "Uri," they shouted.

"Roe claims he went to the wrong room. Or at least that was the story. More likely, Roe was planting the hook in the room, so evidence points to you," Sherry said.

Pep unzipped Charlotte's suitcase. "All they'd have had to do is plant that fishhook in here. One call to Detective Bease to search Charlotte's room, and I would be under arrest. I wish we could find Oxana."

"Do you really think Addison's in bed? Maybe he could help us find her." Sherry handed Pep Charlotte's toiletries from the bathroom.

"Addison is staying two doors down in room one twenty-three. He was very nice to keep our secret after we passed him numerous times in the hall."

Sherry opened each bureau drawer and emptied the contents into the suitcase. When they were satisfied the room was cleared of Charlotte's belongings, they headed down the hallway.

"Made this journey a few times, carrying this suitcase while in costume. Not sure I was fooling anyone, but you never found out, right?"

Sherry came to a halt. "Nothing to brag about, fooling your sister."

"You're the world's best amateur sleuth, so it's a pretty fine accomplishment." Pep put down the suitcase, reached around, and patted himself on the back.

"A slight exaggeration. Listen, you might have fooled me for a little while, I'll give you that. And I'm none too happy about it. Mark my words, your day will come, little bro. I can pull the wool over an unsuspecting victim with the best of 'em."

"If nothing else, this visit back to Augustin is showing me a feisty side of you I've never seen before. I'm liking the new and improved Sherry."

Sherry's grim expression melted. "How do you always manage to stay on my good side, despite frustrating me to no end?"

"Little brother magic," Pep said.

When they arrived at Addison's door, Pep pounded with his fist. "Wanna make sure he can hear me."

Sherry winced. "I think everyone can hear you." She leaned in toward the door and heard nothing. "He can't still be asleep after that onslaught." She cupped her hands around her mouth. "Addison. It's Sherry and Pep. Are you in there?"

Silence.

"Ginger was wrong. He's not asleep. He can't be inside. Maybe he's down in the lobby," Pep said.

"Hey, guys, long time, no see."

Sherry's head swiveled in the direction of the booming voice. "Addison. There you are."

"Do you need me? Technically, I'm not on the clock right now. Ginger only allots me a firm number of hours a day so she can keep my pay in check. And that's no understatement. I need to save up some hours to put the finishing touches on that darn maze. It's beginning to give me nightmares. I can't seem to shore up the walls." Addison shifted the large metal box he was carrying in order to reach in his pants pocket.

"Is that a tackle box?" Pep asked. "Doing some fishing? Maybe for Maine Course?"

"Yes, it's a tackle box, but I'm not fishing. My job with Maine Course is pretty much done. The cook-off's in the wrap-up stages. So is my fishing career." Addison glanced at the box. "This is my last piece of equipment. I'm looking for a buyer. I sold my best tackle box to Roe, and I know he'll put it to good use. I'm out of the fishing business. There's no money in it anymore. Really hasn't been a money maker for a long time."

Sherry detected regret in Addison's voice. "You're so good with your hands. I'm sure you'll find your passion. Ginger must have a million jobs for you."

"I'm here if she does. What can I do for you two? Were you looking for me?"

"We need to get in touch with Oxana. She's not answering her phone. I didn't want to bother Ginger because she's up to her elbows, but someone should make sure Oxana's okay. Vilma was her aunt, you know. First, she finds a dead body in the barn and now her aunt is gone. Has to be tough on the girl."

Addison held a steady gaze into Sherry's eyes. "She works here. She doesn't live here. She's a student and has more than one cleaning job."

"Okay. Figured you might have an idea where we could find her. Has Uri checked out of his room?" Sherry knew the answer but wanted to keep Addison engaged.

Addison edged closer to his door. He drew in a deep breath. "Detective Bease said he wasn't able to conduct certain interviews until tomorrow. Out of courtesy, and for Ginger's sake, I hope, Uri said he won't be checking out until tomorrow."

"Do you know where . . ." Sherry began.

"Uri's in the bar outside the library. When I spoke to him, after I returned from your dinner, he was in quite a mood. Consider yourself warned." Addison inserted his room key into the lock. "Have a good evening."

Chapter
26

The lobby was deserted when Sherry rang the service bell. She admired the historic character of the scratched, dinged wooden desk that housed the bell, a leather-bound guestbook, and an inkwell. A computer sat on the desktop as the only indication the inn was operating in the modern era. The two quilted armchairs positioned alongside the desk had held many a backside over the decades and were a lot worse for the wear. Sherry ran her fingers across the frayed edges and split seams. Behind the desk was a brick statement wall Sherry thought possibly had once been the building's main fireplace, later bricked up. Too bad. It would make for a dramatic welcoming feature for visitors.

Sherry and Pep waited in the quiet of the entryway when suddenly, shouting broke out behind a closed door to the right of the desk. They exchanged glances. Pep sidestepped closer to the door. The angry voices continued until he was within two steps of the door. Sherry waved her arms frantically when she saw the door begin to give way. Out scrambled

Ginger and Uri. Uri's face was beet red. Sherry could see his chest heaving as he tried to manage his rapid breathing.

Ginger pushed up the sleeves of her blouse. "We'll discuss this later, Uri."

Uri shouldered past Pep and tipped his head toward Sherry. He marched past the desk, pounded his clenched fist on the battered wood, and exited out the front door.

"Give me one minute to bring up Charlotte's reservation." Ginger's voice cracked as she tapped on the keyboard.

"Everything okay?" Sherry asked.

Ginger held her gaze on the computer screen. "Uri and I are in a disagreement about saving the inn. His feeling is that we should concentrate on Maine Course Foods for now and hope a third party comes in with capital for the inn. It's been a week of high highs and low lows. I don't have the energy for any more bad news."

Pep handed Ginger a credit card.

"That's what I need. A gentleman with a credit card to pay my bills. Charlotte's one lucky gal. I'll be right back with your receipt." She took the card to the room behind the desk.

"Hope this isn't all too much for her. The inn seems like it's under a curse right now." Sherry shut her lips when Ginger reappeared. She was a moment too late.

"Maybe a curse. Wouldn't be surprised if Clarence Constable were sending a message from the great beyond. Dad doesn't want to see the inn go down in flames as much as I don't." Ginger placed the room

charge receipt and credit card in Pep's hand. She
moved closer to Sherry. "Sherry, I need you to find
the killer or killers. My future depends on it happening quickly and without any more damage to the
inn's reputation. I had a slim hope I could save
the inn, but so much is happening so quickly, I'm
beginning to doubt myself. I have to make some
tough choices."

"I'm doing the best I can. You're not the only one
who needs the investigation wrapped up in a neat
bow." Sherry's sight darted to Pep. "Do you, in all
certainty, think Uri is completely innocent?"

"Don't make me answer that. Please. Don't. Just
see what you can come up with. I'm begging you."
Ginger stepped behind the desk.

"Good evening." A voice interrupted Sherry's attempt to temper Ginger's plea.

Sherry turned to see Roe approach.

"Sherry, when you're done here, I could use a
moment of your time," he said.

Ginger tapped on the keyboard without acknowl-
edging the man who came to rest an arm's length
away. She pulled her phone from her pocket. "I
need to make a call. Don't be strangers, you two.
Roe, if you need me, dial zero from your room
phone."

Sherry inched closer to Pep. "Yes?" was all she
could come up with.

The pleasant grin on Roe's face flowed down to a
scowl. His eyes were bloodshot. He blinked repeat-
edly, as if they were irritated. "Sherry, you've found
killers before. Killers who wanted to destroy lives and
communities. I need you to find who killed Fitz
and Vilma. I know it's the same person. I am one

hundred percent certain. It's someone who wants to see me take the fall." Roe drew in a deep breath. "It wasn't me. I'm no saint, but I'm not a murderer."

Sherry put her hand on Pep's arm. His forearm muscle was flexed, ready to spring into action.

"Why should she help you? You've done some terrible things." Pep's voice rumbled to a near shout. "Sherry and I have put you on top of the suspect list. We just can't quite find the smoking gun. But mark my words, if you did it, you'll pay dearly. Fitz didn't deserve to die. Neither did Vilma."

Sherry's throat tightened. She steeled herself for the words she was about to spout. "The oldest trick in the book is to initiate an investigation, to deflect from being considered the guilty party. Planting evidence on someone else may be the second oldest."

"They do sound like plausible tricks, but, truthfully, I didn't do either. Yes, I was sent up to Charlotte's guest room to place a box on the dresser. No, I didn't do it. I had a change of heart when I saw the prenatal vitamins on the bureau. I want kids one day. I was told the box belonged to Charlotte. I know that's not the case."

"Plead your innocence. Be my guest," Pep said. "You're wasting your time, though. A guy who authors false reports on the quality of a company's products is guilty until proven innocent in my court of law. You're not much of a fishing expert either, may I add."

"The night of the Fall Fest Cook-off contestant meet and greet, I was working the room as Maine Course's sustainable fishing expert. Not my chosen profession, I admit, but to help Uri out I studied the necessary info and recited what I had to say.

The guy's given me employment for years, and I owe him." Roe cocked his head to one side. "I don't want to owe him anymore."

"You were terrible. Worst expert on something I've ever come across," Pep said. "I know more about making the perfect crème brûlée than you know about sustainable fishing, and I've never made a dessert in my life."

"Okay, okay, guys, let's stay on topic," Sherry said. "You say you were at the cocktail party, but that's no alibi. The murder occurred after the party. Any witnesses as to where you were between nine PM and one AM? And your buddy Uri doesn't count. He's as guilty as you, at this point."

"Before the party, Uri gave me an assignment. Warn Fitz to keep a secret or pay the price. I completed my assignment, as I always do."

"If I was recording this conversation, you'd be in prison in about the time it takes me to poach an egg. You realize that?" Sherry pointed her index finger at Roe. "Pep, I'll dial Detective Bease, you hold Roe right here."

Roe put up his hands in surrender. "Hear me out. Fitz knew Uri's had to resort to, shall we say, creative measures to bring the cost of his product down to profitable levels. He'd seen the trucks delivering product from overseas. But a guy's gotta make a living. I mean, sustainable local is one thing, but what dope'll pay forty dollars a pound for Boston cod? Southeast Asia has some wonderful fish for export right now, and we should take advantage of that. Consumers are worrywarts. It's nearly the same product. Besides, Fitz was profiting from keeping a secret. He wasn't completely innocent himself."

Sherry shook her head in disgust. "You sound like you're proud of deceiving your customers. You should be ashamed. The authorities will be all over Maine Course soon enough."

"Uri's reworking the situation, as we speak. The authorities will have a hard time proving Maine Course isn't everything they advertise."

"You still haven't said where you were at the time of the murder and how you can prove it."

Roe's face softened. "Kelly and I, well, we're having a thing."

Pep cleared his throat. "Fitz's Kelly?"

Roe nodded. "My Kelly was never truly Fitz's Kelly, as you so unceremoniously put it."

"That tigress hasn't changed her stripes," Sherry muttered.

"Kelly told Fitz she was going to bed early to rest up for the cook-off. After we took a moonlit walk around the veranda and barn, we headed out. She had gotten her own room here because the old boy, Fitz, snored like a chainsaw. She made sure she told everyone. For convenience sake, we also kept a room at the Augustin Motor Lodge. Ask that spice guy, Lyman. He saw us that night. He was also staying at the Motor Lodge. He even saw us early the next morning when I returned Kelly to the inn. He was packing up his car for an early morning kite surf before the cook-off. Crazy thing to do, I thought."

"So you're judging other people's actions now?" Pep asked. "How much bad karma can one guy wish upon himself?"

"Okay, okay, I get your point," Roe said. "That's my alibi, and it's a good one. Oh, and one more interesting nugget of information."

"What's that?" Pep asked.

"Uri was making regular payments to Fitz to keep him quiet about the late-night fish deliveries received up in Portland from overseas, rather than within a reasonable distance considered local."

"Hush payments," Pep chided.

Roe nodded his head with authority. "It's the truth. Kelly showed me a cancelled check from Fitz. He was bragging about the arrangement to her one day. Said she should keep the check as a souvenir of his good work. Said it was almost enough to pay for a wedding. Joke was going to be on him. There was no way she would ever marry that loser." Roe dusted his hands together. "Moot point now."

"Why is it so important for you to find the killer?" Sherry asked. "I mean, you just admitted you're a cheat, a shady business dealer, and a scam artist. Are you suddenly seeking redemption?"

"I'm not a monster. I'm doing it for Kelly. We've fallen in love. Never in a million years would we have thought Fitz would die before we were able to break the news of our relationship to him. Believe me, I'm not too broken up over his death. Kelly is feeling all sorts of guilt. Plus, I'm pretty sure you'd like to get Pep off the hook." Roe gave Pep his full attention. "He definitely got into it with Fitz that night. Guessing the argument was about the time we first met up in Portland. If only you hadn't taken a walk in the wee hours of the morning and seen what you saw. Maybe Fitz would be alive today."

"Nice try," Pep said. "You can't spin this any other way. You're the lowest of the low. You were planting evidence in Charlotte's room."

"I don't know why you keep saying that. I told you

I didn't." Roe shoved his hand in his pocket and pulled out the gold box. With a flick of his thumb, he popped open the hinged lid. A sparkly gold ring lay inside the box.

"I admit, there was a hook in this box," Roe stated. "I was asked by Uri to put it in your girlfriend's room. I made a show of doing his bidding, but, obviously, I dumped the hook. I gave it away. I really was on my way to Kelly's room with a promise ring to brighten her day. After I made sure Uri saw me go into room one nineteen."

"Ginger *was* covering for Uri. She may or may not have dyslexia. Who knows? I do think she shouldn't have let Uri behind her desk, where he could get at the room keys," Sherry said.

"I don't care. I'm done with Ginger, and I'm done with Uri. If you could help a guy out," Roe pleaded. "I may have done a few underhanded things but never murder. Never. And I've never met such a lovely girl as Kelly. If not for me, do it for her."

Sherry sighed. "I'll see what I can do. No promises, though. If nothing else, how about if you clean up your act, for her sake."

"Hello, everyone." Uri dipped his chin in Sherry's direction. "Roe, care to join me for a nightcap at the bar?"

"I'd like that." He shoved the box back in his pocket.

"If you'll grab us a seat, I'll meet you there in five minutes."

"Yes, sir," Roe replied mechanically, as if he'd uttered the reply thousands of times in the past. "Gin and tonic, with a twist of lime?"

"You know me too well," Uri laughed.

Roe headed down the hall and turned a corner.

Sherry opened her mouth to speak at the exact moment Uri and Pep did. Everyone's words crashed into one another.

"Sorry. You go ahead," Sherry instructed Uri.

"You solve murders. I need you to verify the person I'm sure killed Fitz has enough evidence against him to be locked up. That Detective Bease is on a limited schedule I can't work with. He doesn't seem to care time is money, and both are running out. This is becoming too much for Ginger."

"Everyone keeps telling me time is running out. I've helped out in three murder investigations. I wouldn't exactly say I solved them single-handedly."

Before Sherry could continue, Pep added, "You had a very good reason to kill Fitz. Why are you asking Sherry to speed up an investigation that could very well land you behind bars?"

Uri ran his manicured fingers through his hair. Around his wrist was a thick gold chain bracelet that caught the light as he moved his hand. The last swipe through his hair caught a tangle, and Sherry could see a slight shift in the hairpiece centered on Uri's scalp.

"No worries there. Roe did it. He probably took out Vilma, too. Better sooner, rather than later, to put Roe away, so no one else gets hurt. He's lost touch with reality. I've suspected he did it since the night of the party, but now I have hard evidence."

"Something you can share?" Pep asked.

"Roe wasn't with me at the time of the murder. We left the party together, and I dropped him off at his room. I returned to the lobby to help Ginger with the last cleanup before handing the job over to

Oxana. That was around midnight. I knocked on Roe's door on my way back to my room. No answer."

Sherry considered Roe's description of his visit to the Motor Lodge with Kelly. She pursed her lips and remained silent.

"Of course, I didn't want to wake him, so I gave up. I returned to my room on the other side of the building. The fastest route is outdoors. Who do you think I spotted emerging from the side of the barn? If that's not a smoking gun, I don't know what is."

Sherry and Pep exchanged glances.

"How much longer are you in town?" Sherry asked.

"Ginger needs some moral support. I said I could spare a day or two longer. We're all sunk if I don't keep the Maine Course ship righted, though. I need to get back to work. Our cook-off sponsorship can only keep us in the consumer's mind for so long."

"Did you, by any chance, see the cook-off article Vilma wrote? It was in the paper this morning."

Uri screwed up his face into a sneer. "No, and I'm not sure I want to. We didn't end on such a positive note. Some people take a kind word and misconstrue it for a more intimate expression of feelings. In her case, I should have been a touch more reserved with my compliments. She attacked me verbally for leading her on. Can't a man say something nice these days without being punished?"

"You may want to read it. If for no other reason than to learn how much of a mess you need to clean up. She got her last licks in."

Chapter
27

"Well, that was informative and confusing. Three potential suspects asking me to speed up the investigation and find the killer. And they want it done yesterday."

"Add me to that list," Pep said.

Sherry checked left and right and steered the car out of the inn's driveway. In the passenger seat, Pep leaned heavily on the headrest. His eyelids were sagging. Sherry envied the way her brother could drift off to sleep in a matter of seconds. He must have so much on his mind with the baby, a future suddenly filled with responsibility, and a fiancée. Yet, there he was, a possible suspect in a murder investigation, able to pass peacefully into dreamland, seemingly without a care in the world.

Sherry's phone interrupted the car's quiet. Pep lurched forward and produced an abrupt snore, all the while keeping his eyes closed. She punched the button to accept the call before the second ring.

"I can't do it anymore."

"Ray?" Sherry double-checked the name on the console screen. The desperation in the voice was so uncharacteristic of Ray, she was sure she had read the name incorrectly. She hadn't. "Can't do what?"

"I'm putting in for a leave of absence from the department. I haven't slept in days. My mother consumes every waking hour. The captain's right." Ray's voice dropped down to a near whisper. "I'm not able to do both jobs to the best of my ability."

"Hang on a minute. I have an idea."

"If it's a way to make my aging mother comfortable and positive in the winter of her life, let me have it."

Pep sleep snorted.

"If it's about the investigation, don't waste your time. I admit defeat. Let the young bucks take over. Sorry to have bothered you."

"Wait, don't hang up. It's about your mother." Sherry heard Ray suck in a shallow breath. "Amber writes a family therapy advice column. You remember she was a marriage and family therapist for many years before she moved into retail?"

Ray grunted softly on the other end of the phone.

"I described your situation to her. She told me someone with your exact situation wrote in. She did tons of research on places for elder care facilities, all ranges of care."

"I couldn't send Mom away," Ray stated. "Non-negotiable. Thanks, anyway."

"Hear me out. I'm going to have her text you the name of two facilities in the county. I think you'll be pleasantly surprised at what you find when you visit. Your mother will be happier when she knows you're satisfied resigning yourself to accepting outside help. The caregiver often suffers more than the patient when they try to take on too much. No one wins."

"Maybe you're right. Might be time to give up control." Ray struggled with each word.

"For me to hear you say those words and think it's okay, you have to know I understand what you're going through. I hate giving up control." Sherry laughed half-heartedly. "I'll text her as soon as I get home."

"Thank you."

"In the meantime, switching gears, since you're not taking a leave of absence, Pep and I were at the inn and spoke to Uri and Roe. Both have motives to want Fitz dead."

Beside her, Pep stirred.

"That's not news. And I didn't say I wasn't taking a leave of absence. I'll postpone it for a few days."

"Who are you talking to?" Pep asked.

"Ray Bease," Sherry answered.

"Who are you talking to?" Ray asked.

"Pep's sitting next to me in the car. We're driving back home from the inn."

"I got the recordings from Vilma's car dash camera to review. Not sure if it'll yield any results, but hopeful," Ray said.

Sherry slowed the car and pulled over to the side of the road. She punched the button to turn on the car's hazard warning lights.

"I have a list for you to write down." Sherry smiled when she heard Ray groan. She clicked over to her phone's notepad app. "Ready?" She read the words in a slow, deliberate tone. "Cook-off, recipe, fraud, double-cross, desperation, no other way out."

"Is that it? Pretty thin list." He clicked Sherry off and was gone.

After arriving home, Pep tucked a drowsy Charlotte

into bed. Sherry remained in the living room. With Chutney snuggled up tight beside her, she juggled the cook-off contestant recipe booklet and a section of the newspaper on her lap.

Sherry ran her finger down Vilma's article. She found the spot where Vilma mentioned the brother of one of the best home cooks in the county was her choice as Fitz's murderer. She swapped reading material for the recipe booklet. Opening to Fitz's page, she skimmed over his bio. Property manager. Contest cook. Previous finalist. Nothing outstanding. Except in the recipe itself.

"Too sweet, Fitz," Sherry whispered. "Your shrimp coating was on the sweet side. I don't think the recipe would have made it through preliminary judging, if you had submitted it through proper channels, like the rest of us finalists. Are you trying to tell me the person who killed you was too sweet?"

"Has Chutney ever answered you?" Pep took a seat across from Sherry.

"He's too smart to get into a debate with me."

"Have you given the note, supposedly from Oxana, any thought?" Pep asked.

"She wrote, 'check the box.' What do you think that refers to? Vilma's gold box or a box next to a to-do list that you tick off when the task is complete? What does it mean? Oxana, where are you?"

A muffled voice from the second floor caught Sherry's attention. "Does Charlotte sleep talk?"

"Not that I'm aware of. I better go see what's up." Pep jumped out of his chair and bounded up the stairs. Before Sherry could reshuffle the papers on her lap, he returned.

"My phone woke her up. Now I'm in trouble for

not muting it. Good news is she was back asleep before I left the room." Pep's smile turned to a frown when he read the new text. "Oxana."

"Oxana? You got a text from Oxana? Or about her?"

"She texted if I'm still in the area, could I stop by the barn at the inn at nine tomorrow morning. She doesn't want me to mention this to anyone." Pep studied his phone. "She didn't necessarily write this. How do we know her phone is back in her possession?"

"Doesn't matter who wrote it. We're going back to the inn."

The next morning after breakfast, Charlotte announced she was spending the morning working on her research. She sequestered herself in an upstairs bedroom with her textbooks and Chutney.

"See you in an hour," Pep called up the stairs. "Keep an eye on her, Chutney."

"Good luck," was shouted through the closed door on the second floor.

A bark followed.

"I'll meet you in the car. I want to grab something." Sherry found what she was looking for under the kitchen sink—a small glass bottle with a pump spray nozzle. She dropped the bottle in her purse, collected her barn coat, and headed to the front door.

As she stepped out the door, Pep called out from the car. "Eileen dropped that bag off. I didn't know if you wanted it inside or in the car, so I left it on the porch."

Sherry picked up the canvas bag she'd nearly tripped over and peered inside. She read the accompanying note. "I'll leave it inside," Sherry replied.

"Ginger's going to start charging us a room fee if we keep showing up." Sherry parked the car in the inn's lot. She checked the time on her phone. "Ten minutes to get to the barn. We could have had one more cup of coffee."

"I wouldn't mind if we grabbed one of those lemon Danishes Ginger keeps a fresh supply of in the library. I think I've had one every day since I've been in Augustin. A bonus of visiting Charlotte in the morning."

"Explains why you never ate much breakfast whenever I offered you some," Sherry said.

"Explains why my waistband is so tight." Pep led Sherry into the library. He made a beeline for the tray of Danishes and cookies. "Here's a copy of the cook-off recipe booklet." Pep picked up the colorfully decorated booklet and waved it in front of Sherry.

"We have a huge collection of cookbooks, if you're interested."

Sherry rotated and came face to face with Ginger.

"That entire shelf is cookbooks. Whenever we have a guest who has authored a cookbook, or any book, for that matter, I rush out and buy a copy." Ginger gave Sherry a sly smile. "Speaking of books, would you two like to book a room? You seem to be here so often, you may want to consider it."

"I was afraid you'd say that. We're trying to get to

the bottom of Fitz's mystery, and the inn is ground zero right now," Sherry said.

"I appreciate your efforts. I really do. I'm beside myself about who could have done these awful crimes."

Sherry took a look around the surrounding book-shelves. "Did you know Vilma authored a book under the pen name Granger?"

"Say no more." Ginger made her way over to the corner shelf. She ran her finger along a row of books before stopping midway across. "Stella Granger. *How to Solve a Murder or Die Trying.* The irony of that title. Vilma may not have been my favorite person, but I never wished her ill will. The book itself won't be on the best-seller list any time soon, I'm afraid. Even postmortem. It follows a fictional detective through his paces. Really dry stuff. Not even an ex-citing mystery involved."

Ginger strolled a few steps to the other side of the bookshelf. "Now, if you want a fascinating read, I suggest this cookbook." She lifted the book from the shelf. A thin shower of dust sprinkled down from the binding. She handed the book to Sherry.

Sherry showed the cover to Pep, who was munch-ing on a lemon Danish. "*The Magic of the Meal.* It says it's a nationwide bestseller, and it won three awards. Amazing. I'd love to borrow this. Did the author stay here?"

"You're looking at her." Ginger pointed to the lower portion of the book cover. "I'm Chef Ginny C., one of the original celebrity chefs."

Sherry handed the book to Pep. "Wow. When did you have time to write this book?"

Pep opened the cover. "This is almost twenty years old. You must have been—" Pep stopped short. "I'm not in the business of guessing people's ages."

"I took a year off from college to pursue a passion I knew I would never be able to fulfill when I came back to Augustin. I was slated to take over the inn, and that was non-negotiable with my father. Even an award-winning cookbook wasn't enough to dissuade him from his dream for me."

Sherry watched Ginger's face sag. "Life gets in the way of dreams sometimes."

Ginger managed a slight smile. "Maybe this place going bankrupt is for the best. Who knows? It's not too late to write a sequel. Desserts. I even have a title picked out. *Sweet Temptations.*"

"I'd buy that." Sherry retrieved the book from Pep's hands. He left a smear of glaze on the edge of the book. "Have you had enough?"

Pep nodded.

Sherry returned the cookbook to Ginger. "Would you mind if Pep and I took one more look around the barn?"

"Not at all. You might need an umbrella. The wind has shifted to the east, and that usually means storms.

"Be careful to turn off the lights on your way out. I'm trying to keep the critter population down in there. I think they're attracted to lights. Excuse me. I see my brother." Ginger raced to the library entrance. "Addison?" she called out before disappearing.

"Oxana just texted. She's in the barn," Pep said.

They hustled out of the library and down the hallway toward a set of French doors that led to the veranda and barn. "This is my secret route in and out of the building."

"Look, there's room one ninety-one. Door's open." Sherry poked her head inside the door. "Not a room. It's a supply closet. Why was Ginger sending Roe to the supply closet? Doesn't make any sense. Unless Ginger couldn't think fast enough on her feet to cover for Uri and threw out the first number that popped into her head."

"What does make sense, at this point?" Pep asked. "Let's keep moving. Oxana's waiting."

When they left the main building, Sherry glanced skyward. The weather had followed Ginger's prediction. The swollen gray clouds burst open with torrents of rain. Flashes of lightning, followed by explosions of thunder, filled the sky. Sherry and Pep perched under a slim overhang, considering opportunities to make a mad dash down the path. No such moment came.

Sherry turned to her brother. "We're going to be electrocuted out here." Her words fell flat when Pep bolted for the barn.

Flashback to when Pep coaxed Sherry to the top of a high-dive platform at the public pool. Their parents had warned her not to attempt the jump. Pep talked her into it. Decades later, she could still feel the pain of the belly flop from that height. "Here we go again." She leapt off the protected slate slab the moment an explosion of thunder rattled the ground. She clutched her aching stomach, tucked her head down, and sloshed through the deepening puddles. She traced Pep's footsteps into the barn, where she came to a sliding stop on the moist wood floor. Her canvas sneakers squished water out from the inside when she took a step forward.

"Oxana?" Pep called out.

A boom of thunder cracked. Wallboards shuddered.

"Oxana?" Sherry motioned for Pep to follow her to the back of the barn.

The single bulb over Oxana's desk was lit. It swung with the vibration of the thunderclaps, giving life to the shadows cast by the giant vertical beams holding up the ceiling.

Sherry patted her back pocket. "Can you try calling her? I left my phone in the car."

Sherry's hands curled into balls after a flash of lightning so intense, it filled the interior of the barn with a blinding white light. She shut her eyes in anticipation of the explosion of noise to come. She didn't have to wait long. She lunged forward and dug her nails into Pep's forearm.

He cried out in pain.

Before she could release him, the single light went out. Sherry's mouth dropped open and she felt Pep's arm stiffen.

"Pretty bad storm."

Sherry's stomach iced over. "That wasn't Oxana," she whispered.

"Who's there?"

Sherry's head jerked back with the ferocity of Pep's words.

Pep held up his phone's flashlight. The beam was so narrow that, as he swept the light around the room, Sherry had trouble deciphering what she could make out.

"I said, who's there?"

"It's . . ."

A clap of thunder smothered the reply.

"Let's get out of here." Sherry yanked on Pep's arm.

A flashlight beam emerged from behind the wall separating Oxana's desk and her storage area. The light revealed only a black silhouette of someone walking toward her and Pep. The bobbing topknot of hair gave away her identity.

"Ginger," was all Sherry could manage to whisper.

"We're looking for Oxana," Ginger said.

"We? Are you with someone?" Pep asked.

The lightning was easing up, which left the barn interior unlit for longer periods of time.

"Addison's in here somewhere. He knows this building in and out, even in the pitch dark." Ginger's tone grew distracted and distant. "Recently, he's been spending longer and longer amounts of time in here, like he did when we were kids. I'm afraid Addison isn't taking my plans for the future very well. I'm very worried about him. He puts on a brave face, but I know he's having trouble adjusting to the possibility of the inn closing. He never was good with change. The inn's been his home base for his entire life. Only his fishing trips to Maine get him out of town."

"What about you, Ginger? Are you sure you're giving this situation enough thought? I mean, I'm positive there are alternatives to saving the inn." Sherry squinted to get a better look at Ginger's expression. "Desperation can lead to rash decisions. Take your time."

Heads turned in the direction of the sound of footsteps coming from behind the wall.

"Sherry makes a lot of sense." Addison drew near. "There's a good chance the murders of Fitz and Vilma could have been a result of your decision to sell the inn."

"Sherry didn't say that," Pep said.

"Have you seen Oxana?" Sherry asked. "We were supposed to meet her here right now. The weather may have changed things."

"I'm here," a voice called out from just inside the barn doors. A thin stream of light aimed at the floor approached. Sopping wet footprints illustrated the route. "I'm glad you all could make it."

"Oxana. You invited all of us?" Ginger asked. "What's going on?"

"I've been away." Oxana grabbed a handful of hair and squeezed. Water cascaded to the floor. A remaining drip trickled down her forehead. "Had to think."

"Sounds like she's quitting, like everyone else. Ginger would probably have let you go soon anyway, to save money," Addison said. "Your resignation doesn't require such a big audience, does it?"

"Vilma sent a message," Oxana said.

Sherry's throat constricted. "Vilma's gone."

"Vilma found killer." Oxana's accent strengthened. "I read note in Mr. Trembley's room. I try to work on my English by reading everything. Note was in the garbage anyway. I had to ask Vilma what word in note meant."

Sherry shivered as a flash of lightning illuminated

the barn. The pitch black returned, as did a blast of thunder.

"Ginger?" Sherry called out.

The woman had disappeared under the cover of darkness.

"Oxana, are you sure you want to do this?" Pep asked. "Why don't we take a walk over to the main building?" Pep reached out to guide Oxana forward.

"I'd like to hear what she has to say." Addison peered to his left, then to his right. "I have a pretty big stake in having the killer caught. I'm afraid it's my sister. She's in a tough situation, and I think she took out her desperation on Fitz. He was the one who was taking down Maine Course Foods, and that would, in turn, take down the man Ginger relied on for her future. Am I right, Oxana?"

"Let's go, Sherry," Pep said. "Oxana, we're going back to the main building."

"What's the rush? I have some questions for Oxana. First being, what note?" Sherry's voice took on a tone of urgency. She turned to face Addison. "Ginger didn't do it. You know she doesn't have an evil bone in her body."

"Really? Then where has she run off to?" Addison said.

"Sherry!" Pep grabbed Sherry's arm and pulled her toward the barn entrance.

"What is it? Why are you acting like this?" Sherry demanded.

When they reached the barn door, a crack of thunder halted their progress.

Sherry put her hand on the door to steady herself. She turned to face Pep and whispered, "Just go along with me. I know what I'm doing."

"You guys all right in here? I saw lights that looked like flashlights out here and couldn't believe anyone would venture out here in this storm." The man in the dripping wet raincoat slid the hood off his head. Roe. "Need help?"

Another rain-coated body emerged from behind him. When the hood was lowered, Kelly's face beamed a smile. "We were taking our last walk together before we check out tomorrow. We got caught in the downpour. So romantic, right, Bunny Rabbit?"

Chapter 28

"Was romantic, until we were nearly struck by lightning." Roe fidgeted with his flashlight. "You all look like you're heading out. Hope we didn't interrupt. We were checking to make sure no one was caught in the blackout. Looks like you all were. Thank goodness for flashlights. Anyone seen Ginger?"

Glances were exchanged, but no one replied.

"She was here a minute ago," Addison said after an awkward gap of silence. "Then we started talking about the murders."

Kelly gasped. "I don't want to hear about murders when the lights are out. This barn is chilling enough."

Addison continued. "Oxana was telling us she found a note in your guest room, Roe. In the trash can. She hasn't told us what the note says yet."

Roe eyed Kelly. "Please, don't. I don't want to spoil the surprise." He turned to Oxana. "Please, Oxana. It was only a rough draft. I haven't finished the final copy."

"Surprise?" Oxana cocked her head. "The scribbled note about water and murder?"

Addison took two steps toward the barn door. He cupped his hand around his mouth and bellowed, "Ginger!"

"No, no." Roe pulled Kelly closer to his side. The petite woman was a rag doll in his grip. "I thought you meant my note to Kelly expressing my love."

Kelly hugged Roe with all her might.

"You must be talking about the note I found in the tackle box I bought from Addison. Looked like something he scribbled down. I just tossed that in the garbage."

"I read it," Oxana said. "Instructions to murder someone without a trace. 'Drowning' was circled. I had to ask Vilma to translate."

Addison arched forward, as if he were gut punched. When he straightened up, he had a gun in his hand. A scream caught in Sherry's throat.

"Check the box," Sherry uttered in a choked whisper.

Addison pointed the gun at Roe's head. "I'm holding you right here until I can get ahold of the police. Don't even think about moving a muscle. Kelly, back away. Your boyfriend's a murderer."

Kelly sidestepped toward Sherry.

Roe made a weak attempt to reach out for Kelly. "This is ridiculous. I didn't kill anyone. Get that thing out of my face."

A deafening noise rose from the back of the barn.

Sherry stared into Addison's eyes. "Addison, Roe didn't do it. Put the gun away before someone gets hurt. I want to show you something." Sherry reached into the front pocket of her corduroy barn coat, the coat she always chose to wear when she needed pockets large enough for keys, a phone, and miscellaneous sundries.

Another tremendous thud came from the back of the barn. Roe aimed his phone's flashlight at the noise. Dust was billowing from the floor across the room, where something had crashed down. Before Addison could refocus on Sherry, she pulled her homemade deer repellent out of her pocket. "Look what I brought. Deer repellent for the garden. Works wonders. See?" She pumped the trigger and hit Addison squarely in the eyes.

Addison screamed and swatted wildly at his face with the hem of his shirt. Pep kicked the gun out of Addison's flailing hand. The weapon landed halfway across the room and slid into the darkness.

"Follow me." Pep steered Sherry out the door.

Someone attempted to hold Sherry by the hem of her shirt, but she managed to squirm away from the grip. Outside the barn, the rain had let up, but the saturated ground sucked each step deep into mud, requiring herculean strength to move forward.

"Hurry up," Pep called out to Oxana. He made a right turn into the entrance of the corn maze.

Sherry's stomach somersaulted as she peered over her shoulder. Roe and Kelly were struggling to keep up. Kelly's short legs and ankle-length skirt were slowing her progress. When Sherry rounded the corner of the first maze wall, Pep was clinging to a protruding cornstalk.

"Addison loves gingersnaps," Sherry said to her panting brother.

"I know. I saw him take two handfuls every morning."

"Ginger's one of the best home cooks in the county."

"Again, I know. She just showed us her cookbook." Pep tripped and nearly went down. "Oh! Now I understand."

Sherry heard voices closing in. She winced as the sound of squishy footsteps competed with the sound of the driving rain. Pep put his arm across Sherry's midsection and secured her against the maze wall, out of sight of the entrance. Sherry recoiled when she heard her name uttered by a female.

"Sherry, are you in there?" An airy whisper grew closer.

"Ginger, we're in the corner. Over here," Sherry said.

Ginger, with Kelly in tow, rounded the maze entrance. They tucked themselves beside Sherry.

Roe backed in. "He's looking for the gun. I lost him in the barn."

"I did my best to distract Addison. I'm who's haunting the barn," Ginger admitted. "I didn't want to believe my brother could do what he did. I believe you very nearly were his next victim, Roe. He wanted you gone because you were turning on Uri. You were either going to take the murder wrap or be murdered."

"I'm so sorry," Sherry offered. "This didn't go exactly as planned. If Addison was the guilty party, as I suspected, I had hoped he'd confess, and that would be the end."

Pep caught his breath. "Ginger, how did Fitz know

Addison loved gingersnaps when he wrote his shrimp wrap recipe?"

Ginger shook her hooded head. Rainwater splashed Sherry in the face. "Good chance Fitz read my cookbook. You know, it was a best seller, back in the day. The cookbook has a story about Addison stealing my freshly baked gingersnaps faster than I could make them."

"And Fitz knew Sherry always reads her competitors' recipes," Pep said.

"Addison's pocket fisherman had traces of my car's paint on it," Sherry said.

"Is that what was in the bag Eileen left on your doorstep?" Pep asked.

"Yep. Eileen's note inside the bag said she thought he needed the pole back to finish a job he had obviously started. How right she was."

Sherry pressed her back against the wall. "Addison must have been threatening Fitz for some time now. So much so that Fitz hatched a plan to expose his killer, in the chance the threats turned to violence."

The lines on Ginger's forehead deepened. "Lyman came to the inn looking for information about the cook-off a couple of weeks ago, under the guise of being a spice distributor."

"Obviously, to look into whether Fitz was competing," Sherry said, "so he could serve Fitz. If Addison spoke with Lyman while he was here, Addison may have learned Fitz would soon be legally bound to testify against Shrimply Amazing. But why would he care?"

Pep hung his head. "I've seen Addison a number of times in Portland. The night I met Uri and Roe,

Addison was the one called to escort me off the property. Seems he was as on-call for Uri as Roe."

Ginger frowned. "Addison loves the freelance life of contract work. He works just enough to get by."

"He had your financial support. Makes for an easy life." Sherry hoped she hadn't overstepped with the comment. "Stressful for you, though." She braced for a return attack.

"Huh. That hurts to hear," was all Ginger came back with.

"I'm as guilty as you, not wanting my kid brother to grow up," Sherry said.

"I thought I was instrumental in getting Addison employment as Shrimply Amazing's fishing expert during the cook-off," Ginger said. "Turns out he was already working for them. I knew he made trips to Maine. I gave him money for lodging, with the promise of repayment. Figured he was fishing. That's what he loves. He was so angry when I told him I couldn't afford to fund his trips anymore."

"He was angry at Fitz for potentially taking down Shrimply Amazing. I bet he wanted Fitz gone for some time because he knew too much. I'm also afraid Addison was targeting both of us in the corn maze. Me, for sniffing around," Sherry said.

"And me for what he saw as a multitude of sins, the worst being pulling his financial plug," Ginger said. "But, how did you come to suspect Addison?"

"I began to suspect Addison when I showed him the fishhook Vilma had given Oxana," Sherry explained. "His reaction was so bland to something he cherished. I couldn't get it out of my mind. It would be like me turning up my nose at a gift of European white truffles."

"You're spot on," Ginger said.

"I'm so sorry." Sherry put a hand on Ginger's back.

"This all explains how easily Uri slipped into my life. Uri's courtship was all Addison's doing. My brother wasn't even trying to save the family inn. He only wanted to endear himself to Uri to guarantee his fake contract-fishing job. The plan collapsed when Uri became aware the inn was in financial trouble, and I had no money to offer his ailing business. Out of desperation to keep him interested, I offered all I had left, my retirement savings." Ginger hung her head. "I'm an idiot."

Sherry scanned the space around her. The storm was letting up, but the lack of sunlight made seeing a chore.

"Where's Oxana? She didn't get out of the barn." Ginger's cry was clipped when footsteps neared.

"This is the last the Constable family will see of this wicked maze," Addison shouted as he appeared through the entrance. "Good luck finding your way out." He heaved a sledgehammer over his shoulder and began swinging wildly. He smashed down the stalks that made up the entryway. A growing pile of massacred stalks blocked the escape route.

As Addison worked to deconstruct his masterpiece, Ginger grabbed Sherry's arm. "Run!"

With her free hand, Sherry shook Kelly's shoulder, unlocking the woman's paralyzed stance. The air, thick with shards of plant debris, tightened around the group as they ran blindly into the belly of the maze. Sherry peered back as she stumbled through a sharp turn. She glimpsed Addison, systematically pulverizing anything in his path.

"Keep moving, Sherry!" Pep screamed.

Sherry backtracked to her brother as the others passed her in the slim passageway. "We need to slow him down." Before Pep could reply, she began to kick a dividing wall as hard as she could.

Mud flung from her shoes and dotted her face as she assaulted the maze. Pep joined her and together they brought down enough of the wall to create a formidable obstacle.

"We just bought ourselves some time. Let's go."

Sherry and Pep caught up to the others.

"Guys, this way." Ginger waved the heavy-breathing group forward. She came to an abrupt halt in a matter of seconds. They faced a solid barrier. "Nope. Dead end." She doubled back and had to swerve to avoid hitting Kelly head-on. "I think we take a right here." Ginger jumped a puddle, landing at a fork in the maze. "I have no idea which way. He's got us trapped."

"We can't give up." Roe's voice died off with the final syllable. He began pounding on the wall. "Help! Help! Is anyone out there?"

Pep reached his arm out and pressed a palm on the stalks. "What's that noise?"

"You mean the rain, the thunder, or the sledge-hammer demolition?" Roe asked.

"Over there." Pep pointed at a quaking wall a few feet ahead. "He's got us."

"No, that's a chainsaw!" yelled Sherry.

The tip of the machine's blade pierced the wall.

"Sherry? You in there?"

Sherry stared at the enlarging hole being cut in the wall from the outside. A section of the wall popped out. A head poked through.

"Oxana, am I glad to see you," Sherry cried. "Hurry, let's get out of here before Addison—"

"Don't worry about him. We've got this place surrounded. He's not going anywhere, except to jail." Detective Bease wriggled his way through the hole, gun drawn. He pointed to each person. "One, two, three, four, five. All accounted for. Everyone okay?"

One by one, they crawled out through the hole, until only the detective and Sherry were left inside.

"How did you know where to find us?" Sherry asked.

Ray pulled a handkerchief from his pants pocket and handed it to Sherry. He signaled her face needed a wipe-down. "When you didn't pick up your phone this morning, I was sure you'd be here. Time was running out. Pep was insisting on leaving. He's got the Oliveri stubbornness in his genes."

Sherry inspected the mud-covered cloth. She nodded. "Ginger texted, 'time is running out.' She must have meant for Addison."

Ray continued. "Ginger's way of lighting a fire under you, I'd say. I looked at Ms. Pitney's car-cam footage last night. Didn't show much except a quick glimpse of someone crossing in front of the car, holding something I hadn't seen since I was a boy. Popeil's Pocket Fisherman. One of the first infomercials ever made. I recognized the contraption right away. I remember when I was about nine, I saved up all summer one year to buy one."

"Elvis Purrsley."

"Who?"

"Elvis Purrsley followed a shrimp attached to a

pocket fisherman. That's how he learned to walk on a leash."

"Whoever that is. So, you know what I'm referring to. Anyway, I had a conversation with Addison after I spoke to Oxana a couple of days ago. I found him doing maintenance work on the maze. On Vilma's car-cam video, he was captured wearing the same college sweatshirt as the day I spoke to him. He circled in front of Vilma's car, and I could make out a red cloth with a giant spatula on it in one hand. No doubt it was Addison and the cook-off apron."

"Probably was Ginger's cook-off apron. She received one for hosting the cook-off party." Sherry envisioned the apron wrapped around Vilma's neck. "How awful he used the apron to strangle Vilma."

"Actually, he didn't use the apron. That was just another calling card left at the scene, like the fishhook."

"But you said Vilma was strangled."

"She was. With the pocket fisherman fishing line."

Sherry ran her hand across the front of her neck. A cold shiver traveled down her spine.

"Vilma was an annoying personality, but I feel so terrible for her. She was trying to rejuvenate her ailing journalism career by crafting a fantastic murder mystery with a sensational ending."

"Unfortunately, she was the victim in her own mystery."

Sherry dropped her chin and shook her head.

"Remember the list of words you had me write down?" Ray asked.

"Yes. Of course."

"Cook-off, recipe, fraud, double-cross, desperation,

no other way out. You didn't give me much time to toss all those ingredients into the mixing bowl, add whatever I'd come up with, and see who jumped out. Who had something in common with every item on that list? You wanted me to prove you right or wrong."

"I had a theory Addison might be the missing puzzle piece," Sherry said, "but I wasn't feeling one hundred percent certain. I was hoping if I gave you the bullet points, your street smarts would kick in."

"I went through every Fall Fest Cook-off recipe. Narrowed it down to Frye's and yours. Yours was good, Frye's was very odd, with the whole ginger-snap thing."

"That's what I thought. Your palate is becoming more refined."

"Appreciate the compliment. This morning, while a madman wielding a sledgehammer was chasing you, I hit the jackpot in the lobby when Uri decided to spill the beans. He was a wealth of information when I advised him Ginger was under suspicion, along with her brother."

"Was Ginger under suspicion?" Sherry asked.

"Not exactly. I thought Uri could use a bit of a nudge, so I told him she was. Uri showed a softer side in defense of Ginger's innocence, despite the fact he said he and Ginger broke up. He couldn't afford another cash-strapped business, and she was unwilling to turn her back on the inn. Telling Ginger her brother had made overtures of blackmail to keep Shrimply Amazing's secrets didn't strengthen the already weak bond between the two. Uri was concerned Roe had killed Fitz to keep him from spilling company secrets. Uri gave Roe a box to plant in Pep's room, hoping to mislead the investigation long enough to get Shrimply Amazing back on track. That way, any motive Roe had would evaporate, and he'd be in the clear."

"Why did Addison take it so far?" Sherry asked.

"Addison's plan to solidify a merger between Ginger and Uri was flimsy. He hoped Uri would convince Ginger to sell the inn. Surely Ginger would split the profits. Instead, Uri broke things off with Ginger and terminated Addison."

"Poor Ginger," Sherry moaned. "Addison was trying to sell the inn out from under her."

"Yup," Ray agreed. "Addison lost Ginger's funding, lost his job with Maine Course, and his beloved activity, fishing, dried up. Basically, the way of life he preferred was disappearing."

"Ginger said Addison's not good with change."

Ray's line of sight drifted toward the maze. "Addison's the definition of desperate."

"And Fitz? Why murder Fitz?"

"Addison wanted Fitz gone before he disclosed Maine Course's secrets. That way Addison, who learned the good, the bad, and the ugly about the company during his time in Portland, could blackmail Uri until Maine Course could right the ship."

Sherry flicked a splotch of mud off her coat sleeve. "We owe Vilma some gratitude. Whether she meant to or not, she helped move the investigation along. She wanted to be the first to break the story and peg the murderer. Unfortunately, she tried so hard to get everyone off Addison's scent so she could be the one to break the story, she may have sealed her doom. Addison, obviously, knew she had closed in on him, and he had to get rid of her."

Ray pushed his rain-stained hat up his forehead. "Yup."

"The gold box. The fishhook." Sherry raised her voice. "I also had Roe pegged for a long time."

"That was Vilma's doing," Ray added.

"Vilma, Uri, and Ginger did a good job keeping Roe at the top of the suspect list, along with Pep," Sherry said. "Maybe even when they knew Addison might be the killer. Wonder when Ginger realized Addison was guilty?"

"Uri showed me a framed photo in the library. It was Addison, around twelve years old, at a fishing derby. He was holding up a winning catch. Sticking out of the fish's mouth was the very same hook lodged in Frye's neck." Ray winced. "Uri said Ginger cried when she made the connection. She wouldn't let Oxana clean the bookshelves after that, but she wouldn't hide the photo either. Very strange."

Sherry cocked her head toward her shoulder. "I had every confidence you'd put the ingredients together." Sherry hugged her arms tight to warm her shivering body.

Ray scoffed. "Glad one of us did."

Ray lowered his eyebrows and tucked his dripping notepad in his raincoat pocket.

"Hey, you guys coming out?" Pep stuck his head through the hole in the wall. "You must really like mazes if you want to hang out in there this long."

"I do," Ray answered with no uncertainty.

Chapter
29

Sherry checked her phone for the umpteenth time. She had a few minutes to spare before she had to get home for her lesson. Ginger had been in the Planning Department meeting for over ninety minutes. What was billed as a short information-gathering session seemed to have morphed into a full-blown thorough analysis of turning the inn into a day spa and yoga retreat. Sherry was reconsidering her decision to accompany Ginger to Town Hall as the time ticked by. Moral support was valuable, too, she decided as she slid her phone back into her purse.

A moment later, her phone buzzed with an incoming text. As she read the message, Sherry pushed up the sleeve of her shirt to cool her warming skin.

She typed a reply. Yes, This Saturday sounds wonderful. See you then!!! She pressed send and immediately wondered if she sounded too eager. How would Don interpret the three exclamation points she'd added?

"Great newsletter, Sherry. As always," a voice reverberated from the other side of the oversized waiting room. The rooms in Augustin's Town Hall were so voluminous and sparsely furnished, Sherry was sure even her thoughts echoed throughout the building.

"Eileen. Fancy meeting you here."

Eileen squeaked her way across the wooden floor in her docksiders. "Getting a license for Elvis. Town's probably going to use the fee to put up more ridiculous parking signage that no one can interpret. Can't you do anything about that? I have no idea whether I parked in a legal spot or not. The sign read, TOWN HALL PARKING TUESDAY THROUGH SATURDAY—SUBJECT TO VOLUME—THIRTY MINUTES OR AFTERNOON RULES APPLY." Eileen threw her hand skyward. "What are afternoon rules?"

"I'm sorry. I'm only the newsletter editor. My power is very limited in this case. Speaking of parking issues, did you get a chance to read this week's newsletter? There's a nice recap of the New England Fall Festival and cook-off, written by Patti Mellitt."

"I haven't read it yet. Can't wait." Eileen lowered her voice to a near whisper. "Did she recap the murder investigation? You know, I saw Ginger upstairs when I went to the licensing bureau. Poor dear."

"Sherry, I'm finally done," sang out a lilting voice. "I'm so sorry to make you wait. You're a dear to be this patient."

Eileen gasped as Ginger and Beverly Van Ardan approached. Sherry introduced Eileen to the women. She never lost the stunned look, even as she extended her greetings. Sherry excused her group from Eileen's probing stare. The three women left Town Hall. They took a seat on the bench on the columned porch.

"How'd it go? Do you need a new permit to operate as a spa rather than an inn?" Sherry asked.

"To be determined. No one had done their homework. They were apparently bogged down by a parking debate. The wheels of progress move slowly in this town." The breeze caught Bev's silk scarf. The material blew across her face, hiding her grin. "I think everything will work out just fine. My husband, Erik, and I are putting up a sizable investment to get the project off the ground. The lovely inn lives another day in a new form."

"I can't thank you enough, Bev. I really can't." Ginger wiped a tear from her cheek. "Going to be a fresh start for me and the inn. Negativity is out of my life, and I'm standing on my own two feet."

Bev patted Ginger on the back.

The *clackity clack* of high heels raced up the porch steps toward Sherry. "Sherry Oliveri. Congrats on your win at the Fall Fest Cook-off. I hear the winners received a trip to a winery. That's my dream, if you need company. Great newsletter, as always."

"Thanks, Tia. I'll keep that in mind. Girls, this is Tia, the mayor's assistant."

Bev and Ginger shared a hello.

"Two Oliveris in Town Hall in one week. Couldn't ask for more," Tia said.

"Two Oliveris? Was my dad in for some reason? Probably complaining about the new No Parking sign outside The Ruggery."

"No, actually it was your brother, Pep. Looking into a marriage license." Tia's mouth dropped open. "Uh-oh. Is that a secret? Look at the time. My lunch hour's been over for thirty minutes. Gotta go."

"Your face says that's the first you've heard of that enlightening news. I'm sure Pep will let you know when the wedding is." Bev tweaked her scarf, so it flowed with the direction of the breeze. "Unless he's already eloped."

"The trip you won to Risky Reward Winery would be a great honeymoon for the couple. Just sayin'," Ginger remarked.

"You're right. And a good excuse for Auntie Sherry to babysit." Sherry stood and pitched a wave. "I'll see you gals later. Congratulations again on your successful meeting."

"Want a ride?" Ginger called out.

"No thanks. My car's in the shop. I'm finally having the scratch removed. I'm loving the exercise." She had repeated that answer so many times over the last few days, she'd nearly convinced herself it was true." She swung her leg over the bike seat and pedaled home.

Back in her kitchen, Sherry gathered the ingredients for her Pecan Salmon with Sweet Red Pepper Mayo. Ground pecans, roasted red peppers, mango chutney, and salmon fillets were the stars of the recipe. All the other ingredients were staples in her cupboard. She couldn't wait for her student to arrive.

Chutney's bark alerted Sherry to someone walking up her front steps.

"Oxana. I'm so excited to get started. Come on in."

"Me, too." Oxana handed Sherry a small gold box. "A small thank you."

Sherry's mouth twisted into a half smile as her mind raced back to last week's encounter with Addison in the barn.

"Don't worry. Not a fishhook. Open."

Inside the box was a tiny silver spatula pendant. Oxana held up her wrist and jingled her charm bracelet. "My mother gives me charms for important occasions. This is important occasion."

Sherry's breath caught in her throat. "It's beautiful. Thank you."

"Before we start, need to tell you few things." Oxana positioned herself behind the kitchen counter.

Sherry handed her the Fall Fest apron she'd used in the cook-off. Oxana poked her head through the loop and tied the cord around her waist.

"I found fishhook in Addison's guest room when I cleaned."

"That fishhook sure traveled. From Vilma to you, to me, back to Vilma. On to Roe, who ended its journey by giving it to Addison."

"The same kind of hook was in Fitz's neck in the barn. I saw it."

"I know." Sherry pursed her lips. "Addison's calling card."

"I told Vilma. Addison came in the barn many times and talked to himself about the murder. He didn't know I was in there. I told Vilma. She told Addison she knew he did it. So, he killed Vilma. You see why I went away?"

"Yes, of course." Sherry gave Oxana a hug. "Did you write the note I found in the barn? *Look in box.*"

Oxana gave Sherry a puzzled look. "Nyet."

"He wanted to get caught," Sherry whispered.

Oxana picked up a whisk. "Let's get started. Show me what is mayo."

Please turn the page for recipes from Sherry's kitchen!

PECAN CRUSTED SALMON
WITH RED PEPPER MAYONNAISE

Serves 6

Ingredients

1½ pounds salmon fillets, approximately ¾ inch
thick, cut in 6 equal portions
⅔ cup ground pecans
½ cup panko breadcrumbs
1 teaspoon salt
1 teaspoon pepper
1 egg, beaten
2 tablespoons water
flour for dredging

oil for frying
1 recipe red pepper mayonnaise ***see below**
pecan halves and julienned roasted red pepper
strips for garnish

Preparation

Rinse and pat dry the salmon fillets. In a large bowl, combine the pecans, breadcrumbs, salt, and pepper. In another bowl, combine the egg and water. Dredge the fillets in the flour, shake off excess, dip in egg mixture, and then dip in pecan mixture to coat both sides.

Refrigerate fillets for 30 minutes.

Fry in preheated non-stick fry pan that is lightly oiled, 3 minutes per side, over medium-high heat. Transfer to serving plates and serve with a dollop of red pepper mayonnaise. Garnish and enjoy!

*Red Pepper Mayonnaise

Combine ¼ cup mayonnaise, ¼ cup chopped roasted red peppers, 2 tablespoons mango chutney, 2 tablespoons lemon juice, ½ teaspoon garlic salt, and ⅛ teaspoon cayenne pepper. Mix well.

CRAB STUFFED RED POTATO BITES

Ingredients

24 small red potatoes (about 2½ pounds)

¼ cup butter, cubed

2 tablespoons milk

⅓ cup sour cream, plus 2 tablespoons, divided

¼ cup shredded Parmesan cheese, plus
   2 tablespoons, divided

2 strips cooked bacon, crumbled

½ teaspoon celery salt

⅛ teaspoon black pepper

⅛ teaspoon smoked paprika

½ cup crab meat

caviar for garnish, optional

Preparation

Place potatoes in a saucepan and cover with cold water. Bring to boil. Reduce heat; cover and cook for 17 minutes or until fork tender. Drain.

When cool enough to handle, halve each potato. Scoop out pulp, leaving a thin shell. In a large bowl, mash the potato pulp with butter, milk, ⅓ cup sour cream, and ¼ cup Parmesan cheese, until creamy. Add bacon, celery salt, black pepper, and smoked paprika to potato mixture. Spoon mixture into potato shells.

In a small bowl, combine remaining sour cream and Parmesan cheese with the crab. Top potatoes with crab blend.

Place potato halves on baking sheet. Bake at 375° for 12–14 minutes.

Garnish with a sprinkle of caviar, if desired.

Savory Shrimp Lettuce Wraps with Thai Basil Avocado Aioli
(slight variation on Fitz Frye's recipe)

Ingredients

2 tablespoons soy sauce

1 tablespoon turbinado sugar

1 tablespoon rice wine vinegar

2 garlic cloves minced

½ teaspoon freshly grated ginger

1 pound large raw shrimp, peeled and deveined

1 tablespoon olive oil

4 green onions, diced

1 head butter lettuce leaves, separated, rinsed,
  and dried

Thai Basil Avocado Aioli ***see below**

lemon wedges for garnish

Preparation

In a small saucepan, add the soy sauce, turbinado sugar, rice wine vinegar, garlic, and ginger. Warm over medium heat until sugar melts. Remove from heat.

Coarsely chop the shrimp into ½ to ¾ inch chunks.

Heat the oil in a large skillet over medium-high heat.

Add the shrimp in an even layer. Cook 2 minutes, stirring often.

Add the soy sauce blend to the skillet. Stir well. Cook until shrimp is coated, stirring often.

Remove the skillet from heat. Let the shrimp rest in the sauce for 2 minutes. Stir in green onions.

Serve by spooning 2–3 tablespoons of the shrimp mixture into the center of a lettuce leaf. Drizzle with Thai Basil Avocado Aioli. Serve with lemon wedges.

THAI BASIL AVOCADO AIOLI

Ingredients

¼ cup Thai basil leaves
½ ripe avocado, pitted and skinned
¼ cup mayonnaise
2 tablespoons soy sauce
1 large garlic clove, mashed
salt and pepper to taste

Preparation

Add all ingredients to a food processor and blend until smooth. Transfer to a bowl.

Connect with
U s

Visit us online at
KensingtonBooks.com
to read more from your favorite authors, see books
by series, view reading group guides, and more.

Join us on social media

for sneak peeks, chances to win books and prize packs,
and to share your thoughts with other readers.

facebook.com/kensingtonpublishing
twitter.com/kensingtonbooks

Tell us what you think!

To share your thoughts, submit a review,
or sign up for our eNewsletters, please visit:
KensingtonBooks.com/TellUs.